Genevieve

*Also by Eric Jerome Dickey
in Large Print:*

Drive Me Crazy
The Other Woman
Thieves' Paradise

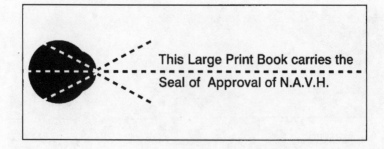

Genevieve

Eric Jerome
Dickey

Thorndike Press • Waterville, Maine

Published in 2005 by arrangement with Dutton, a member of Penguin Group (USA) Inc.

Thorndike Press® Large Print African-American.

The tree indicium is a trademark of Thorndike Press.

The text of this Large Print edition is unabridged. Other aspects of the book may vary from the original edition.

Set in 16 pt. Plantin by Liana M. Walker.

Printed in the United States on permanent paper.

Library of Congress Cataloging-in-Publication Data

Dickey, Eric Jerome.
    Genevieve / by Eric Jerome Dickey.
        p. cm. — (Thorndike Press large print African-American)
    ISBN 0-7862-7870-6 (lg. print : hc : alk. paper)
    1. Triangles (Interpersonal relations) — Fiction.
    2. Married people — Fiction. 3. Adultery — Fiction.
    4. Sisters — Fiction. 5. African Americans — Fiction.
    6. Large type books. 7. Psychological fiction.
    8. Domestic fiction. I. Title. II. Thorndike Press large print African-American series.
    PS3554.I319G46 2005b
    813'.54—dc22   2005012994

for
Dominique

As the Founder/CEO of NAVH, the only national health agency solely devoted to those who, although not totally blind, have an eye disease which could lead to serious visual impairment, I am pleased to recognize Thorndike Press* as one of the leading publishers in the large print field.

Founded in 1954 in San Francisco to prepare large print textbooks for partially seeing children, NAVH became the pioneer and standard setting agency in the preparation of large type.

Today, those publishers who meet our standards carry the prestigious "Seal of Approval" indicating high quality large print. We are delighted that Thorndike Press is one of the publishers whose titles meet these standards. We are also pleased to recognize the significant contribution Thorndike Press is making in this important and growing field.

Lorraine H. Marchi, L.H.D.
Founder/CEO
NAVH

* Thorndike Press encompasses the following imprints: Thorndike, Wheeler, Walker and Large Print Press.

Lust wants whatever it can't have.
Nil magis amat cupiditas, quam quod non licet.
— Syrus, *Maxims*

The gods never let us love and be wise at the same time.
Amare et sapere vix deo conceditur.
— Syrus, *Maxims*

Woman is always a slippery, changeable thing.
Varium et mutabile semper femina.
— Virgil, *Aeneid*, IV, 569

one

She rests on top of my body, naked, wrapped around my leg, her head on my chest. Her skin is still hot, set fire by too many orgasms to count. I've never been with a woman who came so hard, so often. My tongue tastes like her secrets. Her lavender aroma lives on my flesh. She stirs. My leg is sticky where her vagina rests on me. My come drains from her, adds to her wetness. I stroke her breasts, fingers pulling at her nipple, and she purrs. Her hand holds my penis with a never-ending longing, holds my flaccidity as if she wishes it were hers to keep.

My cellular vibrates, hums like her favorite carnal toy, dances on the dresser.

We both jump, startled away from our private world.

Her cellular glows and sings an urban beat, a hip-hop ring tone. Usher. My confession.

We don't reach out to answer, just hold

each other's guilt and wait for peace to return.

We grip our silence as if speaking were the bigger sin.

We kiss. Touch. Her kisses are intense. I whisper, "We should leave."

"Little bit longer, baby?"

"They'll look for us."

She sucks my tongue, bites me with passion. "Please?"

Her tongue finds its way down my chest. Her mouth covers my penis.

Oh, God. Oh, God. Oh, God.

My fingers stroke her hair, hand encourages her rhythm. She looks up and smiles at me, rubs that rigid part of me against her face, glows as if it has healing powers. Her mouth covers me again. She hums. Sounds starved. Heat. Sweet, sweet, heat. The wet sounds arouse me.

I moan, let my hand gather her hair into a fist, keep encouraging her motions, her head moving so smoothly. Every nerve comes alive. I writhe toward an undeserved heaven. My flaccidity hardens. I look down at her. She smiles, proud of the power she has over me inside of this moment. Kisses me and my insanity escalates. She pulls me to where she needs me.

Her legs open and I climb on her. The

lips of her vagina whisper my name.

She takes me inside her and there is a shift in consciousness as we integrate in sin. She moves and I fall into her anxious rhythm, her undercurrents. Her words are soft, her moans are soft, and her skin is soft. They all create a spark. And that spark becomes a raging fire.

I put her ankles around my neck, hold her ass, pull her into me a thousand times. She looks down to witness our connection, then stares into my eyes. My measured strokes go deeper, create madness. She grabs my ass, shudders, tells me she wants me faster, deeper.

Her arms flail side to side. She yanks the sheets, finds a pillow to cover her mouth, give that softness her wild sounds. Her legs shake. I yank the pillow away so I can see her face. Have to watch her. Her eyes close tight. She tremors and grabs her breasts, squeezes them so tight. Her legs spread like wings. Under my every stroke she flies and cries like an eagle.

I turn her over, position myself between the bed and the wall, use that wall to give me power. She can't move. Can only take what I give. She's there. She's coming strong and often.

Oh how she quakes.

Oh how her expressions morph into a beautiful ugliness.

The room sounds like an exorcism in progress.

In between my grunts and moans, I call out to her, say rude and demanding things.

She whispers things to arouse me even more, growls, touches herself then licks her own fingers, touches herself then feeds me her juices, grabs my ass, tells me to fuck her, fuck her hard, whines and moans and squeals and tells me how hard I am, how strong I am, how good I'm fucking her, how deep I'm going, demands my steady thrusting to never stop, goes insane and tells me I can come anywhere I want to, that she will take it in any orifice or drink it like wine.

I turn her over, take her to the center of the bed, suck her breasts while she reaches for my hardness, rushes me back inside her, those hips of hers thrusting upward, taking me with her own measured strokes. I'm not moving, just holding my position, trying not to come, struggling not to go insane. We have breathless kisses, devour and bite each other, so gone, and I'm somewhere else, someone else.

Time stops.

My senses are focused on her.

I lose control of myself.

There is no fear. There is no guilt.

She loses her breath, tenses up, back arches, and she sings my name in three octaves.

She comes. She comes. She comes.

Then we rest. Sweat dripping from our flesh, we fall away from each other and we rest. Minutes pass before I can collect my breath and move. I can barely turn my head to look at her.

She moans. "I think I just had an out-of-body experience."

We look at each other's worn expressions, then we laugh.

She asks, "Ready to go again?"

"You're insatiable."

"I've never been like this with anyone."

"Never?"

"Never."

She puts her face in my lap, hums, then sings part of a love song I don't recognize.

She whispers, her voice sounding disturbed, "God, what have you done to me?"

I don't answer. I could ask her the same, and my question would go unanswered as well.

"You make me tingle." Her voice remains a song. "Make me horny. Think of you and I get wet. You're very intense. The

13

way a lover should be. I find you damn sexy and tender."

Her hand traces my flesh, then I feel her tongue on my skin, licking my sweat. She takes me in her mouth again, does that like she owns me. In her mind I am hers. She nurtures me. I arch, I jerk, get the jitters, but flaccidity remains. That doesn't discourage her, doesn't wane her madness. She is determined to raise the dead, determined for this not to end.

My phone vibrates again.

Her cellular sings again. Usher, still confessing.

She is not mine.

She is my wife's sister.

This is our affair.

two

How does an affair begin?

I think that mine, like most, started un-intentionally. Married or not, it was my first transgression. I'm not malicious, that is not in my nature, hurting someone I love, that is.

My wife. Genevieve.

She is thirty-two. Has been turning thirty-two over and over for the last five years.

Her name has been Genevieve since she turned twenty-one, the day she marched to court and rid herself of the name her mother had given her. In her eyes her birth name was too urban. Too Alabama. A reminder that her ancestors had been slaves and that her family still lived in chains, some physically, some metaphorically, some in the psychological sense.

She is not one of *them*. Not cut from the cloth of people who name their children after cars and perfumes and possessions they cannot afford, or have a home filled with bastard children, each of those bastard children named after drugs the parents were addicted to at the time. She is not one of the people who took a simple name and bastardized its simplistic spelling to the point that it looked ridiculous on paper and sounded ludicrous as it rolled off the tongue, then pretended the name was that of an unknown king or queen, its origin rooted in Mother Africa.

She is Genevieve.

Genevieve.

She loves her name because to her ear, when spoken correctly, Genevieve sounds intellectual. Not Gen. Not Vee. Not any other variation. She will only respond to her name in total, Genevieve. And she is particular about that. She frowns on the Americanized pronunciation, "JEH-neh-veev." She prefers the elegant-in-tone French version, "ZHAWN-vee-EHV." She will answer to both, but only the French version is accompanied with a smile.

She is a precise woman. She is not five-foot-one; she is five-foot-one-and-one-quarter. I suppose, to a woman, a quarter of an inch could be the difference between pleasure and a night of frustration.

She has come up from poverty and, once

again I state, has declared herself an intellectual. Not one that has stumbled out of the womb and continues to stumble through life without meaning or purpose. Not one of the problem children Bill Cosby rants about. She has endless goals. My wife is a planner. A degreed woman who knows what she will be doing for the next twenty years. She has it mapped out, literally.

She says that when she was a teenager, she mapped her escape from a small town called Odenville, from her past, drew a road to her future.

She did that the day her father murdered her mother. Cut her throat. She told me that her mother was a woman who had many lovers. Her father was a man who grew tired of being ridiculed in his small town. A man who lost it, then called the police, and sat waiting for them to come take him away, tears in his eyes, his dead wife in his arms being rocked and sung to, his every word telling her how much he loved her, how she had made him do something bad.

No matter how I have tried, Genevieve refuses to let me into her past. That leaves me feeling shut out in that part of her life. She only gives me part of herself. Thus, my needs are beyond those of the loins. My need is to feel complete. To not have this glass wall between us.

Genevieve's desires are flowcharted, every move thought out like a chess player willing to sacrifice her queen in order to slay her opponent's king. Every move from Odenville to undergrad at Spelman to grad school at UCLA to PhD from Pepperdine University in Malibu, everything that she has accomplished or plans to accomplish is on poster-sized, light-green engineering grid paper, laminated and framed, hung at eye level on the west wall in her office, facing due east. Like a prayer. Her ambitions hang on the wall facing east for another reason as well. That way her map to total domination of the free world will be brought to life and highlighted with every sunrise.

The light of my life, the fire in my loins.

Doctor Genevieve Forbes.

When we married, she kept her last name, the one she had decided would be hers from the first time she picked up a magazine with that title, the new one that sang of richness and power and old money, the name she crowned herself with.

Genevieve.

Not Gen. Not Vee. Not "JEH-neh-veev."

Genevieve. "ZHAWN-vee-EHV."

Write her name in soft italics; cross the ocean and learn to speak it in its native language.

Let it roll off the tongue. Allow it to melt like warm butter.

Genevieve.

I love her because she is an intellectual. Brilliance is an aphrodisiac.

I despise her for the same reason.

three

"Tell her Willie done passed."

"Willie? Who is he?"

"Willie Esther Savage, her grand-mamma."

It starts with a phone call. The caller ID shows area code 256, one that I was not familiar with at the time. It was a call coming in from the Birmingham area, the Pittsburgh of the South. The voice on the other end sounded like that of an old man who took his Jim Beam over ice, his tone Southern and rooted in both poverty and ancestral slavery, a raspy-voiced smoker who had — based on the way he punctuated every other word with a cough — seen his better years. I'm not a doctor, but a deaf man could hear emphysema and bronchitis dancing around inside his frame. When I had answered he had asked for Shauna Smith, a name I was not used to hearing. I told him he had the wrong number. Before I could hang up, he

20

changed and asked for Jennifer. Then tried again, asked for Jenny Vee. Struggled with that name, my guess being that was the closest he could get to the pronunciation of Genevieve. He did not know her as Genevieve.

Cough. "The name she was borned with was LaKeisha Shauna Smith."

He has my attention. "Yes."

"I thank she calls herself Jenny Vee something-another now she done moved away."

I say, "I think you mean Genevieve, not Jenny Vee."

He pauses, then answers, "I reckon so."

My chest tightens as I lean back from my desk, away from the notes I'm looking over, notes regarding the breakdown of the infected enzymes in semen and drugs we've developed, and my eyes go to the clock. It's after eight, close to the time she usually gets in. Genevieve is off work, leaves at five on the dot, but today is Tuesday. Tuesday and Thursday are her Pilates days. Wednesday is an African dance class in Leimert Park, then from time to time she walks across the street and watches poetry at World Stage. She writes poetry but is not one to perform her work. Those are the evenings she gives

21

herself time to do something in the name of self.

I lean forward and ask, "May I ask who is calling?"

Cough. "What was that?"

"Who is this? Who are you?"

Cough. Cough. "Grandpa Fred. Mister Fred Smith Junior. I'm her granddaddy on her daddy side. Need to get her the word her grandmamma on her momma side done passed early this morning. Willie Esther was gone before the cry of the crow."

"She . . . died?"

"Willie Esther lived to see eighty-three last fall."

My lips move in awkwardness. "Sorry to hear that."

"We calling all the family we can find right now." Another rattling cough. Sounded like his lungs were coming undone. "She passed early this morning. Held on as long as she could after that last stroke, but she done been called to glory. We calling everybody and we didn't want to not call LaKeisha Shauna Smith and let her know when the funeral gon' be."

I correct him. "Genevieve."

"Death don't give a rat's ass about nobody name. All Death care about is coming to collect his due, and Death always collect his due. We all gon' die. With open arms, or kicking and screaming, come time, we all meet Death, we all make that trip to the other side."

"Yes, we all will."

"Yessir, I look out my window and see Death's doing every day."

He speaks of death with ease, matter-of-factly, as if it were just a part of life.

I get up from my glass-top desk, roll my chair back so I can stretch my back. My hamstrings stick to the chair's leather. I have on a gray T-shirt and wrinkled shorts, what I wear most of the time I am at home. I look out the window and see our small backyard that has a pool, bamboo trees that give us privacy, the gazebo that houses our Jacuzzi, then glance due east and see parts of downtown L.A. glittering miles away, its smog and lights in the distance. In that same glass I see my gangly reflection. Hair a little too long. As usual I need to shave.

I say, "May I have Genevieve call you?"

There is another pause. The kind that comes when a person's mind is spinning, questions rising. I imagine that old man, his back bent, skin leathery and wrinkled, a road map to days gone by, sitting in a worn and frayed chair, cane at his side, thick glasses on, his free hand dragging back and forth over the stubbles and rough texture in his pockmarked face, maybe shifting his stained false teeth side to side, contemplating me and my accent that rings of education and twenty-five years of living in California, my disrespectful urban way that doesn't add *sir* to the end of a sentence.

He asks, "Who this I'm talking to?"

"Her husband."

Cough. "What her last name now?"

"Forbes."

Cough. "You Mister Forbes?"

"No. Genevieve kept her last name."

"Woman who keeps her last name don't intend on keeping the man she marries."

That is his litmus test for a healthy marriage. Intentional or not, it stings.

"You talk real proper. Where you from?"

"Born in . . . I grew up in Fresno, California."

"You sound the way they talk on television out there."

I chuckle at his Southern drawl and say, "Okay."

"When she done married?"

"She done married . . . uh . . . she done married two years ago."

"You don't say." Cough. "What kinna work you do?"

24

"I'm a research analyst."

"You do what kinda searching?"

"No, research."

"What kinna work is that?"

"I'm a research analyst. I study and analyze cancers, neurodegenerative diseases, and now I'm working on AIDS research training in the form of neurology."

When I finish rambling, he says one word: "Cancer?"

"I'll have her call you. Let me write down your number."

"She know the number. Same number we done had since nineteen-sixty."

Grandpa Fred falls into a coughing fit.

The phone goes dead on his end.

My heart worries for Genevieve's loss. I look at my wedding ring. Her loss is my loss. This phone call has left me the bearer of bad news, a task I do not want.

The phone screams in my ear, lets me know that it is time I hang up.

His call leaves me feeling prickly, the smell of both mystery and death in the air.

Genevieve has spoken of tragedies in her family, reluctantly. Of her murdered mother and incarcerated father. Only mentioned them once. Never gave any details.

I remember my mother. I remember her dying. Remember living with my grandparents. Remember feeling lost and alone. Remember not being able to attach to anyone for the fear of death separating us and leaving me emotionally stranded.

I remember losing unconditional love.

Now I search for the remedy to my inner pain, bask in pleasure to dull its sting.

Grandpa Fred's voice fades as I put my work to the side and look at the television. *The Lover*, the adaptation of Marguerite Duras's novel, is on Showtime. What I see makes me pause. She is beautiful and naked, in one of her erotic scenes with her North China Lover, on top of him, her face sweaty, in the throes of passion. She relishes him as he does her.

I envy them, the sensuality they have for each other, their love.

On the television, the lovers love on, endless pleasure and exploration. She is a teenager, still in boarding school, young and inexperienced. He is in his thirties, a playboy, a master lover. Both characters are nameless. Names, those labels do not matter in the end.

I try to get back to my work, but I cannot.

I smile in appreciation and continue to sigh in envy.

' But in the end, the erotic moments are not why I watch.

It's what is said at the end.

That is what I wait for, the words I wait to hear at the dimming of their day.

I watch to see how she answers the phone, now her body aged and worn, and his voice is on the other end, listen to hear how he tells her that despite them parting ways, despite their separate marriages, despite the grandchildren, despite all the irreplaceable years that have gone by on the breath of time, he loves her still, loves her now as he did then, and will always love her.

That is when my face gets hot, when my throat tightens.

That is what I want. That is all I want. Love eternal.

They loved each other to a depth that they could not comprehend.

Yet their affair was doomed.

All love is doomed.

four

I was born in Pasadena, not the one that is decorated with palm trees and Hollywood-adjacent, but the one in Texas, *the Strawberry Capital of the South*. All I really know about Pasadena, all I remember is that I lived down by Spencer Highway and Westside Drive, not far from where they filmed *Urban Cowboy*, where humidity was king and mosquitoes were queen.

Time to time I try to remember but all I can see in my mind is a lot of used-car dealers, fast-food places, and flea markets up and down Spencer Highway, most of the signs in Spanish. I suppose it is now as it was then, white and Mexican, the latter outnumbering the former.

My momma hated Pasadena.

At sunrise Momma inhaled and called it Stink-adena. At dusk she closed her blinds and called it Klansville, U.S.A. To me, from demographics to culture, Pasadena was just like Fresno.

I was still in elementary school, fourth grade. That was years after Timothy O'Bryan poisoned his son with cyanide and earned the nickname "The Man Who Killed Halloween," but long before Enron and cellular phones and I-pagers and high-speed Internet access.

Momma rode that shopworn strip that would become home to second-rate places like Whataburger and Alamo Thrift Store and Fiesta grocery store. There was a special store down at Allen Genoe, a place near the haven of topless dancers at Fantasy Cabaret. She called the store the boutique. I don't remember the real name of the store, only that EROS was in its neon sign.

It was raining that day.

I remember the rain.

So much water falling from the sky that it seemed there shouldn't be any more teardrops left in heaven. Neither rain nor racism ever kept Momma in the house, not for long. A small town left a big-city woman feeling antsy. Not having a babysitter never kept her restless soul from doing what she wanted to do. That rainy day Momma made me stay in the car while she took some cash from her purse and hurried inside the boutique. Said she had to run in the boutique to pick up a special order. She left me in the backseat, comic book in hand, Tonka truck in my lap. Her umbrella was held high, shawl over her shoulders, a scarf around her face.

When she came out she had a bag tucked under her arm. She laughed and tiptoed through the rain, hurried back to the car, dark glasses on even though the skies were gray. She had on capri pants, the same kind that Laura Petrie wore on *The Dick Van Dyke Show*.

As soon as she got in she put her merchandise in the glove compartment, locked it up.

"What you buy at the boutique, Momma?"

"A girl's best friend."

"A dog?"

"That's a man's best friend."

She laughed, pulled out of the lot like she had robbed a bank. She took her shades off and lit a cigarette, moved her seat belt out of the way. She hated the way it wrinkled her clothes.

I remember that day.

Momma was a horrible driver, most of the time too busy singing and dancing to Motown tunes to pay attention to the road. She squinted to see signs. Even when her

30

glasses were in arm's reach, she wouldn't put them on, not in public. When I look back and think about it, anything that diminished her sex appeal scared her. Refused to wear her prescription glasses because she didn't like the way they made her look. The dents and dings in our old yellow and red Ford told the world to beware of her. She cut people off and blew her horn like a madwoman.

The rain. Sometimes driving in the rain paralyzes me.

Her windshield wipers were working overtime, losing a battle with Mother Nature.

I held on, my eyes on the rain, and asked, "We going home?"

"Let's see. Last week we went to Galveston. Hmmm. Can't let a little rain keep us locked up in the house. Beach ain't happening. Parks are out. Let's be adventurous. This week I think we'll take you to the Buffalo Soldiers Museum. Let's have fun and learn some history."

That was at least twenty miles away. That meant we were leaving the floods of Pasadena and driving toward the tall buildings, toward all the things a kid loved to see.

I asked, "We're getting on the highway?"

Momma mumbled, "Guess we'll take 45 North into town. It's prettier than that old 225."

"Where are the buffaloes?"

"Buffalo Soldiers, not buffaloes."

"Soldiers?"

"We're going to a museum."

"Like on a field trip?"

"Like on a field trip. Shouldn't be crowded on a day like today."

"What are we going to do after that?"

"There's a Family Dollar Store and a Walgreens right across the street from the museum so I can get some batteries for my . . . my toy. And we can look for some school clothes."

"We're going shopping?"

"Mr. Roy loaned me some money to buy you a few things."

Mr. Roy was the principal at Sam Houston High. Mr. Roy was married, had his own family out in League City, six kids, but came by every now and then, always late on a Friday night. The scent of marijuana and tequila would cover up the smell of her divorce and loneliness. My momma was a schoolteacher. Articulate with no Southern accent and the prettiest woman in the world. Slender, dark, wavy hair, green eyes, looked more like she was from

India than Memphis. Never wore a dress that came above her knees or a blouse with sleeves that stopped above her elbow. The most rebellious thing anybody ever saw her do was chain-smoke.

But that scent of marijuana, it still takes me back to Pasadena, back to my momma.

Momma was too beautiful for a place like Pasadena. Too free-spirited. She was meant to be in places like Berkeley or Harlem, someplace where she could rule women like her.

"Think I can go see my daddy for Christmas?"

She snapped, "I wish you'd stop asking me about that mother . . . Lord, hold my tongue."

That killed the singing, stopped the car-dancing. Daddy had ended the relationship, stolen her power when he did that. Women like my mother have to be the one to leave. I'd never see him again. My daddy was gone off to that distant land that daddies go to when they don't want to be a daddy anymore, a land with no phones, no pencil or paper to write letters, no stamps to mail them even if they did. A place where daddies no longer had to be daddies.

"You crying, Momma?"

"God, what has my life changed into?"

"Don't cry, Momma."

"He's gone . . . with that . . . and . . . and I'm buying . . . buying . . . goddamn toys . . . like I'm some sort of a . . . whore . . . shit . . . can't . . . fucking Roy . . . and Charles . . . lonely and . . . using damn toys."

Momma was human. Momma was a woman.

We were on 45, downtown Houston coming into view. Momma wiped her eyes, dropped her cigarette, swerved into the next lane, almost ran a family of Mexicans off the road, then adjusted and swerved to the right, almost hit another car, it too filled with Mexicans.

Momma cursed, so much panic in her voice.

Fear had stolen mine.

The rain. I remember the rain. Remember the day it became my enemy.

I remember hydroplaning, the back end of the car feeling like it was rising and floating, sliding across the interstate like we were on ice, Momma screaming for God to help her, fighting with the steering wheel, slamming on the brakes, then us spinning toward the wall.

five

The security system beeps, interrupting my thoughts. In a soft voice the system announces that the basement door is opening. Genevieve comes up the stairs wearing a black-and-white sweatsuit. When she left this morning she had on a fitted gray skirt, sleeveless pink shirt, black heels, and a low-rise pink thong with a red star on the front, the kind of thing a woman thinks is cute. Her legs are beautiful, flow into her waist. When she puts on a tight dress, with her frame, with her wonderful breasts, it overrules all learned behavior.

My lust for my wife cannot be intellectualized.

My lust for her is not reciprocated, not on the level it should be.

Still, one glance at her and my heart sings.

She has a gym bag over her shoulder, two smoothies, one in each hand, her cellular phone clamped on her hip, her earpiece flashing telling me that her cellular phone is on. Genevieve is chatting away, alternating between laughing and sounding businesslike and serious.

"You don't have any international investments." Genevieve is in the hallway. "Look at all the international products we use in this country. Your cell phone is Samsung. You shop at 7-Eleven and that's a Swiss-owned company. Right. Well, don't feel bad. Not a lot of people know that."

She tells her client the things she told me when we first met. I'm good at making money, not good at what to do with it after the check clears. She is the financial guru in this home.

"Yes, use non-U.S. stock as a diversifier. I'd add between ten and twenty percent international, whatever your comfort level is. Your portfolio is too moderate. Diversification is the key, but you have to have it put together . . . right . . . you're catching on. Performance is the key."

Her conversation, her astuteness, set fire to a man's loins. I am a man stimulated by intelligence, jazz, lattes, and warm conversations. But intellect is the key. Intelligence rises as beauty fades, time giving the former wings to soar while it whittles away at the latter.

Plato knew what he was talking about when he wrote *Symposium* because it's right along those lines, the dialogue showing Socrates' conviction that it is the things not seen which are eternal.

She drops her gym bag outside the bedroom door then leans in and smiles at me. My heart runs hot, has since the first time I saw her sitting across the table. I'm sitting on our bed, naked, white sheet up to my waist, my computer in my lap. I return her smile.

Her skin has a wonderful glow. She looks happy. This moment is beautiful.

I hate the news I have to give.

She whispers, "Brought you a present."

She sets the mango-and-pineapple smoothie on the nightstand, within my reach, takes the banana smoothie and sips her paradise. I snap my fingers to get her attention, then motion at the nightstand, at the note I have left for her, red ink on yellow legal paper.

It only says that her Grandpa Fred has called. When she is ready, the rest of the news will come from my mouth. Death is not to be written down. I have never heard of Grandpa Fred. I have never heard of Willie Esther. I don't know how important they can be if she has never mentioned them. But Grandpa Fred's phone call also told me that I am an unknown as well. If her family does not know about me, then maybe I should ask myself how important am I to Genevieve. What Grandpa Fred said about Genevieve keeping her own last name, it stings.

Still I don't want to be insensitive in this moment. I choose to follow her emotional lead.

Genevieve keeps talking on her cellular as she reads the message.

I watch her. I read the body language of the Taurean woman who never comes unglued.

Her expression changes. Her professional laughter dissipates, but not all at once. What she reads has the effect of a stun gun set on high.

"Your goal is . . . is . . . highest probable consistent rate of return. No guarantees, but . . . minimize risk. That's why you . . . you . . . you pick mutual funds that complement each other."

She rereads the name, stares at each of the words as if she wants them to change.

Her hair is short, wavy, salt-and-pepper with a distinguished and mature appeal. It has more pepper than salt, but the salt will overtake the pepper in the years to come.

Soft breasts that fill out a C-cup. Skin the color of natural honey. Round face with a pointy chin. Dimples live in her soft cheeks, the kind of dimples that make her harshest face seem a little bit pleasant.

She tells her client, "I. Have. To. Go."

She clicks off the phone, stares at me. Wordless.

Genevieve is seldom wordless.

I tell her what she has already read. "A man who said he was Grandpa Fred called you."

She continues to stare, her mouth barely moving. "You . . . you actually talked to him?"

"Yeah."

I put my laptop to the side, swing my body around, put my bare feet on the wooden floor.

She asks, "What, they called to ask for money?"

"He said your grandmother died. Your mother's mother. Willie Esther."

"Willie Esther."

"Yes. I'm sorry."

"When?"

"Today."

She puts her hand over her stomach as if her pain's center is there, then goes blank.

I say, "Genevieve?"

She remains unfocused, eyes flicker, like her thoughts are white noise.

I ask, "Are you having another attack? Genevieve?"

I'm tentative, standing up now, still waiting to see how she will respond, if tears will come, if her knees will buckle, if she will fall into hysterics. I don't know how she embraces death.

Genevieve turns and walks down the hallway. Steps slow and heavy. The sensor beeps three times, then the audio part of the house alarm announces that the door to the patio is open.

I pull on my jeans, walk to the end of the hall, look out the window. The darkness gives me back my own image. Genevieve tells me I'm like the boy next door. That my thin frame makes me more like Jimmy Stewart than Denzel Washington. If that comparison is true, then her being an enigma, her ability to become icy, that makes her more Kim Novak than Sanaa Lathan. Both of us have cute, trustworthy, collegiate features. I run my hand down my narrow face until my fingers get to my goatee. I stare at myself. Don't see that commonplace image in my own rugged reflection. We never see ourselves with the eyes of others.

Genevieve stands at the edge of the pool. Herbal smoke pluming from her head. She has gone into her stash and is indulging in the burning of a bush, its scent spreading, dissipating in the urban air. She inhales hard and strong, its fire lighting up her face, exhales and her stress smokes away from her body. Then the fire goes away. She stands, unmoving. In the midst of the queen palm trees, twenty-foot-high bamboo trees, looks like she's in the background of a painting, a svelte and luminal figure lingering in the murky half-light, her head down, staring at the water, arms folded beneath her breasts, treading in her own thoughts. She starts to rock and continues to rock. Disturbed. No more bush to burn. She takes off her clothes and waits naked at the edge of the pool. She takes a step, goes into the deep end feet first, hardly a splash.

A minute goes by.

I stand there, worry speeding up my heartbeat and stuttering my breath, and watch eight feet of water swallow her the way that mythical whale ingested Jonah.

Another minute goes by. Then another.

She is the master swimmer, the one the local children call Teacher Genevieve, or Coach, or Miss Forbes, or Doctor Forbes, the kind woman who teaches well-behaved neighborhood kids how to swim on Saturday mornings during the summer months. I have a swimmer's build, but my leanness is more hereditary and aesthetic than functional. Next to her, I'm a rock in the water.

There is no movement. No air bubbles. No signs of life.

Panic increases my heart rate tenfold.

I'm about to run out, dive in, and do my best, CPR thoughts and 911 calls and the image of an EMT rushing into my world are running through my brain, but she comes up and breaks the surface, her breathing easy, as if she were sitting on the bottom of the pool, relaxing in an easy chair, contemplating. I back away before she looks up and sees the panic in my face. She can stay underwater four minutes, but that seems like forever, especially to an asthmatic like me.

She swims several laps, moves with the ease of a Chinese water dragon.

She comes back in the house naked, drenched, walks the dim hallway, leaves puddles on the marble floor. Her salt-and-pepper hair is wavy, dripping water down over her breasts. Her nipples are erect and beautiful, dark as raisins and hard due to the chill of the night. Her breasts look heavy, full. She has no pubic hair covering her Mound of Venus. Her legs are shaven. Her feet are small, beautiful, the kind of toes that make a man's mouth water. A clean woman. I see the positive effects that both years of swimming and months of Pilates have had on her body.

Seduction has been on my mind all afternoon. Stereophonic kisses, talking kisses, butterfly kisses, none of that will happen tonight. My intentions now insignificant.

I say, "Genevieve?"

"This will cost a lot. A last-minute airline ticket, even with bereavement discount. I'll have to rearrange . . . I'll have to rearrange . . . my schedule for the next few days . . ." Lines overtake her forehead. She sighs, shakes her head, then nods. "I have to go back to Alabama."

"I'm going with you."

"You don't have to."

"I want to."

"What about your work? You're supposed to go to Boston with the research team."

She stops and stares at me, water dripping from her body like tears.

Her body cries, but her eyes are dry,

43

high noon in the Mojave.

Her mouth opens in protest, then it closes, knowing that this is not negotiable.

Part of me is angry, part of me disappointed at the way she does not include me.

In a voice that reminds her who the man in this house is, I tell her, "I'm going with you."

The dimples in her face vanish, her round face loses its innocence, she lowers her chin. She swallows. *Tsks.* Shakes her head. Her mouth opens. Her eyes darken with wickedness.

White teeth vanish when she closes her mouth. Underneath her dark eyes, she smiles.

She nods, either accepting death or the fact that I'm going with her. She runs her hand over her damp hair as she heads down the hallway, her feet sticking to the floor with each step, a slow and uneven gait that makes her modest ass shift in an almost seductive rhythm, water still dripping from her frame as if tears were running out of her pores.

She whispers, "The bitch finally died."

six

Genevieve packs for both of us, only carry-on luggage, always efficient.

The reservations were made over the Internet, as were the flight plans, as are most of the things that we do. Point and click. That's the world we live in. No human interaction. Point and click. Dinner reservations. Point and click. Theater tickets. Point and click. Single and looking for love. Point and click. Unhappily married and need a new love. Point and click.

I wear baggy jeans, my silver Rolex, a dark blue T-shirt I bought at Heathrow on our last trip to London. *Mind the gap.* Dark brown sandals. Baseball cap.

Genevieve wears Army-green pants, linen-like, a top that has forest greens and blues, blue bra, black thong, bracelets and matching ring, diamond earrings. Her lips are glossy, deep plum with hints of gold, lots of dazzle. Ginger body soufflé on her

45

skin, gold body dust.

She sparkles and glows.

Margaret Richburg picks us up. Our usual driver, Earl, doesn't work for Wolf Classic Limousine anymore. He was an ex-con. I liked him. Genevieve didn't care for him.

On the ride to LAX, my wife is restless. I'm on my cellular calling the L.A. County district attorney, letting him know that we won't be able to come to Lucy Florence for the monthly Urban Policy Roundtable. I tell him that there is a death in Genevieve's family and I regret that we won't be able to listen to a renowned Harvard Law professor discuss today's reparation movement.

When I get off the phone, Genevieve stops rocking and humming along with the Jill Scott CD, music she gave the driver to play on our short ride to LAX, stops and looks at me, nervous.

I ask, "Where are we staying?"

"Tutwiler. It's a historic hotel."

At the gate she falls quiet, checks her watch a thousand times, her mind spinning, still on all the tasks she has to leave behind, on how this inconvenience disrupts her well-planned life.

I ask, "The hotel is in Odenville?"

Genevieve says, "Downtown Birmingham."

"Odenville. Sounds like Hooterville."

I laugh. She doesn't.

I ask, "Where is the Vulcan?"

"You're going to the Mecca of the civil
rights movement and you want to see
Vulcan?"

Birmingham is a steel town and they
erected a statue to Vulcan, who in Roman
mythology is the manufacturer of iron and
armor for the gods.

I ask, "Did you know the family of the
three little girls who were killed in the
bombing?"

"Four little girls."

"How far is Selma, Alabama, from where
we're staying?"

She shifts.

I ask, "And will we be far from the Civil
Rights Museum?"

Genevieve snaps, "This isn't a damn vacation. It's a funeral."

Her stiff tone makes me feel guilty,
makes me remind myself that this isn't a
holiday, this is about more important
things, have to suppress the love of art and
history inside me.

On the plane we barely find room for
our carry-on. We're on Southwest. The

Greyhound bus of the sky. We stand in corrals and are herded on the flight, moving like cattle, hoping that two seats will be available. We shuffle down the aisle, luck up and find an empty row toward the rear of the plane, that section that usually survives in a crash. I become a sardine in a can.

Genevieve says, "It's been a while since I haven't flown first-class."

"I know. This is horrible."

"Sorry. It was either this or a flight with a five-hour layover."

Time and darkness and mild turbulence go by with me reading the *L.A. Times*.

I point at an article. "You know about Deleon Richards?"

"Gospel singer."

"Married to Gary Sheffield. New York Yankees."

Genevieve reads the article. Blackmail. Sexual videotapes of Deleon and R. Kelly.

When she is done, Genevieve shakes her head and says, "That's horrible."

I ask, "Think Sheffield knew before they were married?"

She pauses, swallows. "What if that was me, would you hold my hand and stand by me the way Sheffield says he is going to

48

stand by Deleon? Is your love that unconditional?"

"It's not you."

Her voice is soft, distant. "We all have
things in our past."

I look at my wife and she looks away.

The flight attendant finally makes it to
our row. Genevieve asks for two glasses
of Pinot Grigio, which they don't have.
She settles on Sauvignon Blanc. Both
glasses of wine, plastic cups actually, for
herself. She finishes those, goes to the
bathroom, and comes back with her
third glass. She rings the call button and
when the flight attendant brings her
glass number four, I take it from her the
way a parent takes candy from a child.
She doesn't protest. I've never seen her
take in more than two glasses of wine.
She's fidgety, adjusting clothes, going
from looking at magazines to filing her
nails. She wants to swim her worries
away. She wants to self-medicate.

I sip the wine and pull out a book. *In the
Cut* by Susanna Moore. The story starts on
page three and when I get to page nine,
start reading about the main character in a
place where she can see a red-haired
woman giving a shadowed man a blow job,
the description arouses me.

Genevieve interrupts me. "What else did Grandpa Fred say?"

I blink out of that world, put the book down. "What you mean?"

"When he called, what did you talk about?"

"Nothing. He said Willie Esther was dead and coughed a lot. He's a sick man."

She lets her seat back. "He's been sick for a long time."

She is nervous. When anxiety runs through her blood, she complains, anger rises for no reason, and she vents. Maybe she really isn't complaining, maybe that is only my perspective.

Still I look in her eyes and I see the little girl inside the woman. She is five years older than I, and sometimes I imagine her with crooked teeth and in pigtails and hot-combed hair and skinny legs decorated with dark spots that come from being bit by a thousand mosquitoes.

With every passing mile, every fleeting minute, I see her fear blooming. I try to think of something to talk about, some-thing to distract her. Going to Alabama is all that is on my mind.

I ask, "You okay?"

"Head hurts."

"Three glasses of wine. Not one cup of

water. You're dehydrated."

"No."

"You're going to be constipated."

She tells me, "Side effects from being on the patch."

I say, "Might be time for us to start a family."

She does not respond.

That is one of our pink elephants. Children. To have or not to have. Before our marriage becomes vapid, evolves into a white elephant, something of little or no value.

We're both restless, marinating in our own fears and desires.

I want a family. Need that stability or I will crumble.

I want to know about the mystery of her family, the family I inherited when we stood in front of a preacher in Vegas, the family that became mine as I slid that ring on her finger.

I want to ask about Willie Esther and Grandpa Fred, but part of me is waiting for her to mention her family. We talk about the news, about Major Jim Hahn having an uphill election with former LAPD chief Bernard Parks and Councilman Antonio Villaraigosa in the mayoral race. A white, a black, and a Latino elec-

51

tion will polarize the city, all of them looking for African-American support. Blacks want a black mayor but are more comfortable with the Spanish politician.

Genevieve says, "Parks only has a hundred-thousand-dollar war chest. You can't run for mayor with a hundred thousand dollars. Plus Villaraigosa has personality, is more exciting."

"Hahn?"

"Oh, please. White. Deceptive. He lied. The fifty-five blocks that make up Skid Row have been neglected. The black community has been neglected. There are areas in Latino communities that have never been touched by urban planning. Hahn is a done Tom Turkey."

She's a good communicator. She knows how to receive, not just transmit, the downfall of many women I dated before I met her. Genevieve listens when I talk, then I listen as she talks, the art of conversation. Not a woman who babbles incessantly about things that do not matter.

The flight attendant passes by, bumps into my leg, apologizes with a glance, keeps going. She has erotic curves that sing, a smile that reminds me of that beautiful woman on KTLA morning news, Michaela Pereira, golden skin and long curly hair in a chic ponytail.

I watch her, fascinated.

The flight attendant has a high waist with nice legs. Her walk has an exotic sway and she has subtle feminine gestures that arouse my interest, that make me watch her. And her lips are full, so beautiful. She yawns, her mouth wide, her eyes tight, as if she were willing to give and receive. In that instant I imagine her in the shadows, on her knees, taking my penis in her mouth, taking me deep into the back of her throat, looking down on her lips as she strokes me while she licks and sucks my shaft, pleasing me to the point of orgasm, then when my legs start to stiffen, when my eyes tighten and breathing shortens and my moans rise, as I'm about to come she backs away, drives me insane, sucks my balls, knows the wonders of anatomy and sexuality.

"Baby?"

I shift and look at my wife. "Yes?"

"Let me see part of your newspaper again."

Genevieve eyes the flight attendant a moment, takes in her attributes, sees no threat. My wife cuts her eyes at me and yawns, starts talking about the front-page dramas.

We talk about Scott Peterson and his

guilty verdict. His death sentence, well deserved.

Genevieve says, "It's eerie how that Peterson thing reminded me of *A Place in the Sun*."

"Is that a play?"

"No, an old movie. Shelley Winters was pregnant by Montgomery Clift. But he wanted Elizabeth Taylor. Montgomery Clift took Shelley Winters out on a boat and had planned on drowning her. He wanted to kill her because she was pregnant and he had met someone else."

I turn to sports and end up talking about Kobe Bryant's case.

She says, "I still can't believe your fallen hero."

"Because there was no crime. Laws of morality were broken, but no criminal act. Denver police ran in with smoking guns before a crime was established. Kobe hadn't committed a crime."

In her world, he who holds the dick is the bastard villain.

In mine, never trust the bearer of the clit.

Both of us want the final word, both of us want to win a winless battle.

My wife frowns. "You're incredible. Guess you're just happy Kobe can go back to the Lakers. Would hate for him to mess up the Lakers' chance at a championship ring, right?"

"Anyway. The whore went to a married man's room to engage in congress. Kobe's only crime, adultery withstanding, was not having an attorney present with a contract for her to sign."

"Why do you have to call her a whore?"

"She had DNA in her underwear from three different men. That's what she was."

She shifts, ignores how I tried to lighten a serious situation with a slice of my humor. I'm no Dave Chappelle, can barely tell a joke-book joke in a way that will get a chuckle.

I ask, "What about her accountability?"

"I'm done with it."

"I'm not through talking."

"This conversation was over five minutes ago."

Her voice is intense enough to tell me that, no matter how Mars sees the fiasco, Venus is riled, to back off before the gods declare war. Her words have the power of lightning, punctuate our conversation, then with a thunderous move she stuffs her magazine into the back of the seat, gets up, and walks the aisle, resisting the desire to storm the aisle in high dudgeon, walks to the front of the plane then comes back, goes into the bathroom with her arms folded.

I watch her. She knows I'm watching her. Her eyes never come to mine.

Minutes go by. This silence, this burning hush being the hallmark of our rising tension.

She goes to the flight attendant, says a few words, then has a nice laugh with her, and comes back with two small bottled waters, hands one to me, her peace offering.

We're back to where we were. Back to pretending nothing is wrong.

She lets up the armrest, puts on her headset, listens to her Angie Stone CD while reading an Andrew Klavan novel. *Man and Wife.* She doesn't read books sold by Black Expressions, nor does she do Chick Lit. She listens to R&B, only the singers who aren't accompanied by rappers. When it comes to books, her literature-shopping list is published in the *New York Times,* and she will only read the top five, the Harry Potter series included. But no Chick Lit. Too contrived.

I fire up my laptop, pop in a DVD, *Chappelle's Show,* first season.

She looks at my screen, sees Chappelle in beaded braids, smoking a joint, licking the side of a white woman's face, and Genevieve *tsks*, a brusque sound that tells me what she sees is offensive. I ignore her, laugh, watch Dave Chappelle and Charlie Murphy satire Rick James.

Genevieve runs her hand over her salt-and-pepper mane, its curls so sweet and sensual, leans against me, her head on my shoulder. Her hair smells fresh. I'm aroused by her touch.

Arousal. The weakness of man. So easily achieved by the stimulation of the senses, sight being the most prevalent. One glance and a chemical reaction makes us rise.

I whisper, "That headache you have . . ."

"Stress."

"It's a scientific fact that an orgasm can alleviate that."

"Pervert."

"When I'm eating your pussy you don't think so."

"Hate it when you talk like that."

"I want to fuck you until fucking goes out of style."

"Stop talking like that."

"You don't like the way I fuck you?"

"Don't talk to me like I'm a slut. I'm not a whore."

"When I take you from the back and you can hear my balls slapping against your ass?"

She stares me down. Defiant, I lick my lips like I have her ass in my hands and I'm feasting on her clitoris, or like I'm on my back with her kneeling over my face, my tongue moving in and out of her vagina, tracing the edges of her goodness. My wife frowns, but her eyes tighten.

Talking dirty makes her uneasy, but I want to believe it excites her at the same time. There are a lot of things I want to believe that at the end of the day I know will never be true.

She says, "People see you as the epitome of an urbane gentleman: meticulously groomed, faultlessly polite, always poised and gracious in every situation."

"How do you see me?"

"As my husband. The king. The nabob of this marriage."

I back down, modify the language of Mars to fit the need of Venus.

I say, "Do you think we have enough intimacy in our marriage?"

She shifts, her stern expression telling me to cease and desist.

I wait.

"I think we make love enough." There is a decent pause, she purses her lips, shifts, opens and closes her novel. "Considering our schedules, how long our days are, yes.

So far as other married couples, we're on track."

My truth is restless as I wait for her to ask me for my opinion. I want to tell her that we do not, that I want to make love to her until my lingam is tender and my tongue is swollen, until we collapse into each other's arms and slip into a coma, warriors at the end of a wonderful and erotic battle, one that leaves bites and scratches, but no losers. Then wake, eat, and battle again.

And that the intimacy I seek goes beyond the bedroom. Yes I desire that. I am built that way. But I also need a deeper connection, the kind that comes from wanting to know about her. That is why I am on this plane. That is why I'm going to meet her past.

She goes back to Andrew Klavan.

Genevieve asks, "Would you make love to the flight attendant?"

"I don't love her."

"Would you engage in congress with her?"

I answer, "Only if we did it together."

"You keep staring at her. Maybe I'll just go up and ask her for her damn number. She could be your whore. Would you like that? If I went out and brought us back a whore?"

"I wasn't staring at her."

"You were transfixed. Licked your lips and made that sound."

I ask, "What sound?"

"That sound you make."

"She has nice breasts."

She asks, "Nicer than mine?"

"Nobody has breasts nicer than yours."

"You like mine?"

"Love yours." I nod. "Go ahead. Get her number. It would be fun."

She *tsks* and frowns. "Sometimes I look at you and I just want to scream."

"Feeling's mutual."

She shifts, her lips tight and defensive. "Could you handle me being with a man and a woman at the same time?"

I ask, "Have you ever been with a woman?"

"You've asked me that before."

"You never answered."

She asks, "Have you ever been with a man?"

"Hell no."

"Did that upset you?"

I say, "I'm not upset."

She chuckles, shakes her head. "This is so fascinating to me."

I ask, "What is?"

"How it's so easy for men to dialogue about girl-on-girl sex. Amazing how it's become this sexual ideal. Almost another rite of passage. Yet men — straight men — always blow their stack if women press them to imagine which men they could picture themselves with."

I laugh.

She doesn't.

She asks, "Is that what your Ecuadorian *whore* was into? Group sex?"

"Don't go there, Genevieve. All I'm saying is that it's normal."

"Normal? Since when?"

"Women — professional women — have those kind of fantasies."

"Well, all I know is I've never heard a guy go 'I'd love to get head from Boris Kodjoe.'"

I tell her, "I don't appreciate that image."

"I don't hear men saying they'd want to experience Enrique Iglesias because he's *exotic*."

"You're upset."

She makes another disgusted sound. "You're sickening. Sometimes I hate that I married you. Of all the men I met that night, you were the one I dated and fell in love with. I hate that."

61

That stops me. I look in her eyes to see if that is her truth.

She says, "How would you feel if I insisted that you fuck one of my male friends?"

"This conversation is over."

"Or if I kept suggesting that we went someplace and found a man?"

"I've never suggested that."

"What if I insisted you let him shove it up your butt because that was my fantasy?"

"I'd say you were insane."

"What if I just used my vibrator? You're always trying to coax me into doing anal, maybe we could trade sodomy for sodomy. Fair exchange is no robbery."

My hands open and close, then I rub away the tension that is building in my eyes.

She says, "Oh, now you don't have anything to say."

I push her too far and she attacks me. She attacks me and the part of me that is ruled by Cancer knots up, withdraws, starts moving side to side and fleeing like a true crab.

She is a true Taurus woman. No games. No fantasies. No false modesty.

I am a Cancer. Born to be an emotional

and hopeless romantic fool.

I get up and walk away, pace the plane, anger cruising my veins like an open freeway.

I don't pace for long. Can't because we hit turbulence and the seat-belt sign comes on.

I have to hold on to seat after seat as I go back.

Genevieve has the face of a scared little girl, her knuckles turning white.

As soon as I sit, I take her sweaty hand. She shivers.

The plane dips and rocks. People are troubled. Silence means horror. Genevieve holds my hand, her grip as strong as her fear of dying like this.

We cling to each other. It doesn't show, but I am afraid and powerless too.

When the turbulence wanes, she takes a deep breath.

I wipe my damp palms on my pants.

I loosen my grip. She keeps her hand on mine.

Genevieve says, "I'm sorry. What I said, I'm sorry."

No response from me.

She shifts awhile before she whispers, "Angelina Jolie or Salma Hayek. It would have to be one of them. She'd have to be exotic. Not Penélope Cruz. Too skinny. Not a black woman."

At times Genevieve becomes someone else, a person both electrifying and terrifying.

I ask, "Genevieve?"

"Yes?"

"Who are you?"

"I'm your wife."

She goes back to Andrew Klavan. I go back to Dave Chappelle.

We touch each other but at the same time we fall into our separate worlds.

seven

Almost three years ago. When I started dating Doctor Genevieve Forbes.

Before I knew that she used to be someone else. Before I knew about the attacks.

I was planning to go see the Fresno State Bulldogs battle the Grand Canyon Antelopes on the basketball courts. Genevieve had never been to Fresno. I doubt if Fresno was on her list of top one thousand cities to visit. I asked her if she wanted to ride with me. She said yes. I drove her three hours north to see Fresno and its entire nothing. Drove her places she had never been, beyond the tumbleweeds in Bakersfield and the raisins in Selma.

There is a Selma in California, just as there is one in Alabama. Ours with the present of brown-skinned men picking raisins. Theirs with the history of dark-skinned men picking cotton.

I was nervous. I was in my car with Doctor Genevieve Forbes. A woman who had let places like Paris and Jamaica become her playground. And Fresno wasn't a real city, just a small town.

She said, "I grew up in a small town."

I said, "People joke that if you take away Cal State Fresno, Fresno is Bakersfield North."

She laughed at my lame attempt at humor. She always did. Always so kind and sparing of my feelings. The roads leading to my old town were agricultural, cows and horses, cotton fields and strawberry patches, trailer homes and dilapidated structures with clotheslines in the backyard. Turn on the radio and clear reception came from either country music or gospel. Integration was legal but segregation was practiced. Whites lived in the northern part of the town, blacks huddled in the west, Mexicans on the east side, and the Asians were in the south.

Genevieve said, "What you do is impressive. Not a lot of black people go into research."

"I could have gone to medical school, but I was burned out, it was expensive, and I could make the same amount of money in pharmaceutical and drug discoveries, if not more."

"I heard that."

"So here I am. It's always good to start in academia and then go private."

She asked, "What have you been up to at work?"

"Things are pretty cool. I'm working on getting a two-point-five-million-dollar AIDS training grant and they're trying to kill me. Hard work, but we're doing some excellent research. I've been busy proof-reading the application. I have a lab assistant testing a drug we've developed. If the test comes back okay, we will inject the drug into the infected mouse and wait for the results. You have to come down and tour our laboratory sometime."

She shook her head. "I have a disdain for needles."

"So do the mice."

We both laughed. I realized I was being long-winded. Being with her did that to me.

I told her, "This is different. Very nice."

"How so?"

"Usually when I start talking about my job, when I mention neurodegenerative diseases and genetics, women look at me like I'm talking in Spanish mixed with Swahili."

She laughed again. "Since you brought it up, do you date a lot?"

"Nah. Not at all. That's the only setback in research; you never have time to do anything but study and work. Sometimes I feel like I want to quit and get a regular job. I need a life."

"You're doing something important. I admire that. You have ambitions."

"Thanks."

"You'll be famous one day."

"Afraid not. We develop the drugs but don't get any credit."

"Really?"

"It all goes to the principal investigator of our lab."

"No credit whatsoever?"

"None. We have to sign a statement stating that anything we develop in the lab, they get all royalties. So if I find a cure for AIDS, I'll be assed out. Unless I develop it in my garage."

"That's pretty crazy." She shook her head in disbelief. "But it's still important."

I nodded and sighed. "That's the only thing that keeps me there."

"Too many black women are dying. It's disturbing. Has to feel good knowing that you are trying to develop a drug that could cure a lot of sick people. It requires total dedication. I understand that. You must have a goal in life. We all should have goals. Or we are lost."

I nodded. "My goals have taken me a long way from Fresno."

We were on highway 99, Fresno County, coming up on Selma, *The Raisin Capital of the World*. A barren town. Two-star hotels at best. Genevieve stared around at all the nothingness.

Genevieve asked, "You said your grandfather was a truck driver?"

"Sure was. Drove an eighteen-wheeler cross-country."

"And your grandmother?"

"Worked at hotels. Food service. And when she had a day off she spent most of her time out at Table Mountain Casino or Chukchansi gambling away my college tuition."

"Gambling?"

"On sacred Indian grounds. She'd run three slot machines at the same time."

"Good Lord. That could be a problem."

"It was. Grandparents always fought tooth-and-nail about the finances."

"Physical fights?"

"Time to time. Mostly screaming. They slept in separate bedrooms. Doors locked."

"So you were alone a lot."

"Pretty much. Nobody cared if I was there or not."

She chuckled. "That's how you and your Ecuadorian lover were able to hook up."

"I was a latchkey kid. Grew up over by the intersection of Fresno Street and California Boulevard, not too far from Maxey Park, over where the homeless and transients congregate on that strip of grass they call a recreational area and play dominoes all day. Surprised I didn't end up in a gang. Or dead."

She whispered, "Or in jail."

"I was one of the fortunate ones."

I wanted to ask her what it was like having a mother and a father. Every parental figure in my world was dead or missing in action. I didn't want to resurrect ghosts. Just remembered my own mother. Us in Texas. Riding through Third Ward, Fifth Ward, Acre Homes, riding with the radio up loud and the windows down low. Eating catfish and spaghetti in the summertime.

We checked into the Radisson, next to the Fresno Convention Center, the only hotel in the area that had more than a three-star rating. A woman like Genevieve, you couldn't take her to a three-star hotel. The way she took slow steps into the room let me know that our room was borderline. She went to the bed, pulled back the sheets, inspected, didn't like what she saw, called housekeeping and requested they change the sheets and clean the room again.

She was critical, inspecting the bathrooms, commenting on the smallness of the tub, the furniture in the sitting area, vented that she could hear people in the next room or above us taking a shower, pretty much disliked everything, ranted, "And these sheets are thin. Would think they would have better quality sheets at a four-star hotel. Especially in the executive suite."

The way she called downstairs and complained I found it hard to believe that she was a Southern-born woman who grew up on biscuits and molasses and ate buttermilk and corn bread.

That turned me on. How she refused to settle for less than the best.

That unsettling wench was here with me. That said a lot about how she felt about me.

From our eighth-floor window in the executive suite, our views were second-rate clothing stores, traffic on 41, and on the other side of Selland Arena were railroad tracks. Over on Tulare Street, Amtrak's screaming whistle woke up this cow town at sunrise every morning. Trains were symbolic. Their cries and rattles let you know that you were in the ghetto. Every day six trains came through here. Six chances a day to leave the Central Valley and see the world.

No trains ran through Beverly Hills. No Greyhound stations on Rodeo Drive.

I looked at the disheartening view and told Genevieve, "This is what I left behind."

"Bet I would've liked this better than Odenville. Odenville only had six hundred people."

"Six hundred?"

"Twenty years ago. When I . . . when I left. Six hundred people. If that many."

"Don't fool yourself. I grew up in Fresno and I've yet to meet anyone from Fresno who does not hate Fresno. Did you know how low Fresno is on the terrorism totem pole? How irrelevant does a city have to be to get its antiterrorism funding revoked? Bin Laden is not interested. This cow patch is a bus stop."

"Odenville is a truck stop. You put your thumb out and catch the first thing going."

I took her to River Park, up 41 to the

north side of town. An area that had nice streets and restaurants, no parks with transients, no homeless congregated over a domino game.

I wore jeans, black shirt, black leather jacket, black shoes.

Genevieve wore a gray pin-striped button-down shirt. Long black skirt. Crystal necklace. Small stud earrings. Everything about her was always so balanced. Red lips that broke up her dark colors. Michael Kors perfume. Silver rings and bracelet. The way she wore her hair, short and wavy with her gray unhidden, she was classic. I looked at her and wondered how could a woman that smart, that beautiful, that classy be single. How could she be here with me?

We went to the Elephant Bar. We sat on opposite sides of the booth facing palm trees.

Our tones were still tight back then, almost formal, guards still up.

But alcohol loosened the tongue and diminished inhibitions.

Somewhere along the line, between drinks and Thai dishes and jambalaya, she stopped smiling and fell silent. My nervousness made me ramble, made me talk about people and relationships, about the three-minute dating environment that had landed us where we were.

I said, "We meet each other and we are mysteries. We see what we want to see. We idealize each other with our own fantasies. When we meet, at first we are blank slates, we have no knowledge of each other. We're virgins in each other's eyes. We're perfect. Perfect because you choose the colors you desire and paint the picture you want to see."

She winked. "I think when people know too much it taints the relationship."

"Knowledge enlightens."

"And ignorance is bliss."

"Promoting ignorance." I chuckled. "That's strange coming from a woman with a PhD."

"When a man knows too much about a woman, he holds it against her."

"Is that right?"

"Of course. And women are taught to accept men 'as is.'"

"As is. You're saying that we're damaged goods."

"One could argue that we are all, in some ways, damaged goods."

I nodded. "But you think that ignorance, in that sense, will manifest bliss?"

"This is personal. Truth be told, I'd

rather you remained a virgin in my eyes."

"I've already told you a few things about me."

She nodded. "Amazing how . . . that you lost your virginity at thirteen."

"How did we get on that conversation?"

"I have no idea. Oh, think I mentioned that I went to Brazil and wanted to visit Ecuador."

"Right, right."

"And you took that as an opportunity to tell me about your Ecuadorian friend."

"Amongst other things."

She smiled but her words didn't. "And, to be quite honest, it was disturbing."

"Disturbing? So, I've said or done something that turned you off?"

"Maybe we shouldn't talk about our old relationships."

"Four weeks, Genevieve. You never talk about anyone you've dated."

"Why should I relive my past?"

"It's conversation. It's what people do."

She ran her hand over her hair. "That conversation would serve no purpose."

"I'm curious. Tell me about someone."

She laughed. "Wouldn't you rather see me as a virgin?"

"Are you? Over thirty-five and still a virgin? In Los Angeles?"

"As far as you know, I am."

"I doubt you are."

She ate, sipped. "Besides, when I'm done with something, I'm done. I don't look back."

I said, "So you rebalance your portfolio and move on?"

That made her laugh. "Exactly."

"Who was the last man you dated before you met me?"

She raised a brow. "Why do men always need to know about ex-boyfriends?"

"Because we are curious."

She chuckled. "Because you are insecure. Because you are little boys. Because everything remains a competition, even if the former lover remains unseen and unheard."

"Because we're not afraid to take the red pill."

"Be careful what you ask for. Once you take the red pill, there is no going back."

I told her, "I'll tell you about mine, if you ask."

"I don't ask because it doesn't interest me. I'm more interested in moving forward."

"Are you afraid I'll ask you the same?"

"It wouldn't matter. Asking does not generate an answer. Your curiosity is just that, your curiosity." She sipped her wine. "Besides, and I repeat, when people know too much it taints. Some of the things you told me, like I said, they can be disturbing."

"What have I said that's disturbing?"

She hesitated. "Allow me to see you as a virgin as long as I can. And don't expect me to destroy my chaste image too soon. Let's enjoy the effects of the blue pill while we can."

I shook my head and smiled. "You're a mystery."

"You're kind of pushy, you know that?"

"Am I pushy or are you evasive?"

"You are indeed pushy."

"That offends you?"

"I'm not sure."

"Then I apologize for asking about your former lovers."

She shook her head. "FYI. I don't need to know anything like that."

"Is it because it makes me less than ideal or because you don't want to share any of your past with me? We've been talking almost every day for three weeks."

"Four weeks."

"Exactly. How long will you keep me behind this glass wall?"

"Glass wall?"

"You have a glass wall up. I can see you. But I can only get so close."

She pulled back. "Like you said, it's only been three weeks."

"Four weeks."

She laughed. "Are you trying to get close?"

"Am I allowed to?"

"Neither of us can walk on water. Let's leave it at that."

I sighed.

She said, "Frustrated?"

I shrugged, asked her, "So, Doc, a month later, what do you want to know, if anything?"

"Don't call me Doc, please."

"Didn't mean to offend you."

"No, I mean . . . don't make it impersonal between us. That sounds too professional."

"So, Genevieve, what do you want to know, if anything?"

"Knowledge is our salvation, but it can also be our enemy."

"WYSIWYG. What you see is what you get." I motioned at Fresno as if to say this town, everything it gave or took away, it was part of me. "If I take away any of my experiences, no matter how you see them, then I would not be who I am now. I

78

would not have met you."

She pulled her lips in and looked at me as if I were still a child, as if I had a soupçon of edification but there was something indispensable I had missed in life. She told me, "I wish I could touch you and make all the bad things go away. And I wish you could do the same for me."

"What bad things, Genevieve?"

She looked out the window, her eyes toward highway 41, not blinking, her mind deep in thought. Then she blinked rapidly, came back from wherever she had gone, and smiled.

She asked, "Do you outsource your affection?"

"Outsourcing affection? What does that mean?"

"Do you cheat?"

"Where did that come from?"

"If we were to take this relationship to the next level, should I expect you to be unfaithful?"

I asked, "Will you please me?"

"Don't answer a question with a question."

"Of course I'm going to say no."

"You're right. I phrased that incorrectly. Have you ever outsourced?"

I said, "Thought you didn't want to know anything."

"A woman's prerogative is to change her mind."

"Sounds like you have your own insecurities."

She stared out the window again, went off to some faraway place.

I asked, "What's on your mind?"

Genevieve asked me, "What are you looking for?"

"What do you mean?"

She asked, "Are you attracted to me?"

"Of course."

"You don't act like it."

What I knew about Genevieve then: she held a PhD in business administration, concentration in organizational behavior. Taught at UCLA. Was well respected. Dream was to be the president of a university. And have a financial planning business on the side. Ambitious and well put together. Did consulting for major companies on the side, volunteered with small black-owned businesses, rendered her services pro bono to some of the community, those who didn't waste her time, and helped them train to be successful, also went to major companies and helped train them for success. Loved swimming. If she could, she'd swim a zillion laps every morning. And loved to teach young children how to swim, loved to give them structure and discipline, loved to nurture their minds with positive things and goals while they were young.

She was beautiful. Simply beautiful.

I confessed, "I'm a little . . . maybe a little . . . actually a lot intimidated by you."

"Intimidated?" She laughed a little. "You have to be joking. You're so damn smart."

"Not like you. You know all about qualified and nonqualified assets, macroeconomics. It blows me away how you talk about how the economy performs in geopolitical situations."

"Oh, my God." Then she looked embarrassed. "I bet I sound like an idiot."

"No, I like it. Really, I love listening and learning."

"I talk about that crap because I get shy and nervous around you. So I babble about what I know. Keep thinking that everything I say sounds really, really stupid."

We paused.

She said, "So you can't be intimidated by me and have me feeling shy all at once."

We laughed together, soft and easy.

I sipped my wine. "Good point. We have

to get by this awkwardness."

"And trepidation."

I nodded.

She said, "I like straight up honesty. I'm typically a black-and-white person. I'm working on developing my gray area. But for the most part with me it's yes or no, right or wrong, good or bad. This dating thing is hard for me because I'm not good at beating around the bush. I can be vague when I'm not sure of my footing, however. But once I'm grounded, it's all good."

"Okay."

"At the risk of getting my feelings hurt, do you . . . God this is so damn high school."

"What is? Just ask."

She took a sharp breath. "Do you like me?"

"Yes, I like you."

"In what way?"

"On many levels, and I do want to sleep with you. Have since I laid eyes on you. Now, here is the problem I have, as a man. Well, here's the problem with a woman like you."

"A woman like me?"

"Not like you, with you. With a woman that I'm totally infatuated with."

"I don't know if I should blush or leave before my feelings get devastated."

I told her, "If I give in to my attraction, that primal and physical part of me that yearns to touch you in so many ways and go for sex, I risk your getting turned off, possibly getting mad and starting to pull away because then you think I'm objectifying you and ignoring your brain."

"True."

"If I remain on an intellectual level, if we keep talking about stocks and chemistry and news and other bullshit, then I risk you backing away because I don't make you feel attractive."

"You're right."

"So my dilemma is this, Genevieve, I can't win."

"So in other words, it's my call."

"Isn't it always the woman's call? Do you like me? Which way do you want this?"

"I'll be one of the first to admit that we, as women, sometimes want it both ways."

"Sometimes?"

"Okay we want it both ways, period."

I laughed. "How fucked up is that?"

She laughed with me, but not in chorus.

"And that thing about me being so damn smart, geesh, if I had a dime for every time I've heard that . . . well . . . anyway, my dilemma is this."

"Uh-huh."

"You . . . we've been out and each time . . . I . . . I . . . I feel as if you like me, but the vibe I'm getting is like I'm your little sister or something. Feels like you're going to kiss me on my cheek or reach over and pat me on my head. If I do or say certain things, you might see me in the wrong light. I mean you invited me to Fresno. I'm here with you and I still don't know what to make of it."

I chuckle. "Well, Fresno is not exactly the Bahamas."

"But it can be. If you want it to be the Bahamas or the South of France, it can be."

I nodded that I felt the same way. We both backed away and sipped our wine.

She said, "With that said, what are you looking for? A good time? Something serious?"

"God, this is going to sound corny."

"If it's from the heart, corny is nice. Very nice. Everybody wants to be a pimp these days. All that posturing and chest thumping. For me, corny feels refreshing."

I took a shallow breath. She sipped her

84

wine. She was so beautiful, so radiant, everything that I had imagined when it came to intelligence, and she was wonderful on the eyes.

I asked her, "You familiar with solutes and solvents?"

"Chemistry?"

"Yes. Solutes and solvents."

"Vaguely. Haven't had chemistry in years. Not my best subject."

"Sugar is a solute, what dissolves. Water is a solvent, what dissolves the sugar."

"Okay. And all that means . . . ?"

"I work a lot. Twelve-hour days. Have a lot of friends, all at work. But loneliness is a solute. My solute. I'm looking for a meaningful relationship; want a woman's love as a solvent."

She stared at me a moment, then she laughed.

I said, "I just blew it huh?"

She reached across the table, put her hand on mine.

She got control of herself and said, "No, that was nice. Made me tingle. It just . . . it just . . ."

I asked, "Okay, what's the joke?"

"Talking about solutes . . . that made me remember taking this biology class when I was at Spelman, and Professor Davis was discussing the high glucose levels found in semen."

I smiled.

She went on, "And this freshman, country girl with crooked teeth, raised her hand and said, 'If I understand what you are saying, there is a lot of glucose in male semen, as in sugar?' "

"Uh-huh."

"Professor Davis told her that was correct. Then the girl raised her hand again and asked, 'Then why doesn't it taste sweet?' "

I laughed.

Genevieve sipped her wine. "First everybody was quiet, then the room, I'm talking the whole class exploded, burst out laughing. That girl turned bright red because she realized what she had implied. That girl picked up her books and, without a single word, hurried out of the class. Never went back. And, oh, as she was going out the door, oh my God, Professor Davis, her reply was classic. Totally straight-faced, she said, 'It doesn't taste sweet because the taste buds for sweetness are on the tip of your tongue and not in the back of your throat.' "

We laughed hard.

I asked, "Was that red-faced girl you?"

"No comment."

The ice had been broken. We'd become real people to each other.

We talked a little more, our tones and words warmer, not so distant. She moved over to my side of the table. Leaned against me. We sat there drinking and holding hands.

She said, "This is our fourth date."

"Okay."

She whispered, "Since this is our fourth date . . . I think we should . . ."

"Should what?"

"It's the wine. I should've stopped at one glass of wine."

"Say it."

"Don't make me say it."

"Say it."

She blushed and sipped her wine again. "Guess."

I raised a brow. "Go to church together?"

She laughed. I smiled.

"You are so silly." Her voice turned sweet and husky. "We should engage in congress."

"Congress."

"Sex."

"I know what congress means."

I smiled wider, my insides turning, erection rising like I was a sixteen-year-old again.

She sipped her wine. "What do you think? Or is the fourth date too soon?"

"You're the virgin. You tell me."

"Already using my words against me."

"Genevieve, you're brilliant, you're drop-dead gorgeous."

"Let me know. I ordered this little Victoria's Secret thing over the Internet. Black, gold, and red kimono-style thing that has a big split, flower prints against black. I brought it with me."

"You planned on seducing me? In Fresno? What kind of woman are you?"

She laughed.

I said, "I don't want to do anything that will make you feel uncomfortable."

"Would you like to see me in it?"

"I'm imagining you . . . and I'm . . . speechless."

"I've asked you two questions and you haven't answered either one."

"Yes. And hell yes."

She reached over, rubbed her fingers across my hand. "I'm going to the ladies' room."

"I'll get the check."

"No, leave the check. I'll get the check. You paid last time."

Miss Independent took a few steps away, my eyes on her petite wonderment, then she stopped where she was, turned, and came back, her head down, hand rubbing across her hair.

Genevieve sat in the booth next to me and said, "Things are out of order."

I asked, "How so?"

"We're talking about . . . doing that."

"Engaging in congress."

"Yes. And we've never kissed. Second date. We should've kissed on the second date."

I put my hand on her face and leaned toward her. She leaned her head, met me halfway. Our lips touched over and over, then mouths opened as eyes closed. Her tongue spoke to mine, said kind and hopeful things. We ended that kiss, stared into each other's eyes, and kissed again. Then again. That out-of-character move surprised me. Her last kiss was brief, but it was strong and promising, tongue-sucking, intense, lip-biting. Combined, they left me feeling dizzy and light.

She was heady, it showed in her eyes. And she looked relieved.

Wished I had the power to TiVo that moment. How she softened as she gazed at me. How my expression did the same. How she shifted like my smile had created a fire that ran from her heart to her vagina.

How her eyes closed like she was willing to give me her heart to break.

I kissed her again. Gave her the kind of kiss that healed all wounds from lovers past.

She whispered, "Having achieved everything you ever imagined and not having a man in your world, it's like having all your fingers on one hand but missing your thumb."

She kissed me again.

She asked, "What are thoughts made of?"

"Why are you asking me something like that?"

"Because I can't stop thinking about you. Since I met you . . . can't stop."

And I hadn't stopped thinking about her. Her résumé, outstanding. Perfect on paper. More desirable in person. Imagined her coming from a family of cerebral kings and queens.

When a man was ready to propagate the species, he desired a woman with certain qualities, both professional and uxorial. He still needed a woman who knew how to be a woman. But he also wanted what was not visible to the eye, what he could not see. Her beauty appealed to me on that aesthetic level, her conversation stimulated me on an intellectual plane, but I was a man concerned with hereditary transmission. With family history. Yes, before the first kiss I pondered what type of children we would create, what information we would pass on as individual traits. What perfections. What imperfections. Those qualities were important because when a man was ready to abandon the dating game for something on a higher level, he too fell into Mendel's breeding lab and played *What if?* All that to say that in the end, we all looked into the eyes of our lovers and we searched for the qualities we wished upon our unborn children.

I wanted the best. I wanted the next generation to surpass all I had and would achieve.

What I wanted to see in my son's and daughter's eyes, I saw all of that in Genevieve.

And what I needed for myself, as a man who needed lust and love, I saw that as well.

Again we kissed; soft and easy, lip-tasting, no tongue at first, then she sucked my tongue, over and over, nice and stimulating. The two glasses of wine had dissipated her shyness.

Her staccato breathing, the rise and fall

of her breasts betrayed her arousal.

She whispered, "We'd better leave before we do something wicked."

I wanted to slide my hand between her legs, massage and feel the heat from her sex.

Then she got up and led the way, her head up, her sultry stroll no longer professional.

Another version of Genevieve had emerged, a woman with erotic eyes and wet lips, legs ready to be spread. The jiggle in her breasts was sensual, a little sassy, and very sophisticated.

No matter how high a woman stacked her degrees, she still had the needs of a woman.

At every red light, we stopped and kissed. Kissed until horns blew for us to move on. It was the most overpoweringly romantic thing I'd ever experienced. Genevieve could have enslaved me at that point. The lack of concern for the cars behind us, the way she made me feel.

I was the center of the world.

Inside our hotel room, velvet touches and butterfly kisses as clothes fell to the floor.

We never made it to the silk kimono, not that night, not right away.

The first time a woman stands before a man naked, he does not know if it will enhance what he feels, or if he will be disappointed, if the visual will diminish the fantasy.

She was beautiful. Toned. No visible scars.

I stared at her with her clothes off. Doctor Genevieve Forbes. Naked.

I saw her vagina. Saw how she took care of her sacred spot.

She gazed at my penis.

I gazed at her breasts.

Mysteries were revealed and evaluated.

A penis, a man's lingam, in some ways it can be judged, evaluated by sight.

The same goes for a woman's breasts. You can see how they hang, which is larger, the nipples betraying desire, even if that desire is not shown in their eyes.

But a vagina. A man knows nothing until he moves across those fleshy folds.

She gave me her body to worship. I took my time getting there.

I was erect and nervous. She was wet and shy.

She lowered her head, tilted her face to the side, gave me an impish smile.

I said, "Move your hands. Let me see you."

She did.

The first time a man sees a woman's bare breast, the first time she gives them to him to kiss, to lick, to squeeze, the first time she allows a man to pay homage, that is Christmas.

I ordered fruit, painted her skin with strawberries, and licked away the sweetness. I showed her how clever I was with my tongue. Five-foot-one-and-one-quarter underneath my six-foot-plus frame. My weight, hers plus at least ninety pounds. I fit inside her. There was no sigh. A foot taller and a hundred pounds heavier and I fit inside her without a sigh. It surprised me how she took all of me without a sound. Surprised me how she could squeeze her vaginal muscles almost as if she was adjusting her vagina, her sacred space, to fit what was given.

Doctor Genevieve Forbes climbed on me and moved in a nice rhythm.

I remember wanting to come, but willing myself not to. Maybe even praying not to come. That heat growing in my belly. Felt as if my penis had doubled in size, was enormous and hot.

She asked, "Would you like me to give you a blow job?"

Genevieve. The woman who plans things. This was an option. The logical woman. Sometimes, even the most logical among us lose the ability to reason when it comes to sex.

I answered, "Yes."

She stopped and took me in her mouth, took in both of our scents, both of our flavors, the satin flesh of her tongue first licking me, then her mouth opening and swallowing me. I fit. Her movements were gentle and pure, like a child sucking her thumb, automatic and without thought, natural. But still as graceful as a ballerina, even when she was sucking enthusiastically.

I looked down on her. Watched until my eyes glossed over and madness arrived.

I told her I was coming and she moved her mouth away.

Kissed me while she stroked me, gave me gentle kisses.

I came. An orgasm that took forever to seep out of me. I came forever.

She whispered, "Let me get a towel."

She came back and cleaned me.

She asked, "Would it bother you if I smoked a joint later?"

"So you do have vices."

"We all have vices."

"You smoke weed. That's surprising."

"When . . . sometimes. Would that bother you?"

I lied and I told her it didn't.

I asked, "Did you come?"

"Almost. It was good. I enjoyed it."

"I want you to come."

Then I licked her again. Licked her until my jaws ached. Licked her like I was on trial and her orgasm, or lack of orgasm, was the verdict, what determined if this would happen again.

It took some time to get her flushed, to get her breathing irregular, to get her to move from making love soft and gentle to fucking, to get her hips bucking, to get her to let go of her PhD, be honest with her primal desires, to seek pleasure. And I was proud to make love to her.

A woman not having an orgasm while congress is in session, in the land of Eros, as the impulses to gratify basic needs take over, that was a nonnegotiable.

That is my selfishness. The need to please and be pleased.

That night she came once. She smiled and said that was good enough for her.

She went to the bathroom, brushed her teeth and showered, came back and cuddled.

Sleep found me, and my dreams took me

to my teenage years. To another woman. To Maria. To my Ecuadorian lover. She comes to me in my dreams as a lover, but as a mother figure as well. I turn my back on her now, as she did to me then, when I was no longer useful.

The sun was rising when I woke up, in bed alone. Genevieve was across the room. She was sitting in a chair, in her kimono, back straight, legs crossed, hands on knees, dignified and sensual, staring out at Fresno. Clouds faded over my head. The room held the scent of ganja.

Her nostrils curled and a ribbon of smoke snaked from her mouth. I asked, "What are you looking at?"

"The railroad tracks. I grew up by railroad tracks. Could hear the train."

"You miss it?"

"No. I don't ever want to wake up to that sound again."

Genevieve suddenly looked like a saturnine woman with a permanent frown.

Then she smiled, came over and kissed me, as beautiful as the sun over Malibu.

And she remained obscure in so many ways, enough of a mystery to electrify me.

No matter who Doctor Genevieve Forbes was, I loved her then, as I do now.

Six months of dating and two years of

marriage have flown by on the wings of time.

Her mysterious ways didn't trouble me back then.

Now I long to unravel the secrecy of the woman I married.

eight

It's late when our flight descends into Birmingham. The final leg of our journey is filled with turbulence, enough to make this feel like a roller-coaster ride into the arms of Lady Death.

For a while I jerk around and stare at the rain, think about my mother. Sweat blooms in my palms. The rain. Our accident. My heart speeds up, my breathing shortens.

Genevieve touches my arm. "You okay?"

I nod, manufacture a smile, a lie to calm her worry, then I create a yawn and look away, my five senses drifting back outside the window, back to a rainy day in Pasadena, Texas.

Outside my window, gloom and trees. No tall buildings like cities such as New York or D.C., no grids and endless traffic like LAX. In the darkness I stare at land I've never seen before, try to imagine when this was the land of slaves. Of forty lashes.

Of bombings and lynchings.

When we leave baggage claim it feels like I'm breathing through a damp blanket.

I ask, "It's this tropical all the time?"

"Tropical is sexy." Genevieve says that in a voice that can barely be heard, already wishing she were somewhere else. "Beaches and Spanish drinks by a pool. This is not sexy."

A Town Car is waiting for us at baggage claim, the driver holding a sign with Genevieve's last name. The driver is thin and white, his black suit not crisp, the pants and jacket two different shades of black. He is smiling but exhausted from his long wait. I smell the cigarette smoke in his suit, smell the cancer as it rises from his pores, permeates the airport, the city.

The driver asks, "How was y'all flight in from Los Angeles?"

I wait for Genevieve to answer, but she ignores him.

I say, "Started off smooth then got pretty rough near the end."

"Sounds like my first marriage."

He laughs. I laugh a little too.

He says, "You and the missus picked a heck of a day to come to town. Tornado done already carved out some parts down south then went through Atlanta, now

100

looks like it's turned and is heading this way quick, fast, and in a hurry. We was about to shut down, thought the airport would do the same, but they sent me to make this run before the weather turned on us."

As he loads our bags he talks incessantly, his Southern accent strong and redneck, an offspring of *Deliverance,* not rooted in slavery and at the same time reminding me of those pale-skinned people who used to own dark-skinned people. His demeanor so different from all the Hollywood people we just left behind, all of his interactions peppered with no, sir or yes, ma'am.

The driver takes I-20. The skies become the blackest of all blacks. Traffic crawls at a civilized pace, as if they respect the weather, something that does not happen in Los Angeles.

Rain. Highways. Everything I fear greets me.

Genevieve is tense, staring at the city, posture tight, as if her heart is heavy, sighing off and on, as if this were land she had never intended to see again.

She frowns upward, mumbles, "She knows I'm here."

I swallow my own fear and ask, "Who?"
No answer.

She clears her throat and says, "Driver, can we get some more air back here?"

"Yes, ma'am. How's that, ma'am?"

"Better."

"Got some cold water up here, if you like."

Genevieve says, "Please. Thank you."

He passes Genevieve two bottles.

I say, "Could you not drive . . . you don't have to rush."

"Yessir."

Genevieve takes my hand again, squeezes it as if to say everything will be okay.

Lightning illuminates the sky as soon as we get off I-20 downtown, thunder booms as we drive by the lights of the Sheraton Hotel toward the courthouses. The driver is lost, the way his face is tense and his lips twist speak of confusion, but he is not saying. He's not a city-dweller. Probably drives in from his own poor white ghetto to clock in. His teeth have a smoker's stain and his hair is greasy. Moustache crooked, slants down to the right. I don't care. The longer we drive down this maze of one-way streets, the more I get to see of Genevieve's old world.

I say, "So this is Birmingham. Wonder why Europeans moved here and named the cities after the cities in England. Seems like they would've come up with new names."

Genevieve frowns, thinks I'm making a statement about her changing her name.

The driver responds, "There is another Birmingham over in England?"

I clear my throat. "Yep. The original one, as far as I know."

"You don't say. That's strange. I knew Alabama got its name from an Indian word, means to clear the thicket, if I remember correctly. Assumed Birmingham was Indian too."

"Wasn't aware of the etymology of Alabama."

"You wasn't aware of the which-a-what?"

"The origin of the word Alabama. Didn't know it was Indian."

He asks, "Y'all been over there? To England?"

I answer, "Twice. Once for our honeymoon. My wife has been several times. You?"

"No sir. Ain't never been on a plane. My wife's always getting on a plane. I ain't getting on one. And don't plan on getting on one. More people get killed by donkeys than die in plane crashes, but I'll stick to a donkey just the same. Just like I ain't getting on the Internet. She's always on that too. Had to get an extra phone line because she's on the doggone Internet all the time. Last week she was up every doggone night going to all those Internet Web sites looking at pictures of some ten-year-old grilled cheese sandwich that's supposed to look like the Virgin Mary. Can you imagine what a ten-year-old grilled cheese sandwich looks like? All that mold."

Genevieve shifts, shakes her head.

I ask, "What's your name?"

"Smith. Bubba Smith."

"Like the football player."

"Only I can't play football. Yessir, Alabama is the reason God invented football. I can't play, but I love to watch it. Yessir, Bubba Smith. People used to tease me about my name, especially when them *Police Academy* movies was on, but I likes it."

Bubba Smith talks on and on, asks me if I'm a college football fan. I tell him I'm a die-hard Raiders fan, not big on college ball. He tells me that he only watches collegiate football games, favors Auburn over Alabama, the latter being the extent of his political concerns.

Bubba Smith starts to smile, says, "I met Dale Earnhardt."

"Who?"

"Dale Earnhardt. You know. *Dale Earnhardt*. You not up on NASCAR, are you?"

"Oh. Dale Earnhardt. Did you?"

"See my moustache? I done cut mine just like Dale Earnhardt's moustache."

"Is that right?"

"Took some trying, but I did it."

"And you met him."

"Sure did. Was a volunteer at Carraway, saw them wheeling Dale into the hospital after his wreck at Talladega. Had cut my hand and was down there getting stitches."

"Is that right?"

"Waved at 'im with my left hand. He stared at me and blinked two times, which is the same as waving back. Wish I could've got his autograph or something. Or taken a picture with him all banged up. Yessir, met Dale Earnhardt. And my wife got yelled at by Loretta Lynn."

"While you were meeting Dale Earnhardt?"

"That was a different time. Yessir, she met somebody famous too. Got yelled at."

"For what?"

"Being too loud at a concert. She looked

105

right at my wife and told her to shut up."

"Is that right?"

"Made her day. Yessir, Loretta Lynn told her to shut her trap."

"What happened after that?"

"Oh, the missus got put out of the concert. Yessir, they carried her out kicking and screaming. She was Loretta Lynn's number one fan, now she has started up an anti–Loretta Lynn Web site. Obviously Loretta was not amused at her jabbering and yelling, none at all. My wife has an oral problem. Don't know how to shut her trap, if you know what I mean."

I say, "Most women have that in common."

"Don't they? No offense back there, ma'am."

Genevieve shifts. "You two good old boys go right ahead with your misogynistic chatter."

"Just running my mouth with your husband. Man talk. Don't mean no harm by it."

Genevieve groans.

I smile and stifle a little laugh, one directed at my wife.

Silence covers us followed by more lightning, then more thunder. Rain starts to fall in pound-size drops. The windshield wipers screech back and forth, struggle to slap water away.

I ask Bubba Smith, "What's a good place to eat around here?"

"Milo's, now they have the best hamburgers. Remember Milo's. If you lucky, you get a good-sized extra meat chunk hidden underneath the patty. Now that's a good day. Get one of them burgers then go on over to the Nick and get a beer, that's what a lot of people likes to do."

The driver turns, sighs, looks like he has his bearings and turns right by the Alabama TelCo Credit Union and the Greyhound station. A park and a library appear when we cross Twentieth Street. Then we are at the Tutwiler. Bubba Smith pulls into a U-shaped parking lot that is tiny and stacked with cars. Hotel looks full. A young bellman runs out with an umbrella, another runs out to get our luggage, both black. We wait for Bubba Smith to let us out.

He says, "If you need a driver tomorrow, be sure to ask for me."

I say, "Not sure. We might get a rental car. Haven't decided."

"Be careful in this weather. My cousin wasn't paying attention and the car tumped over."

"Tumped over?" I smile, having no idea what he means. "Is that right?"

"It sho did. Tumped right on over."

"I'll be careful."

"If you need to know the hot spots to go have fun, everybody goes to the Blue Monkey and Bell Bottoms. I hear Workplay has good music, that's over on Twenty-third Street."

"Thank you."

"Some people congregate by the water fountain over at Five Points. You eat Thai food?"

"Yeah."

"Gives me gas. But there is a good Thai food place up there in Five Points, Surin West."

"Thank you."

"The missus loves to eat there. She likes that place and Ruby Tuesday's real nice too."

I give Bubba Smith a tip, then shake hands and we go our separate ways.

As soon as we get inside the Tutwiler, the thunder and lightning increase. Rain falls in sheets, like the sky has been cut open. Still I look around at its history, all of it rooted in either Southern or European design, dark woods and golds and deep-colored leathers. There are three people in front of us, all checking in or trying to extend their stay due to the pending weather.

The slim blond girl behind the counter is busy giving a middle-aged couple directions, telling them to "Take 31 to 459 to 280 to 76 to 21 and you'll be there."

"Uh-huh. We from Little Rock, honey, so we'll be needing to write that down."

Genevieve clears her throat, her message that she is tired and wants them to hurry up.

The wife in the couple is doing all the talking, overweight and tight-fisted, dressed in Wal-Mart. She knows people are in line waiting yet she continues, "Where is the Statue of Liberty?"

"Across the street on Liberty Parkway. It's nice."

"Is it like the one in New York?"

"Not as big."

This is ridiculous. Genevieve sighs, shakes her head. I hold her hand. She tells me, "Sorry. If I had known I would've made reservations at either the Sheraton or the Pickwick."

Genevieve does not whisper. Her irritation sounds out in bold letters that have been underlined three times. Everyone in front of us turns and looks at us like we're strange and rude visitors from another planet, with patience and tact below those of mortal men.

That is what Genevieve wants, for them to challenge her. The tourist looks at my wife. Genevieve stares her down despite her size. I expect Genevieve to hold her hands out, to make herself look bigger, the way you're taught to do with animals in the woods. The woman's lips curl in, veins pop up in her neck, but all she wants to say is kept on the other side of her lips.

I have been here two minutes and a race war is about to start. One call from that woman and Bull Connors, the police, and fire departments will be outside with water hoses and dogs.

The woman makes a huffy noise and goes on. "Like I was saying, can you tell me how to get to the Last Chance Barbecue? And do you know exactly where Courteney Cox grew up?"

I rub my eyes and look around, my own impatience rising, damn near matching Genevieve's. I drift away from the counter, leave her to go it alone, walk up the three or four steps to the next level. The lobby is small, marble and chandeliers and gold trimmings, leather high-back chairs, a piano to the left of the front entrance on the library side of the hotel, everything very aristocratic. I feel too hip, too California for this room. Genevieve handles checking in while I head for the men's room. It's across the marble floors to the left.

I hear her first, her voice is lower, her whisper rugged.

"Fuck you, Deuce. Fucking fuck you. Why did I? Because I had to see for myself."

Then I see her.

She is in the hallway, in a leather chair, her head down, cell phone up to her mouth.

"What did you do to my charge card? Don't act stupid. I told you I have not seen no damn U-Haul truck. If somebody stole your truck it ain't my fault. Maybe your friend took it for a ride. You're unreal. Do what? You expect me to come back after that shit? You fucking freak."

She hangs up her cellular and stands up.

Light-blue faded jeans, fitted and low-rise, black belt, green and white sleeveless T-shirt that has been cut to stop right below her breasts. Red letters across her breasts read I'M A SCREAMING ORGASM WAITING TO HAPPEN. She has on lace-up sneakers, bangles on the right arm, stud

111

earrings. Light gloss on full lips that remind me of Lauryn Hill. A sorority umbrella is at her side, but she is soaking wet from her waist down. She is not dressed for this weather. She stands there with her arms folded beneath her breasts. Trembling. The downcast eyes, the knitted brow, the fretful countenance — all the body language of a wounded heart.

I say, "You okay?"

Her eyes carry pain and dried tears. She's been crying for days. For miles. She looks at me but gives no answer. Bad time to speak to her. She is riled, used to men in a bad way.

Dark skin. Tall and lithe, with distinct feminine curves that are generous, but not excessive. She looks directly at me in a way that is pointed, yet far away, like she can see what I am thinking. It is the kind of look that gives hope and, at the same time, takes it away. I should have paid more attention to her hair. She was Medusa, hair of snakes and evocative stares.

She shakes her head. "No, I'm not okay."

She sees me. Pauses with her destructive thoughts putting lines in her face. Sees this tall and gangly older man, skin that could use some sun, sees this short curly hair that needs trimming, sees me dressed in sandals, not close to being trendy, yet far from being bohemian.

When her mouth opens her tongue ring shows itself. Tattoos decorate her skin: a raging leopard on her right shoulder, a blazing sun on her belly, a shiny navel ring in its center.

I ask, "Anything I can do?"

Her head tilts back, gives her an air of haughtiness. "You kill people?"

She looks like she is suffering from insomnia, an aching back, and a fractured heart. Hard and fragile all at once.

Then I say, "Afraid not."

"Know anybody who does?"

"What's wrong?"

I ask that, not knowing why, more out of awkwardness than true concern.

Her head tilts forward, a quizzical and defensive expression. "You ever look at the people in your life and ask yourself, where did these people come from? These are my friends? This loser is my fiancé? You think you know what you want then wake up one morning and you don't want any of it. Your life. You hate everything about your life. You just hate it."

"Hate is a strong word."

"And it's in the dictionary for a reason."

"Can't be that bad."

"How the fuck would you know?"

I let her words settle while my mind rotates. It is time for me to walk away, but I stand where I am, stare at her full lips, ripe lips that curve up even when she is living in anger. I imagine kissing her would be like eating ripe chilies, the kind of kisses that take time to burn.

She turns to walk away.

I ask, "And what do you feel when you feel that way?"

My own voice surprises me. It's strained. Somewhere between my heart and my lips most of my voice has evaporated. My lips move but my words are like shadows in the light. Throat feels dry and I expect dust to fly out in the place of each evaporated word.

She stops and looks back before she turns and faces me.

I'm nervous. My insides become tumbleweeds.

She is tall with keen features. The hips of a goddess. Aphrodite in brown skin, a soft voice that is like the whispering of girls. She has the kind of beauty that is disturbing, the kind that can cause misery and bloodshed for anyone who tries to possess what they see.

She takes a cigarette out of her purse,

lights it, inhales deeply, blows smoke out of the right side of her lips, fans the fumes away from her face, puts her free hand on her hip, legs almost in a ballet dancer's first position, some classical training beneath that hard exterior.

She takes another pull, blows smoke away.

We stand in the hallway, regarding each other. I struggle to keep my eyes away from the letters on her T-shirt. She knows that and smiles, understands her power as a woman.

She motions at my wedding ring. "I was supposed to get married next month."

"What happened?"

"Well, when you witness your man fucking somebody else . . ."

Lightning flashes.

Again her eyes go from my face to my wedding ring, then back to my face.

She skips answering my question and asks, "How do you like being married?"

Her voice, the way she says that is so simple, makes truth rise.

I shrug. "Sometimes . . . sometimes I miss being single."

"Same way I feel when I'm in a relationship."

"We always want what we don't have."

"Ain't that the truth."

I nod. "We all want an idyllic existence."

"Where is your wife?"

I swallow, resisting an urge to look behind me. "Around the corner, checking us in."

She almost smiles. "You're bold."

"I haven't done anything bold."

"Too bad."

"Why?"

"With my mood, as long and tall and cute as you are, I might've done something bold."

Thunder roars.

I ask, "Where were you born?"

She gives a one-sided smile. "I was born in a manger surrounded by liquid crackheads and chain-smoking alcoholics who had been displaced from their motherland, physically and mentally abused to the point that would create a warm smile on Willie Lynch's racist face, a tear of happiness in his racist eyes as his spirit watches us devour ourselves with self-hatred, a smile that turns into a never-ending laugh as he sees us living day-to-day with misdirected aggression, hopelessness raining from above as prayers go up and come back unanswered because the savior's phone is off the hook and He is not

116

accepting our I-pages."

I look at her body art, her hair, her neo-soul style, say, "You're a poet."

She asks, "Did you understand it?"

"Not really."

She laughs a little. So do I.

Her cellular phone's ring tone interrupts us.

She holds my gaze, gives me an innocent smile, the kind that can turn a wise man into a fool. Without taking her eyes from mine she lowers her smoke from her face and answers with a snap, "Deuce, stop calling me. What the fuck you want? For the last time, I told you I haven't seen no damn U-Haul truck. None of your business where I am. What is the problem with my charge card, asshole? I'm trying to get a damn room, that's why. None of your business where or who . . . You know what? Fuck you. No, fuck you, your bitch ass."

She turns and storms away, still arguing, heads down the hallway into the bar.

She is familiar, the incarnation of the women I grew up with in Fresno, the women who frightened and excited me all at once. The women who looked at me and saw nothing.

I take to the men's room, but the water

won't come. My mind is elsewhere. Still in the hallway. When I'm done trying I fight the urge to hurry back to the lobby toward what is right, and instead I walk to the door that leads to the bar, circle the room looking for the crass woman.

There is a door that leads out toward the streets facing the library.

I move in that direction, then stop when sanity taps me on my shoulder.

Near the back of the room an interracial couple is laughing over whether or not he should use Viagra. A dim light is over their heads and candles are on the table. I stop where I am, looking out into the rain for the girl and eavesdropping all at once. The couples at the table are not old; she just wants more time on the meter. He is heavy and European, glasses and a thin beard, wearing Dockers and a Polo shirt. The woman he is with is Indian. She has large breasts, plenty of cleavage, has a pleasant face, borderline full-figured, her skin as dark as the night is long. Next to them, a heavy-set Spanish woman and an Italian man. He has on jeans and a white button-down collar shirt. She wears a green blouse that has no sleeves, open enough to show off her pearl necklace.

I walk the perimeter of the room,

searching for the woman with the untamed hair.

My eyes go back to the two couples.

The interracial couple lean closer, no longer laughing, now kissing slow and easy, the sensuality between them igniting the room. Next to them the Spanish wife and the Italian husband are touching, his hand on her breasts, foreplay on a dark and dreary night.

Both couples are close, the women next to each other, tables touching as if all four are in the same party, and all are well-tanned, look well-to-do, like old money and plantation-sized homes, sitting in a cozy darkness surrounded by the sounds of a rampaging Mother Nature.

At first I don't understand, then I do. The Spanish woman's movements tell the story of the unseen. Her Italian companion has slid his hand underneath the table and his finger is stroking the wet folds of her vagina. She trembles and coos, jerks as if he is lifting that finger in a come-here motion, shifts as electricity is surging through her body, holds the edges of the table as if she is pushing her hips against his finger, her eyes looking greedy, daring him to do more.

I envy them, wish I could bottle their in-

119

tensity and bathe my wife in their passion.

The Spanish woman shifts, moans out something in her native tongue, then she laughs.

The white man protests in a rugged whisper, "What are you doing to my wife over there?"

The Italian replies, "What do you think I'm doing? I'm finger-fucking your wife."

My mouth drops open as my curiosity shoots off the meter.

The Spanish woman laughs. "Honey, mind your business. Go back to talking about whatever you were talking about. I'm drunk and I need to come, so mind your own business."

"I'll have to finger-fuck your beautiful wife then. See how both of you like that."

The white man frowns. "You've got big fingers."

The Spanish woman purrs. The Indian woman moans.

In between moans the women dip their fingers in their alcohol, feed their lovers, that hard liquor smell and sex permeating the air in this dark chamber. The two women stare at each other and smile the smile of true vixens. They lick their lips like they want to take this to another level.

I sneak away, the same as I did when I was a child.

I want to be like that with my wife, finger-fucking her in a room filled with people, pleasing her underneath the table. I look at the women and make them Genevieve, make the men me.

The Indian woman sings her victory. The Spanish song of orgasm comes in as a chorus.

A symphony of moans sends chills through my groin.

Back at the front desk, Genevieve is just getting to the counter. She still doesn't have the room key. Computers went down for a moment. The thunder and lightning.

Genevieve turns away from the counter, sees me standing next to her.

I am disturbed.

Genevieve asks, "You okay?"

"Yeah."

"You vanished."

I hesitate. "Bathroom."

"Stomach okay?"

Again I hesitate. "Yeah."

I take her hand in mine, run my fingers across her palm.

She looks up at me with a weary smile.

121

She loves me. Her love should be enough.

Minutes later we get on the elevator, the bellman in tow. Before the door closes, a huge hand catches the door. The Italian man from the bar. His friend staggers on behind him. The Spanish woman and the Indian woman get on next, high heels clicking against the marble floor. The elevator is small. We're all shoulder-to-shoulder. They reek of alcohol and the stench of love. Genevieve's eyes are down, preoccupied with her own impenetrable thoughts. The men argue about the war in Iraq, the Italian man being for Bush and his friend against Bush's policy.

The white man says, " 'Beware the leader who bangs the drums of war in order to whip the citizenry into a patriotic fervor, for patriotism is indeed a double-edged sword.' "

"Quoting Shakespeare will not change my mind."

"Your problem is that you are, my friend, a sore loser."

"I'll agree, not everyone who praises Allah is a terrorist, but all terrorists worship Allah."

"Is that right? How soon we forget about

Timothy McVeigh. I believe he was Catholic."

"Sore loser."

"I am not a sore loser. Ask your wife."

"Maybe I'll ask yours."

The women are talking with their hands and ranting about Martha Stewart being in jail, joking about her wearing Blahniks with her prison garb, both laughing about it.

They push the button for the second floor and the elevator hums before it rises at a slow pace. At the second floor, as the door eases open, the Italian man looks at my wife in an evaluating way, smiles and winks and me, does all that before he gets off.

I hold my wife closer.

nine

As soon as I get to the room I head for the shower. Genevieve gives me space, starts unpacking a few things, getting her laptop set up so she can get on the Internet and check e-mail. I'll do the same in a little while. We're both workaholics and tech heads. But I need some space. After traveling there are certain things a man needs to do without a woman in the bathroom. I ease my bladder and bowels, then shave my body with my electric shaver. Genevieve hates pubic hair, hates hair underneath my arms. I've come to agree with her, love the cleanliness. Hair traps odors. I do the same with a few rampant nose hairs, and make sure no hair is growing on my ears. Then I take a cool shower, stay in until my body temperature is regulated.

Twenty more minutes pass before Genevieve comes back to the room. She is glowing. Sweat on her brow. She fans herself and, without looking at me, complains about the heat.

I ask, "Where did you go?"

"Went to complain. Look at those plantation shutters. They're coming apart. And this carpet, see how it bunches up by the door? I went out on the balcony and it's been overlooked."

"Genevieve, don't give these people a heart attack."

"The carpet is atrocious. Have you looked over the bed?"

"For what?"

"Are you blind? Can't you see the smoke detector is hanging by the wires?"

I inspect the room with her. A creature of detail, she points out the things she complains about. As usual she is right. The lobby of the hotel is wonderful but our room is bleak. Like a woman who looks pristine on the outside, her soul in need of renovation. Hotel Genevieve.

She continues to protest, says, "And I had to see what we could do for food."

"You could've called room service."

"No room service."

"No room service?"

"I went down there and gave it to them good. For two hundred a night, you would think they would've told us the kitchen was closed for renovation before we made our reservations. The Pickwick doesn't have room service, but it's in Five Points, plenty of places to eat."

I open the plantation shutters, then open the door to the balcony. Our seventh-floor view is four lanes of empty street and Energen Plaza. I step out and spy toward downtown, watch the rain falling hard and wind blowing mercilessly outside. Thunder adds sounds to the background. A fourteen-foot U-Haul comes down the street, being beaten by the tempest. There is no traffic, so the U-Haul stands out. Since that bombing in Oklahoma, in this post-9/11 world, every moving truck looks suspicious. The driver struggles with the weather, looks like the truck is about to crash. The truck pulls over, emergency blinkers on. Then I hear a siren. The sudden wail pierces the darkness, and like the rain the scream comes from all directions. The city is terrified.

I hurry to the bathroom door, ask Genevieve, "Is that a terrorist alert?"

"Tornado warning."

"What do we need to do?"

"Unless you're Thor or Storm, nothing we can do."

I ask, "You call your family?"

126

"No need waking anybody up."

I raise a brow. "You think they're sleeping through the Armageddon?"

She firms her voice. "In the morning."

"Let them know we made it in."

"In the morning. In the morning. In the morning."

The siren dies. The rain falls strong and steady. We get in bed. I can tell that she is exhausted. I'm exhausted too, but I'm wired. What I saw downstairs has left me with fire in my belly. I move around like a restless kid. My mind alive with the excitement that comes from the chance of experiencing nirvana someplace new. The rain and the thunder and all the danger outside, even the possibility of being struck by lightning as I come hardens me. Being in a place where countless others have had sex turns her off, but it stimulates me to no end.

I am on a strange bed that holds the memory of countless hours of lovemaking. Countless illicit fucks. If a hotel room could talk it would speak in orgasmic moans. The walls whispering for all who come here to come here. While rain falls from the heavens, I imagine that in every room congress is in session. That the thunder is their orgasms, lightning their spasms.

I touch my wife, rub my flesh against her flesh.

She gives me a gentle moan. That is her yes.

I kiss her, pull her T-shirt away from her body, lick her skin, take her breast in my mouth.

She says, "Turn the air up."

"Magic word?"

"Please."

I do.

When I come back she's on her belly, ass in the air.

I say, "Turn over."

"From the back. I like it from the back."

Her saying she likes it from the back has deeper meaning. That means she doesn't want me to make love to her sacred spot with my tongue, doesn't want me to lick around the edges and create figure eights, that she's tired but accommodating, ready to get down to the nitty gritty.

I touch her from the small of her back down over the curve of her rising backside. Her ass is modest, very nice, very toned, very well proportioned, as is everything about her. At times she seems so tiny, as if sex with me, when I'm in that final moment, the one that takes us back to being primitives, as if those thrusts should hurt her, as if, if I let go, I could kill her with my passion.

I ease on top of her and she reaches down, takes me, puts me inside her.

She's not as wet as a river, but her vagina isn't a desert.

I kiss her back, touch her skin, start to move in and out of her hollow.

She whispers, "Wait."

I stop moving. "What?"

"Turn the TV off."

I shift around, slip out of her, hand patting the covers, until I find the remote, fumble for the off button, give us blackness and create the silence she needs to focus on the task at hand. That moment, that coitus interruptus breaks our momentum, makes me too aware, almost dissipates my desire. I hold in my sigh, one that is heavy with disappointment, the fallout from my own expectations, happy she's on her stomach and can't see the cold expression in my face. If I stop it will be an issue. So I go back and try to recapture the moment before.

She puts me back inside. She's wetter this time. Not a river, just wetter.

I hold her waist, move slow, stay in first gear, massaging her insides.

Tingles rise and my disappointment

melts from my expression.

Genevieve doesn't moan, not at first. Never does. Never feels like I fill her up the way a man wants to fill up a woman, never make it into uncharted territory. Or maybe I don't make it into territory that has not been charted by me. Makes me wonder about the men who came before me, how big they were, how they stirred her from the inside, how I compare, if others gave her better pleasure, if they made her hysterical, made her back arch, made her yell things and become sensually barbaric, if she went insane and did things to them that she doesn't do to me.

I'm good. Have multiple techniques and more than enough passion to prevent me from coming across as a technical fuck. Genevieve is so damn sexy to me. I love her and I love making love to her, love the bonding that sex brings, love pleasing her and relishing in the shared pleasure. I've read all the books on pleasing a woman, everything from Kama Sutra to books by lesbians. I can use my tongue and make her float, I understand how to listen to her body, I know all that. But I want to dip into her emotional well.

Our libidos are unequal. Mine runs at about a nine. It's been that way lately,

130

humming along in fourth gear. My awakening. As if my body were going through some change, this fire inside me never dying. Genevieve hums at about a five. That means I crave her twice as much, need her twice as often, leaving me feeling rejected and neglected.

Yes, I know that there is more to loving than sex. Much more to a relationship than putting my dick in her hole and stirring, stirring, stirring. But intimacy, those erotic moments I crave, that is part of the foundation, one thing that can turn a marriage into a house of cards.

I love being on top of a woman, her legs apart, ready to experience my predilection for pleasure. Love to feel her heat underneath me, being able to see her face, touch her breasts, have her hands on my back and ass, her warm vagina so wet and slippery. My penis easing inside her, deep and strong, moving across her wetness, feeling her surround me. Listening to that sigh that comes as I break the skin. As I go deep. As I stroke. Love the scratching to mark territory, the biting, the onomatopoetic sounds, grabbing her hair above her ears and giving her a deep and never-ending kiss, all the wild and spontaneous things that happen during congress.

But the sigh. That *first* purr that lets me know a woman is melting.

I live for that sigh.

When two become one. When souls start to dance. When she submits.

When she is mine.

That moment is magical, when a man becomes king.

Genevieve grunts, "Hold on."

"What?"

She shifts away from me. "Let me move my . . . yeah . . . like that."

"You okay?"

"My leg was awkward."

"Better?"

"Better."

When I make love with Genevieve, most of the time I'm conscious of every stage that we're in. Most of the time. Maybe because she's so dramatic and meticulous, as well as predictable. I climax, but I rarely get to that over-the-top endorphin high, never fall into that euphoric state. I'm never lost in the abyss of pleasure. I am aware of every move. Aware of time. Aware of my own breathing. Aware of things that I have to do later. I watch her face, watch all the porn-star faces she makes, listen to all of her dramatic moans, sounds that sound more manufactured than spontaneous, and wonder if she is aware too, and at times I think that she is.

During foreplay, when I think she's in the zone, she can go from a heated exchange to rubbing her nose and casually telling me to get the condom. In her eyes lust is just a phantom.

I crave that uncivilized zone.

If you're that hot, if you're in that zone, you can't control your tone like that. You don't go from being barbaric and on fire to being less-than-smoldering, to a place of calmness and clarity and logic in the next breath. I want to blame her, but I don't. I take it personally. That tells me that I don't make her opiates kick in and get her where she needs to be either.

But she never complains.

I dig into my bag and remember all I have done with women, how I have pleased them and been pleased in that way since I was a teenager. I've learned a lot in the art of pleasure, and since college I've taught twice as many as have taught me.

I remember being in that zone. In that special place between life and death.

I turn her over. Kiss her face. She puts her hand on my ass, asking me to stay on task, ride the road to orgasm. She is tired. She is jet-lagged. I stroke her in a steady rhythm, go deep as I can go, come back to the tip of my penis, go deep again, again, again, like I am famished, greedy, want her clitoris to swell, breathing to thicken, want her legs to tense, want her to come.

There is pleasure in giving pleasure, in not being selfish. Pleasure in making a woman have more orgasms than she can count. Pleasure in watching a woman set free sounds and come like she's losing her mind.

There is no sigh.

That zone. I crave it. It's my drug of choice.

Need to get into a state where you're oblivious to the clock ticking on the wall, where you can't hear Luther singing anymore, where all of your body feels like an open nerve set on fire. When you shudder and howl out your orgasm, then collapse, drenched in sweat, so close to death, but feeling so alive. Where you see a thousand colors and the sounds coming from your mouth that are unstoppable, unrecognizable, and you're floating like a dancer, suspended above the rest of the world, having an out-of-body experience and staring down on yourself.

I get to the point of coming and try to stop. I control the fire inside me.

I stroke I stroke I stroke I stroke I stroke.

My legs tense, I grip her waist, give her all of me.

She yields, her face an orgasmic expression, very few sounds.

I stroke I stroke I stroke I stroke I stroke.

I want her to scream, want her to let loose and go insane.

My mind drifts. I see a mouth. The flight attendant from Southwest. Her image comes to me. She's underneath me, legs open for me, moaning for me, those full lips crooning for me. Her feminine gestures arouse me. Her skin feels smooth against mine. Her clitoris swells, her breath grows short, her legs stiffen, back arches, she strains to come, makes greedy sounds, and under a thicket of kisses gives me moans in that poetic language of onomatopoeia.

I fuck her good. Her hands hold my ass, her hips move against me and I fuck her good.

That fire consumes me. I strain to not come, then give in to that overwhelming feeling, work with it. I stiffen, swell, move with reckless abandon, stroke to heaven without her.

Then self-consciousness returns.

Face damp, lines of physical and mental

exertion decorating my forehead, I gaze down on my wife. Her face is moist as well, her expression that of travail, the same as mine. I pant, sweat blooming on my flesh and I stare at my Genevieve. Her skin is sultry, but there is no glow.

My wife.

My partner.

The woman who is supposed to be my last lover, the one that leads me into eternity.

She whispers, "You came hard."

"Been a while."

"Guess we've been off schedule."

"Did you come?"

"I came."

"Couldn't tell."

"We came at the same time."

There is kindness in her lie. But even with kindness, it is still a lie.

She smiles, but there is no glow. No transition from insanity to common sense.

Then, in a clear voice, she says, "You're getting heavy."

She shifts to get from underneath me and I roll over, sweat dripping.

She fans herself, says, "Had forgotten how oppressive it was here in the South."

"Oppressive ain't the word."

She wipes my sweat from her breasts,

licks her fingers, looks so sexy, so erotic.

She whispers, "Turn the TV back on, please? Want to keep up with the weather."

"Okay."

"Hot as hell."

She goes to the bathroom. Limping.

I ask, "You okay?"

"Cramp in my leg."

"All that wine. You're dehydrated."

I hear the water running, imagine her cleaning herself with a warm towel, then she comes back to my side of the bed, still limping, takes my penis, and wipes me down.

I ask, "You okay?"

"Lot on my mind."

"Willie Esther's funeral?"

"Yes. Are you going?"

"I don't want to look at dead people, not if I can help it."

"What are you going to do?"

"You know I don't do funerals."

"Why not?"

I emphasize, "Because they are funerals."

"Why not?"

My mind goes back to a rainy day in Pasadena, Texas.

I readjust, make my memory and demons go back into the darkness, say, "I'll go with you and meet your family, will be at the repast, but I can't go to the funeral."

We all have our issues, our fears, our phobias. Looking at dead people is one of mine.

Genevieve takes the damp towel and tosses it across the room, toward the bathroom. This is a hotel. Here she will not be meticulous. She will make sure the maids earn their pay.

I ask, "You okay?"

"You want a blow job, don't you?"

That husky voice is not the voice of the Genevieve I know. Her tone is distant. The look in her eyes is as foreign as the crass language she uses. She never sounds like a whore.

Her voice thickens. "Want me to be your slut?"

"Yes."

"I married you so I wouldn't have to be a slut."

"I married you to make you one."

"Is that what you want? Me to transmogrify into your personal whore?"

"Transmogrify?" I chuckle. "Yes. I want to transmogrify you."

"You're a pig."

"I'm a man who loves the woman he fucks and fucks the woman he loves."

138

"What if I told you I was a slut before I met you?"

"What if I told you to prove it?"

"Then would you think I was eminently qualified for the job?"

"If you were, prove it."

"What else can I do? Suck your dick? Swallow? Gargle your protein? Allow you to sprinkle your come on my face like it's a religious ceremony? Is that what you want?"

Her raffish tone affects me, disturbs and erects me all at once.

She rubs her hand over the length of my erection, eyes tight, as if she's in some kind of an altered state. Then she pushes me back on the bed, takes the fullness of my penis in her mouth, does that in a way that is more political than lustful, a way that tells me she is using pleasure to keep me from talking, from asking questions, that maybe the conversation we had on the plane has put her into a different frame of mind. Created insecurity. She is being a good wife to her husband. Her mouth covers my penis, consumes its entire length, makes it vanish into her face with ease. Has mastered her gag reflex and allows me to go deep down her throat.

She is good. So damn good.

The first time she took me in her mouth, that night in Fresno, when she bewitched me this way, I must admit, she gave me pleasure that made me want to cry. No biting. No pain of any kind. I want to turn her ass around, bring the sweetness of her vagina to my mouth, do the same thing to her that she is doing to me, but she resists, won't let me pleasure her in sixty-nine ways.

She stops her slow and steady rhythm, begins moving her head like a maniac.

Tingles race through me. Toes curl. Breathing thickens. I strain, come in heated spasms. She continues until the well is dry, until I'm so sensitive I have to beg her to stop, as if she is telling me to be careful of what I want, what I ask her for, because she will give it tenfold.

She should put this on her résumé. Highlighted. Bold. Italics. Underlined three times.

She sits on the edge of the bed, watching me return to sanity.

She wipes her lips in a motion that reminds me of a vampire after its feeding, and looks away. Her breathing evens out. Back to being the other Genevieve, the one who intellectualizes the world, back to a veiled and rigid expression. As I always do, I ask if she is okay.

She says, "Willie Esther finally died."

"You never talked about her. Never mentioned her name, not once."

"I only speak of positive things."

In that voice I use at work, I say, "You repudiate her."

She answers like a witness on a stand, a woman on trial. "Yes."

"What's up with that? I mean, you hated her because . . . what?"

She snaps, "She was an evil woman."

"You repudiate your entire family."

"Don't badger me."

I don't respond to her harsh voice, one that has more disdain than grieving, not right away. I want to ask her a million questions, but I also want answers without having to ask. When I do seek to peel back her layers there is a disturbing change, I see it in her face, how her face changes to concrete. Her memories create thunder and flood her senses, give her brain its own electrical storm, the lightning showing in her eyes.

Genevieve goes to brush her teeth. Always does that after oral sex. It disturbs me. While I relish in the taste of her magnificence, she rinses mine away and spits it into the sewer.

She pulls her panties back on, does the same with her T-shirt, gets in bed. She rarely sleeps naked. Her panties are her shield, she told me when we first met. As if my six-foot frame isn't enough to protect her, but panties by Victoria's Secret can. Genevieve moves around until she gets comfortable, then as an afterthought she leans over to me and kisses me on my lips, then she returns to her side of the bed, either content or hoping that I am in such a state of being.

Plain and simple, in the darkness, she whispers, "Good night."

She's done her marital job.

I've come.

The itch has been salved and I should be satisfied.

I'm still restless, squirming.

There is an imbalance here. At least there is in my mind. In the beginning, our erotic life was different. After Fresno, we used to see each other once, maybe twice a week. The dam was broken and we had sex each time I saw her, each time she came over or I went to see her.

In my mind we made love every time we saw each other.

In my mind, she saw me as her desirable Adonis.

After marriage, like most men, from time to time I have to engage myself to release the pressure. If masturbation is an art, then I am Renoir. Masturbating while married, while sleeping next to a woman you desire, oh the resentment that builds up. Once I reminded her that we used to make love every time we saw each other, lived for each other's touch. But she was quick to remind me that we've always made love once or twice a week, that we are still on task. Every time we saw each other was how I saw it. Once, maybe twice a week was her point of view, the way she has her marital duty mapped out.

I assume that two years from now, when her biological alarm sounds and she wants my sperm to dance with her egg for the sake of procreation, the patch will come off her arm and we will make love more frequently as she ovulates, we will be dutiful and fuck like rabbits until the mission is accomplished. Then back to business as usual, that alarm sounding again two years later when it is time for the second child. No child should live alone.

At times I think of how we take ski trips and the jazz concerts we go to where all of our friends see us laughing and enjoying life and see us as the couple of all couples.

Not being desired as much as I desire the one I love, the woman I married, makes me feel like I'm some sort of freak. As if I'm abnormal. Hard to explain how I feel at times. Like I'm a straight-A student who does his best only to get a C grade. A failure. As if whatever it takes to stimulate her loins is not in my possession. It feels as if my duties as a man, as a husband, have been reassigned, that moving from boyfriend and lover to devoted and faithful husband has been some sort of an emotional and sexual downgrade, the kind that is tantamount to a demotion.

We live longer. Death might not invite me for a cup of coffee for another fifty years. I ask myself if this is the best it will be between us, can I deal with this until they etch my name and final date in a tombstone. All that to say, I worry about the quality of our relationship. I don't want to start living in a dysfunctional comfort zone, where marriage becomes a prison. If something isn't working I need to know now. Not in divorce court.

A moment passes. I ask, "Do I satisfy you?"

"I don't orgasm all the time."

"You said you came."

"Must I have a mind-blowing orgasm every time?"

"That would be nice."

"I repeat, I do not orgasm every time I have sex."

"You come if you use a vibrator."

"It's a stimulator."

"Well, you come when you use your stimulator, right?"

"Well, yes."

"Every time, right?"

"Sweetie —"

"Or if I pull out and you masturbate, then you can come."

"Where is this going?" She shifts. "Why are we having this discussion?"

I rub my hair. "What if I didn't orgasm with you?"

"What are you talking about?"

"How would you feel if you couldn't make me come?"

She shifts some more. "I don't have to come for it to feel good."

"What if the only way I could come would be to *pull out of you* and *jack off?*"

"Fine. Then I'll start faking orgasms. This is why women fake orgasms. The male ego is so fragile. You have to control everything, even a woman's orgasm."

"Don't start that Gloria Steinem bullshit."

My tone shuts her down.

I say, "I just want to please you. I'm feeling . . . saw these people downstairs . . ."

"What are you taking about?"

"The two couples who got on the elevator with us."

"What two couples?"

"Nothing. Maybe I'm . . . nothing."

"No, say it."

"Guess I'm feeling incompetent."

My vulnerable moment rests between us, staring at her, then at me.

She sighs. "It wasn't a big one, but I had an orgasm."

"But you don't come all the time."

"What is this about, my orgasms?"

I take a breath. "Maybe . . . maybe this isn't about you coming."

"What's the issue?"

I swallow. "Remember the movie *The Lover*?"

"What?"

"Humor me."

"Yes. Another movie with a wretched pedophile."

"He wasn't a pedophile."

"She was a young girl and he was a grown man."

"I'm talking about the love he felt for

her, the love she felt for him."

"Why are you talking about that movie right now?"

"At the end when he calls her and tells her that he still loved her, tells her that he would love her until his death . . . do you feel that way about me? About us?"

"What are you talking about?"

I think, and what word comes to mind is strange. *Equinox.* I want to ask her if we have a sexual equinox, or if we will continue to be as different as night and day. That seems shallow.

Instead I ask what makes sense. "Are you happy?"

"What?"

I tell her, "I'm asking about our marriage as a whole."

"All because of an orgasm?"

Despite the fact that she adopts a forward attitude when confronted, I firm my voice and press through her barriers, let her know I am the man in this bed, say, "Answer the question."

"Get some sleep."

"No, answer."

"If you're asking me if you satisfy me, that means that I'm not satisfying you."

I snap, "Don't do that."

"Do what?"

"Don't do that reverse-psychology bullshit."
Silence.

She whispers, "I'm here to bury a relative."

"Talk to me. Tell me . . . tell me something."

"Please. Don't do this to me. Please? I have enough grief and stress as it is. If you're going to become a burden, if you're going to badger me, go back to the airport."

"You'd love that, wouldn't you? If I went back home. What are you afraid of?"
Silence.

I get close, smell her hair, then ask, "Where did you vanish to?"

She pulls away, knows what I'm asking. About her habit of vanishing to set fire to an herbal shrub. She struggles with herself, then says, "Stop sniffing me like you're a damn dog."

"I hope you didn't bring any of that bullshit on the plane."

"Don't talk to me like that."

I shift around. "It was code orange today. See how they were searching people? They were searching eighty-year-old white women, making them take off their orthopedic shoes."

"Do I smell like I've been getting

high?" she snaps. "Do I?"

"Last thing we need is to get pulled to the side, get busted and treated like terrorists. Something foolish like that could be damaging to our careers." Then I lighten my stiff tone. "Or worse, we could get banned from the airlines and have to ride Greyhound next time."

"Last time, get off my case."

"Where were you?"

"I went to cry. I needed some space and I went down to the lobby, couldn't find anywhere to go, so I went into the library, found a corner, and I cried. Is that okay?"

Her shattered tone rocks me. Makes me feel distant to her emotions. I've never seen her cry. I wish she did not sequester herself with her sadness, wish she threw her arms around me and let me dry her tears. But she cries, evokes sadness under her own terms.

Just like that I feel bad for thinking her to be so stolid. Things affect her but she's not good at expressing them, not like I am. I wear my heart on open display.

I feel shallow for bringing up that issue when the air has been seasoned with death.

I remind myself of what I already know. Of what I have read. Of how Plato described loving the beautiful soul, that

149

which is unseen. It might start off with the physical, but under the influence of true love, we are drawn nearer to the vast sea of beauty until at last we perceive beauty itself, not existing in any being, but beauty alone, absolute, simple, and everlasting.

We become the friends of God. To that consummation we are led by love.

I remind myself that I am flawed. That Genevieve is beautiful.

I love her.

I whisper, "Sometimes I just want to get lost in you. But it feels like you're guarded. Like I've told you before, you're on the other side of a very clean, very sterile glass wall."

"You say that like I'm . . . like I'm in a goddamn prison."

"Exactly. Only it's not Plexiglas. Glass so clear that I can't tell it's there until I reach out to you, not until then do I feel how thick it is, not until then does it get in the way."

"So that's how you see me."

"I know you're there, but I just can't get to you. And it hurts running into glass."

Silence.

She asks, "So you're trying to say that you think I have a sexual dysfunction?"

"All I know is that I get rejected a lot. If

I didn't jack off, I'd have blue balls. If you have hypoactive sexual disorder syndrome, Intrinsa refuels sexual desire."

"Don't insult me."

"You should be at your peak. Don't you think your desire level is low?"

"No."

"Then maybe I just don't do it for you."

"And if I did have hypo-what-the-hell-ever it was, I'm not poisoning my body with pills that cause acne and weight gain, not to mention liver damage. Would that make you happy? Having a fat, horny wife with horrible skin and a bad liver?"

Regret makes me shift. I rub my temples. I try not to, but set free an aggravated sigh.

She asks, "Would it? Is that what it would take to make you happy?"

I don't answer that ringing bell. Leaving her question unanswered irritates her.

I say, "Good night, Genevieve."

She sits up and snaps, "Maybe the problem isn't me."

"What are you saying, it's me?"

"Maybe you need to stop looking out the window and look in the mirror."

"Is that right?"

"Maybe I'm not hypo, you're just hyper. Maybe you need to take saltpeter."

"Saltpeter?"

"What they give men in prison to reduce their desire to fuck each other in the ass."

"Saltpeter is not an *anaphrodisiac*. It's a reagent in analytical chemistry."

"Whatever."

"Get your facts straight, Doc."

"What-the-fuck-ever."

"And if it is, maybe that's what you need to take out of your diet."

Silence.

She lies down, back to me.

She whispers, "You were abused. That's why you are the way you are."

"Abused? What are you talking about?"

She repeats, "You were abused as a child."

"Where did you get that from?"

"A thirty-year-old woman took your virginity, stole your innocence. She was a predator. A pedophile. She took you to the mall and bought you presents, treated you kind, but in the end there was sex. If she had done all those things without sex, she still would be questionable."

I sit up, stare at her silhouette. "Where did this come from?"

"Maybe that's where your addiction, your satyriasis, your behavior stems from."

"Addiction? What addiction?"

"That sexual addiction you have stems

from you *romanticizing* and *glowing* over being abused by a sexual predator, having all types of illicit sex with a damn pedophile."

"Pedophile?"

"That's why you worship movies like *Lolita* and *The Lover*, films that praise sexual deviants."

"You're joking, right?"

"Am I lying? Oh, I'm sorry. Since it was dick getting pussy there was no crime."

"Where is all of this coming from?"

"If you had a thirteen-year-old daughter and a thirty-year-old man was buying her presents, seducing her, having sex with her, even if she called it love, what would you call it?"

"You sit around reading grisly serial-killer-of-the-month novels and you want to chastise me? What does that say about you, somebody who sits around reading novels about killers?"

She persists, "What would you call it? Love or statutory rape?"

"Okay, Genevieve, where are you going with this?"

"The sad thing is that you *romanticize* your exploitation."

"I wasn't exploited."

"Of course not. I'm the stupid one. Why

is it when a man gets laid, if there is *pussy* in the end, why is it in his mind that he has won the battle? Do you fail to see what it has cost you?"

"What it cost me?"

"*Innocence.*"

"I lost my fucking innocence in Pasadena. On a rainy day. When my mother . . . if anything took my fucking innocence it was the rain, it was the streets, it was that fucking city. That fucking accident changed my life and left me living with two people who couldn't give a shit about me."

"You watched your mother die. I saw my mother get murdered. That is no excuse."

"Why in the fuck are you . . . what is your fucking problem?"

"You were exploited as a child. As a teenager. When you were . . . thirteen."

"Was I?"

"By a pathetic and desperate thirty-year-old woman in Fresno."

"You're insane."

"And you're so fucked up that you fail to acknowledge the crime against you."

Silence smothers me. I have to stand, have to pace, have to come back and face her.

I say, "You always have to win, don't you?"

"Me? You can't win a fair fight, so you attack me —"

"I didn't attack you."

"You attacked me."

"I did not fucking attack you."

"Attacked my womanhood."

"I did not attack your womanhood."

"Told me I need . . . unbelievable how you just . . . I suck your dick . . . swallow your jism . . . then you say that I'm not sexually competent —"

"That is not what I said."

"That made me feel . . . like shit."

Silence.

She says, "All because you are incapable of making me come the way *you* want me to come. Don't blame your incompetence on me, sweetheart. *Your* shortcomings are not *my* fault."

That coldness stings. Stings hard.

I get in the bed, stare at the ceiling, knowing that words are not enough. Primal thoughts rise and I think about choking my wife to death, then standing over her body, beating my chest, making Cro-Magnon sounds. But I don't want to end up playing dominoes with Scott Peterson.

She's bouncing her foot. Making disgusted sound after disgusted sound.

I wonder what her thoughts are, if she is pondering my unexpected demise.

I try to become Zen. Still my mind drifts, shifts away philosophical thoughts, and this physical vessel refuses to ignore what stirs in its restless soul. Conflicts play out in my mind, create their own mental movie. Polaroid images of my next sixty years, of our next sixty years, and I stir and wonder what time will do to us, that great healer and destroyer, wonder if what is now, what is certain, wonder if this is the best it will get between us, wonder if that is good enough for me, wonder if my restless soul will settle into a state of complacency.

Genevieve cuddles next to me, as if reading my thoughts, erasing that movie in my mind.

She whispers, "I'm sorry."

I put my arm around her. She kisses my flesh, then settles herself.

I say, "Sorry, too."

Her glass wall becomes thinner. My shield eases down.

But her words, her excited utterances that were meant to damage me, I feel the pain.

She does not understand me. I do not understand her. She does not see the world the way I see the world. But no two people see the world with the same eyes. We have an animal instinct to go after what makes us happy. Right or wrong, we go after what makes us happy.

I convince myself that I was not abused. That when I was thirteen I searched for love.

I close my eyes and drift. The sound of the rain stalks me; humidity continues to smother me, both demons following me into my dreams. I land in a place where my ancestors work for years, blood on their fists, work from sunup to sundown without release, without respect.

The hotel phone rings.

Like at home, the phone is on my side of the bed. I jump to answer before Genevieve wakes up. But she is not asleep. Our conversation left her disturbed. Genevieve turns to me, a stressed-out silhouette breathing roughly in the darkness. She shifts as I answer, listens.

I say, "Hello."

There is a pause.

"May I speak to . . . to . . . Doctor Forbes?"

"Who's calling?"

"Kenya."

"You're calling from Africa?"

"No. This is . . . who am I speaking with?"

"Her husband."

"This is her sister."

I hand Genevieve the phone.

She covers the receiver, looks confused, asks, "Who is calling me here?"

I tell her.

Genevieve sits up, wide awake. "Kenya?"

Just like Grandpa Fred and Willie Esther, another name I have not heard before.

My wife is not breathing. She takes the phone and moves away from the bed. Her conversation doesn't last five seconds, but that seems like forever.

I ask, "What's going on?"

"Says she's in the lobby."

"Your family is here?"

"I don't know who she's with. Maybe . . . maybe they have come here."

Genevieve pauses, stares out the window at the never-ending rain for an eternity.

I say, "You never mentioned anyone named Kenya."

"I never mention my brothers either."

"Which one of your sisters is she?"

She doesn't answer, just rushes to put her clothes on.

Body lethargic, I'm moving at half her

pace, doing the same.

She tells me, "Could you let me . . . I want to . . . maybe I should go alone."

"You sure?"

She becomes jittery, overwhelmed. "My hair."

"Your hair is fine."

"Makeup."

"It's the middle of the night. Nobody cares."

"I smell like sex. You're still draining out of me."

"Then shower. I'll go and tell your family you'll be down in a minute."

She snaps, "No."

I look at her.

Genevieve takes a deep breath. "You smell like sweat and sex too."

Her voice sounds cagey, disturbed, owns a darkness that only a shadowed past could bring. As if something that she has been running away from is tapping her on the shoulder.

Her eyes don't blink, voice trembles. "Wait up here."

I stand for a moment, thinking, then give in to her wishes and sit on the bed.

She dresses, after she brushes her teeth again, after she washes her face, after she cleans her sex. She kisses my forehead, whispers, "What I said, I didn't mean that. I was angry, more with myself than at you. You satisfy me. I love you."

She combs her hair, puts on lip gloss as she walks toward the door. Then she freezes.

Stands there, a life-size statue of herself. Her past breathes down her neck. She takes a reluctant step toward her memory, then stops, now a felon being subpoenaed, forced to go.

I say her name; ask if she's okay.

My wife whispers, "I'm not ready for this. Not sure if I can handle this."

She bounces her fist against her leg in a stabbing motion, killing memories.

Her eyes widen. Her steps falter. She stabs her leg. Those memories rise, will not die. An electrical storm is raging inside her brain. She's not ready to face anyone from her past.

Her voice trembles as she looks at me. "Go downstairs with me. Please?"

She needs me.

That makes me feel good. Validates my existence in this marriage.

I follow her, my Alice taking me deeper into her rabbit hole.

ten

We get off the elevator and see a few people at the front desk. The storm has chased weary travelers here for the night. A flight crew is checking in, no doubt their plane grounded.

I ask, "Where are they?"

"How am I supposed to know?"

"Don't snap at me."

The lobby has a sitting area; three steps up from the reception desk. We know that she can't be waiting outside toward the circular driveway, not in the storm, so we take those three steps. I see a woman standing across the marble floors, beyond the chandeliers, waiting near the front door, resting in a high-back chair, head down, legs crossed, one bouncing like an erratic heartbeat.

The woman raises her head.

My breath catches. I slow down. Genevieve keeps walking.

The same wild hair and low-rise jeans I'd met not too long ago. Same black lace-up sneakers, same tattoos, body piercing, and bangles on the right arm.

Now I know her name.

Kenya.

Her panicky expression turns into shock when she sees us coming toward her, me with her sister, and that astonishment changes into a smile, creates slits of dimples in her cheeks.

She stands when she sees Genevieve, says, "Sister."

Genevieve nods, says, "Kenya."

At first there are no hugs, just that single word and the nod of heads.

Genevieve asks, "Who are you here with?"

"Just me. I'm alone."

Genevieve's body relaxes some, enough to show fear has left her heart.

They measure each other with their eyes. There is an understanding. Then they hug and bits of the past dissipate. They retreat back to their spaces, outside of each other's personal bubble, like two people who were taught to avoid bodily contact with strangers.

Genevieve owns a nervous smile. "This is my husband."

Kenya doesn't smile. "This is a surprise."

162

Kenya reaches to shake my hand, polite and brief, her few words a song. I'm ready for her to tell Genevieve that we met earlier tonight, but Kenya acts like she's never seen me before.

Kenya keeps her distance, regards me with curious eyes.

Genevieve says, "Look at you."

"You've lost weight."

"You have breasts."

"Yeah. Cool, huh?"

"When did you . . . ?"

"Last year. Got tired of being an A-cup."

Genevieve touches her hair. "Where did you get all those tattoos?"

"Frog's. Atlanta. New York. Other places I've been."

"Most people just buy postcards and magnets."

Kenya laughs off Genevieve's criticism, says, "Married? Sister, you're married?"

Genevieve nods, holds her impatience on her tongue. My wife shifts and her eyes widen, a strange look covers her face, some sort of guilt, and for a moment she looks so young.

Kenya asks, "Was there . . . why wasn't I invited to the wedding?"

"There was no fairy-tale wedding. I don't believe in wasting money on ceremony."

Kenya's phone sings Usher. She doesn't answer. Her eyes come back to Genevieve. She smiles. Her surprise shows at the right corner of her lips. Her teeth are straight and white, a wonderful contrast to her beautiful skin, skin that still has that youthful glow, a glow that will become dulled by that bastard we call Time.

Now she shows a different kind of interest. She asks me, "What do you do?"

AIDS researcher is the general term that I use to describe my work. I skip telling her that I have degrees in both molecular and genetic biology from UCSD, don't tell her that I work at Nicolaou Laboratories, just say my research is on human immune deficiency cell growth.

She acts as if she has never seen me before.

Kenya's cellular rings again. Usher ring tone. She doesn't answer.

Genevieve asks Kenya what she is doing here, which means how did she find her.

Kenya says, "Grandpa Fred figured you'd stay in downtown Birmingham. Only three good hotels here, so it wasn't too hard."

"When did you talk to Grandpa Fred?"

"Right before I called you. Did you

know J-Bo was back in jail?"

"For what?"

"Burglary. He stole a shipment of frogs down in Galveston."

"Stupid." Genevieve shakes her head. "So he won't be at the funeral?"

"Please. He won't get out for two years."

"That's enough. I don't want to hear any more bad news."

Kenya takes a hard breath. "Understandable."

"So, Grandpa Fred told you I might be here."

"He figured you'd be staying at the Sheraton. Guess he was halfway right."

Genevieve redirects the tête-à-tête, does that like she's a businesswoman in a board meeting, the CEO of this conversation. "Why are you out in this weather at this time of night?"

Kenya tells us that she was driving in from Stone Mountain, Georgia. The storm came in strong, she had to stop several times, eventually made her way into downtown Birmingham.

Genevieve shakes her head as if what she's hearing doesn't make sense. She tells Kenya, "You had to pass the exit for Odenville and drive thirty minutes to get to Birmingham."

Awkwardness rises, builds a wall between them.

Genevieve asks why she was driving alone. Kenya says that she has been living in New York for the last three years, but moved back to Stone Mountain a few months ago.

I ask, "New York?"

Her cellular sings Usher again. She ignores the call, then she answers, "Yes, New York."

She hands me one of her cards. The front has her beautiful face, a face that no camera will ever do any justice. I flip it over. I should not have flipped it over, should've been content with the innocent smile on that side. The other side disturbs me. Pictures of her in bikinis and other sensual garments, everything from elegant outfits to pink leather pants and cowboy hat.

She says, "As I said, Stone Mountain is a temporary thing."

Genevieve asks, "What were you doing in Stone Mountain?"

"Went to take care of my daddy."

There is a long pause. "How is he?"

"Prostate cancer. He passed six months ago."

The past settles between them. Something is said in the silence.

Genevieve makes a hard sound, then asks, "And you're still there?"

Kenya nods. "For the moment."

Genevieve asks, "Are you going back to New York?"

"Not sure. But I love New York. I finished my BA at Sarah Lawrence College last May. My focus was literature and creative writing."

Kenya has a surreal, dreamlike way of talking.

I clear my throat. "New York and Georgia. You should be used to this humidity."

"Actually, you'd be surprised about how little humidity we get in New York. Besides, the pluses of New York far outweigh any damage the humidity would do. Loads of cultural stuff: the ballet, modern dance, opera, Philharmonic, plays, musicals, jazz clubs, restaurants, museums."

Genevieve watches her. Listens. Reads between the lines.

Kenya. Her jeans are tight and wet. My eyes follow her curves to her small waist, her apple butt, and I look away, toward the front desk, toward the storm outside, a storm that refuses to end. The sky rumbles like it has an ulcer. And we stand here, *they* stand here, in the middle of the night, in the eye of the storm and have a conversation as if there was no disturbance.

Genevieve asks, "Your father leave you anything?"

"Debt. No insurance. You know how we do it."

"He owned a home?"

"Was still staying in an apartment off Memorial Drive."

Genevieve asks, "What are you doing to support yourself in the meantime?"

"My last job was an office assistant. That was out in Marietta, by the Big Chicken."

"And now?"

Kenya answers, "Looking for something with educational benefits. Had thought about trying to get on at Delta, but they're cutting back over seven thousand people."

"So you're done with school? You're stopping at an undergrad degree?"

There is a pause between them. More measuring as the sky rumbles. Genevieve's eyes say *I've pulled myself up, raised the bar, gone from Odenville to Spelman to UCLA to Pepperdine. There is no excuse for failure and I don't want to hear any excuses for slacking.*

Kenya smiles, a mirror of Genevieve's expression.

Kenya's phone rings again. She becomes

168

uneasy, does not answer her summons.

Someone is desperate to find her.

Once again my wife shifts, has a strange, edgy expression on her face.

Genevieve yawns, asks, "Why did you wake me up at this ungodly hour?"

She laughs, tells Genevieve, "Well . . . I couldn't drive anymore, not in this weather."

Genevieve says, "Didn't you know that it was raining before you started your drive?"

"I wasn't going to fly in this weather."

"But you'd drive through floods and a tornado?"

Kenya retorts, "For family, yes."

Genevieve loses her faux smile. Her dimples cease to exist. She shakes her head. She doesn't believe her sister. In her eyes I see a history of lies and deception.

Kenya licks her lips, pauses as if she is trying to maintain her cool.

She says, "Look, Sister, the reason I woke you . . . I was trying to get a room."

"Here?"

"Yes. Here."

"How did you even know I was here?"

"Didn't even know you were checked in here. Not until I called up."

"Uh-huh."

"So, God has his hand in this. Divine intervention."

Genevieve snaps, "Don't do the God crap."

"What do you have against God?"

"I have God in my heart, don't need God shoved down my throat."

"I understand."

"It's late. I'm tired. What's going on, Kenya?"

"Problems with my charge card."

"What kind of problems?"

"Think Deuce canceled my card."

"Who is Deuce?"

"Friend of mine."

"And his name is Deuce?"

"Guy I'm kicking it with."

Genevieve gives her a rugged smile. "How could your friend do that?"

Kenya folds her arms, unfolds her arms. "We had a joint charge card."

"Why would you do that?"

"You know, getting married, already had started combining charge cards."

"Oh. So you're engaged?"

"Was."

"So you're not engaged."

"No big deal."

"Why would he have that control over your credit?"

"Just a charge card. Only have one. We had started combining incomes, consolidating our lives. Actually the card was mine, but he got it for me and I paid the bill. I know how you are when it comes to money. Not trying to stiff you like everybody has done. I have enough to cover this in my ATM. First thing tomorrow, or today I should say, I'll take care of this."

Genevieve's hand rubs her hair, her head drops. "Let me get my purse."

We abandon Kenya, leave her where she stands, wet, arms folded, jeans hugging her vanity, and we hurry back to the elevator, quick steps under a rumbling sky.

Genevieve's eyes are down, head shaking. I glance back before the elevator door closes, see Kenya's stiff face, her gray eyes now slits. As the elevator rises Genevieve is mumbling unkind things about Kenya. Pathological. Unorganized. Self-centered. Manipulative.

I say, "You're shifty."

"I'm shifty because your protein injection is dripping out of me."

I laugh.

She says, "God, feels like a river of tapioca pudding is running down my leg."

Back to our room.

Genevieve's sense of probity overflows

like a volcano, her frustrations with those who do not have their lives highlighted on a wall facing east makes her pace awhile before she gets on task, finds her purse and rants, "She could've said all of that over the phone. Every job she has, the best she can aspire to be is something that has the word *assistant* preceding it."

I'm at the window facing the patio. I tilt a broken plantation shutter and spy outside. That U-Haul is still in front of the Energen Plaza, emergency lights flashing. A slim figure appears, its darkness battling the forces of nature, dashing through the rain to the truck. She runs through the storm, her colorful sorority umbrella losing a battle with the wind. It's Kenya.

Genevieve hurries into the bathroom, begins cleaning herself, water running as she continues to seethe, "Dental assistant. Office assistant. And you know what they say: *assistant* is just a nice way of saying *instant ass*."

"Assistant. *Instant ass*. An anagram."

"Almost, but not quite."

The television is on in the background. Seven dead. A half-million without power. Flooding in more than fifty counties. Expecting up to eight more inches of rain.

Kenya gets in the U-Haul on the driver's

side. With the darkness, the distance, and the low visibility, I can't tell if anyone else is in the cab. She stays inside long enough to grab an overnight bag and turn off the emergency flashers. She gets out, alone, lets her umbrella get blown away. She looks up and I assume she sees me. Her eyes stop on our window. She stands in the storm watching me watch her be clumsy. Lightning booms, lights up Magic City. Kenya runs through puddles and rivers, fights the wind and races back to the hotel.

Genevieve is still talking, my five senses have moved away from her.

Kenya is driving a U-Haul through a storm, through floods, a whirlwind of downed trees, dodging tornadoes to get to a funeral, no money in her pocket, not a single charge card.

I clear my throat and say, "Your sister . . . she's . . ."

"Great. Now she's a model. And a writer. A model who isn't working and a writer who isn't writing. Handing out zed cards. Always has been so conceited. So unfocused, looking for an excuse to not be successful. She's smart but still sells herself in order to further herself."

I ask, "More siblings?"

"Two of my five brothers were taking a

173

vacation out in Elmore last I heard."

"What's Elmore?"

"Jail. With J-Bo locked up for stealing some damn frogs, that makes three on vacation."

"Your dad, same facility?"

"One big family reunion."

I've never seen Genevieve riled like this. Have never heard her talk about her siblings.

She repudiates her old life.

The door closes as she rushes back out of the room, not waiting for me to accompany her. The zed card is still in my hand. My sweaty hand. I read the stats across the bottom.

Height five-eleven. Thirty-six C. Waist twenty-six.

The phone rings. It's Kenya.

She says, "You played that off like a pro."

I swallow. "Sounds like things are rough between you and Deuce."

"I don't want to talk about no damn Deuce."

"No problem."

"Didn't mean to snap at you like that. It's just . . . relationships start off like a Norah Jones song, smooth and melodic, full of flowers and romantic longing and sexual passion. Then end up like a DMX cut, a lot of *motherfuckers* and *bitches* being shouted in the air."

"Been there, done that. Hope I don't end up there again."

"This is surprising. You're not the kind of man I'd imagine LaKeisha with. You're down to earth. She thinks she's better than everybody. So arrogant, like she thinks she is the shit."

"Maybe we shouldn't talk about Genevieve either."

"Part of the reason I came back here was because I was looking for you."

"Were you?"

"Because of the way you looked at me in the hallway."

"How did I look at you?"

"Like you didn't know whether to wind your watch or howl at the moon."

"How did that make you feel?"

"Like I didn't know whether to wind my watch or howl at the moon."

Another pause.

Kenya says, "Then I call her room and . . . when you stepped off the elevator I almost fell on my ass like Michelle from Destiny's Child did on 106th and Park."

Six images, my eyes stay with the toned frame in the bikini, the one that is ninety-five percent naked, the one that shows all of her curves, and I watch those curves as if they were the roads to heaven. I'm suffocating. I'm not breathing. I cough and come back to life.

I swallow again, ask, "Genevieve down there yet?"

"Did LaKeisha tell you her history, our history, about how violent her father was?"

I think of what Genevieve has told me, about their mother being unfulfilled, having many lovers, about her father being humiliated, his ego not being able to take any more, and, how like Othello, he killed his Desdemona, killed what he loved in order to preserve his image as a man.

Thunder. Lightning. Wind strong enough to uproot a tree.

I say, "You don't look old enough to be out of college."

"I'm twenty-two, if that's what you're asking."

I ask her, "When is your birthday?"

"June thirteenth."

Gemini. Restless. Gregarious. Needs change of scenery as stimulation.

She asks, "And you're . . . ?"

"Thirty-two. Born on the Fourth of July."

I accumulate things, would rather eat at

home, for me lovemaking is seldom repetitious, varies with the moon's waxing and waning, intensity varies with the ebb and flow of my emotions.

My eyes remain on the U-Haul. I ask, "What did you do?"

"What do you mean?"

"The U-Haul."

Her breathing thickens.

She says, "Sister . . . she tell you her father killed . . . that her daddy murdered . . ."

"She told me."

More thunder and lightning punctuate her grief.

I ask, "Where were you when it happened?"

"Was there. Standing next to LaKeisha Shauna Smith, crying and screaming."

In that instant she digresses, her accent modifies and takes her back to her youth, sounds extremely Southern, extremely pained, as if she too were ridiculed by her past.

Kenya calls out, says, "Sister. Didn't see you come back down."

Her voice is all smiles and love, her accent as suppressed as her Southern past.

She hangs up.

Kenya leaves me uneasy. Pacing is futile.

177

As futile as winding my watch or howling at the moon.

I sit on the rented bed, my mind going through a Rolodex of thoughts in search of memories that have not yet been cooled by the passage of time.

Lights off, I lay back, arms folded across my chest, and close my eyes.

I center myself, my heartbeat, my breathing.

My mind takes me away from Kenya.

Back to Genevieve before she was my wife.

Oakland. Claremont Resort and Spa.

The weekend after we were engaged.

Six. Nine.

I smile.

69.

Slang term derived from the shape of the numerals.

Slang term for mutual, simultaneous oral sex by two individuals.

I am the six to Genevieve's nine.

She is the six to my nine.

The cacophony of consecutive orgasms fills the room as *Dr. Phil* comes on.

On the nightstand are erotic oils. Books on Kama Sutra. Silk scarves.

We catch our breaths and spoon. The

sandman teases me as I float through cloud nine. Genevieve falls away, leaves me be. I hear her in the bathroom brushing her teeth. My eyes are closed when she comes back, turns up the volume. Dr. Phil's guests are a married couple. Young. Barely married. Already staring at that evil bastard known as divorce.

So it goes.

It buzzes into my dream, that story of pending bankruptcy where Cinderella had to have it her way. I drift away and Dr. Phil is in the room with me. Asking me questions I cannot answer.

"Her husband took loans against his 401(k) to get married?" Genevieve says that and I jerk awake. "Major no-no. He'll never recover. His financial advisor needs his butt kicked."

I yawn and listen. "Sounds like . . . they started their marriage in this financial hole."

"Don't mistake a hole for a financial abyss. The wedding was a money pit. She had the man cashing in his 401(k), giving massages and spa treatments to the brides-maids. Good Lord."

I watch in silence. "Looks like they've been together less than a year."

"And they're broke. Did you hear what

she said a minute ago?"

"Think I had drifted off."

"She's moved into another bedroom."

I yawn again. "Change the channel anytime you feel like it."

"Listen to how she's bitching about how she can't get what she feels she deserves. I think she wanted the wedding, not the marriage. Her warped sense of entitlement is unreal."

We listen to that wife complain like a five-year-old child. She doesn't want to work to help fix the mess they are in; working is not in her plans. Blames all of the failure on her husband.

Love is in his eyes. Disdain colors hers.

Eyes closed, I listen to the husband say he was doing fine before he met her. Now his income is divided by two and the bills have shot through the roof, he is no longer good enough for her. She counters and says she needs a man who can finance her hobbies and fantasies.

Genevieve gets up and runs to the bathroom, calls out, "Turn the volume up."

"Can I change to the Sci-Fi channel?"

"Don't you dare change the channel." She laughs. "Turn it up."

I lean up on one elbow and do what she asks, give her what she needs.

I listen to the disillusioned housewife vent about *her* plan. Her dreams of doing what she wants to do to fulfill herself, and working would mean she has given up her dreams. With her every complaint a devastated and drained look paints the poor man's face, his inner thoughts jumping out at the world. *What about my fucking dreams? Think I planned to be living like this?*

Genevieve yells, "Why did he marry a selfish bitch like that?"

That assessment surprises me. I yell back, "Love makes a man weak."

"Oh, please. Maybe he was just a weak man."

"Surprises me you said that."

She *tsks*. "He has no spine."

"He has a spine. She was a pathetic woman who needed to be rescued."

"Do you think I need to be rescued?"

"This isn't about you."

Genevieve laughs. "Has to be horrible being a man."

"Actually, it's the best thing going."

"How confusing it is for a man to be with a woman who doesn't need to be rescued."

"Believe it or not, Genevieve, we all need to be rescued."

"I don't need rescuing."

"Has to be horrible to be a woman. Look at your fine ass. Smart. Strategic. Professional. You've had to learn to fight like a man and prove you're better."

"Is that right? Now you think you're Dr. Phil."

"Men are still men. Women are the ones in search of an identity that amalgamates masculine power with femininity. That, if anything, has to be confusing for women."

"Is that right?" She laughs. "So I'm bewildered because I don't need rescuing."

"Even if it's from loneliness. Even if it's from ourselves. Admitting your weakness, the part of us that seeks comfort and pleasure, that doesn't make you weak. Makes you human."

She yells, "Let me tell you what I think of your chauvinistic theory."

"What?"

The toilet flushes.

We laugh.

Genevieve comes back, gets under the covers.

My hands find her breasts, her nipples.

She asks, "Do you ever get enough?"

I kiss the back of her neck. "You ever been in love?"

"Once. When I was in the seventh grade."

"Seventh grade?" This time I laugh. "That doesn't count."

"Then maybe you'll be my first real love."

I move closer to her. Rub her back.

She watches Dr. Phil, listens like his words are the equivalent of her Holy Grail.

I give in to the sandman.

She nudges me. "Honey?"

I wake up.

She hands me her purple friend. "Please?"

I smile.

Back then the purple man was my friend.

We were a team.

Magic and Kareem.

Things change.

Now me and the purple man are as sociable as Shaq and Kobe.

Downstairs. Same evening. Jordan's restaurant. View of the San Francisco skyline.

Seafood, vegetables, and chicken dishes. Wine for Genevieve.

Genevieve says, "Women should prepare for the type of man they want to meet."

"Well, you're an exceptional woman."

"I can't be in a relationship and have it based on financial gain."

"That's nice to know. Not a lot of women, at least the ones I've met, have it like that."

She asks, "How is it for a man? Dating, I mean. Be honest."

"Exhilarating at first. Not easy in the long run. I love romance, but some women want romance constantly. The wrong woman can be like having an emotional vampire on your neck. It's expensive, financially and emotionally. And can get to be tiring as hell."

"Tiring. How is it tiring?"

"The energy. Like that woman who was on Dr. Phil. She's another full-time job."

Laughter. "Why do you say that?"

"Has to be a living hell to try and keep her lazy butt happy all the fucking time, busting his balls trying to get her what she needs, the way it gets tiring trying to keep a child entertained."

"Well, men shouldn't start what they can't finish."

"Same for women. Like that woman, if that was the man complaining, I wouldn't be able to call him a man. So, with that in mind, I fail to see her as an emotionally mature woman."

"Interesting."

"You disagree?"

A moment goes by. "I believe a woman should be honest with herself and look at her résumé. Her job résumé. Her financial résumé. Her credit rating. Her goals, if she has any. Even the number of abortions she has had. Write down how she feels about herself. About life."

I ask, "So, once a woman has all of that information, all of those résumés . . . then what?"

"Then she should ask herself if she met a man and he handed her that résumé, would she want to be with him. Would he be her dream man? Or someone she would . . . walk on by."

I nod. "Good point. But people aren't like that."

"If you look in the mirror and don't like what you see, why should a woman want to be with you? Whoever you're with, you inherit what they bring to the table, and vice versa."

"Hadn't really looked at it that way."

She rubs her temples. "I think the alcohol is creeping in and making me babble."

"Well, what you said, all of that goes against the Cinderella Theory. Poor woman gets rescued by a prince, taken to castle, given jewels, and lives happily ever after."

185

"As long as she's beautiful, thin, and pure white."

"So you're not into the fairy-tale, happy-ending thing?"

"Fairy tales are fiction. Fiction is the untruth. The untruth is a lie."

"Therefore?"

"Therefore fairy tales are lies. Therefore there are no happy endings."

Her inner landscape shifts. The sensuous light in her eyes dims, her own history blowing out its candle. She falls into a dark moment. She disappears, leaves her hull behind. Her breathing shortens, lips move into a slow frown. I don't know that she was gone inside a nightmare. I think that she is pissed off, has turned bitter by something that I had said.

I ask, "You okay?"

She jerks a little, like a solider with post-traumatic shock. "What's that?"

"You vanished on me."

"All the fairy-tale talk made me think about Blanche DuBois."

"Who is she?"

"This movie. *A Streetcar Named Desire.*"

"Heard about it. Never saw it. What's it about?"

"Blanche DuBois. A Southern belle. A faded beauty that ended up broken down."

"You want to rent it?"

"No. I've seen it enough to last me a lifetime."

The light clicks on.

I wake up to Genevieve's smiling face, the light a halo behind her head.

She whispers, "Take your clothes off."

"Everything okay?"

"It will be."

We undress.

We get in the bed.

She clicks the light off.

Sleep finds us.

eleven

Bubba Smith says, "Smokey all over the highway. Must be quota time."

"Smokey?"

He catches me off guard. I look over at Genevieve. She is staring out the window, watching her old world go by on I-20. My mind is elsewhere too. On my new world. On Kenya. Saw her at continental breakfast this morning. Her tongue. The silver ring in her pink tongue.

"Highway Patrol," Bubba Smith answers, changing lanes. "Like *Smokey and the Bandit*. I still call 'em Smokey. Not many people do, but I still call 'em Smokey."

The Highway Patrol has drivers pulled over every ten feet.

I say, "Guess the city needs revenue."

"I reckon. I sure could use some more revenue."

We do not pass by German and Italian cars, automobiles that cost more than small houses in some cities. The highway is not cluttered with Hummers or Escalades or SUVs and off-road vehicles that will never go off road. I do not see twenty-four-inch rims that spin.

Traffic here is a breeze. Not like Los Angeles, where sixteen million people ride the grid of freeways every day. Get on the 405 the wrong time of day and a ten-mile ride takes an hour.

Bubba Smith gets caught at a red light as soon as we get off I-20 at U.S. highway 411 in the city of Moody. He rambles that Moody, Branchville, many small towns buffer Odenville from the rest of the world. It's calm and the world looks polite when we take exit 144B. Gas stations and fast-food businesses. Winn-Dixie. Cracker Barrel. Krystal hamburgers. Krispy Kreme. Pizza Hut. A cluster of artery-clogging eateries. Like a last-chance exit for truckers.

There are no Starbucks with cappuccino and wireless connection, no Jamba Juice to get my daily shots of wheatgrass, no Baja Grill to get a broiled chicken burrito.

This is the end of civilization as I know it.

I smell her on my hands. She saturates my pores and my consciousness.

Bubba Smith keeps talking, "You hear

that Tim Burton is remaking *Willy Wonka?*"

"Who?"

"Tim Burton. Did that *Edward Scissorhands* movie. Loved that movie. He's doing another Willy Wonka movie, re-making it with that Depp fella being Willy Wonka this time."

I force my mind to not drift, make myself say, "Hadn't heard."

"With that Johnny Depp. I likes him. Good actor. Was in that *Edward Scissorhands* movie. Heard that Gene Wilder was making a cameo in *Willy Wonka*. Can't wait for that one."

Across the street sits Frog's Ink House, the word TATTOO across its roof in huge black letters, as if they want every passing plane or helicopter to know this is the spot to get inked.

Kenya remains on my mind. Her scent rises from my skin. Feel her tattoos under the tips of my fingers. The provocative words that were on her T-shirt moan and orgasm in my ear. The way she looked at me the moment we met. That wicked smile. And that hidden U-Haul.

My mind pulled me back to continental breakfast at seven this morning, while

190

Genevieve was still asleep. I stepped off the elevator and saw Kenya there. Her hair was in one single braid. Long pink floral skirt with blue flowers, matching necklace, black high-heeled shoes that made her taller, leaner, made her have an apple bottom. Her skirt had a lace opening at the knees, an opening that continued to display skin to mid-shin, showed off her long legs. Her skin glistened. She had herself together, looked more stunning than her zed card, not worn like she was last night, but like the model she wanted to become. Her goddess heels gave her height, added three inches to her five-eleven frame, more definition to her backside.

She saw me looking her way and smiled, came over to me.

She laughed.

I smiled.

Just like that we were in sync.

There was enough erotic chemistry to drown a nation.

While we filled up plates with fruit and croissants we talked about the weather, my eyes transfixed on her mouth, watching the way her tongue ring moved and clacked against her teeth.

I said, "Your tongue ring, did that hurt?"

"Considering what I can do with it, it

was worth the pain."

That changed the temperature, set the tone. Simple conversation was destined to be more than simple conversation. I stared at her and knew that I was ill equipped for any kind of conversation with a woman like her, someone who had an absence of inhibition and propriety on any level. I loathed her as I inhaled, admired her as I exhaled. Loathed her because I didn't understand the recipe, what it took to get a woman to behave like her, how to bottle what she had. Loathed her because she had a freedom that I wished Genevieve possessed.

She said, "I have one more piercing."

"Where?"

"Curious to see?"

She smiled and walked away, went to the beverages, picked up a cup of orange juice.

Her eyes invited me to follow her. I found my way to where she was.

"Genevieve wasn't too happy about your tattoos."

"I noticed. I have two tattoos you can't see."

"I'm scared to ask what you have hidden. Okay, what?"

"Let's see. I have a colorful tattoo of a Christmas tree on the right side of my pussy. And I have a tattoo of turkey and dressing on the left side of my pussy. You know why?"

I asked, "Why?"

She leaned in closer, coyly slanting her head, lowering her voice, then staring intently into my eyes. "Because the best eating is between Thanksgiving and Christmas."

She walked away, her Pickwickian smile leading her sashay, looking back to see if I was pursuing her tattoos and body piercings. She headed down a hallway, away from the elevator. I caught up with Kenya, took her arm and led her inside an empty conference room filled with more aristocratic furniture and books from the era of *Gone With the Wind*. I expected her to try and get away, call off her bluff. Or to snap at me because of the abrupt way I took her arm. She didn't. As soon as the door closed, she stood in front of me. Nothing was said. Not for a moment. Her hand touched my face, rubbed down my neck, to my chest, toyed with the hair on my flesh.

My hand traced from her neck up to her jet-black hair. Her face felt so soft in my hands. I touched her cheek, felt her warm skin. My hand moved across her lips, down her neck, to her breasts. She closed her eyes, closed her eyes and sighed, trembled, inhaled, and sucked in her bottom lip, the thing a woman did when she was swallowing emotion, eating her own desires.

Kenya asked, "What are we doing?"

"This is wrong."

Kenya didn't pull away, didn't stop touching my face, my neck. She knew her power over men, I saw it in her eyes, a feminine supremacy she had grown accustomed to, a control she relished and still downplayed with a simple turn of her lips, a movement that created innocence.

I told her, "We. Need. To stop."

She nodded. "You are Sister's husband."

"And you are my wife's sister."

She leaned and brought her lips to mine, moved in slow motion, put her lips to my lips, eased her tongue inside my mouth, gave me her tongue ring, and our tongues danced and danced and danced, danced until her hands began to wander and touch and feel and explore the length and girth, until I wanted to explore her insides. She moaned. She sighed. She gave me all the sounds I longed to hear. Sensual sounds, a song of promise. We did that until pleasure felt inevitable, until kisses tasted and felt like hot honey, until nature's lotion begged to flow.

Voices were in the hallway, loud enough to kill our momentum.

We backed away.

My erection was as obvious as the hardness of her nipples.

Without taking her eyes off me she moved to the other side of the room, her fingers first caressing her breasts, her nipples, then touching things as she passed. She cleared her throat.

Her coy smile. Her gray eyes. Her tongue ring.

She asked, "How did you meet LaKeisha?"

I almost stammered. "Genevieve."

"Whatever." Her voice remained a soft whisper. "How did you meet Sister?"

I took a hard breath, readjusted to this new mood, told her we met over the 'net, were invited to a speed-dating service, one where a group of professionals who were either too busy to date, or had no dating skills congregated and gave each other three minutes to impress.

She asked, "How does something like that work?"

I told her. A dark room with candles and wine. Soft jazz. Sensual setting at a mansion in Bel-Air. Everyone dressed in black, a few men in tuxedos. Women were at tables. A bell rang. The men changed tables, went to the next woman. Three minutes. Bell rang. Men moved on to the next table. At the end of the evening you filled out forms, checked boxes, who you wanted to get to know better, and if they felt the same, then information was passed on.

What was good about that evening was that you had an idea of who you were sitting across from. People who were not into infidelity, lowering their partner's self-esteem, people who were financially responsible, had at least a bachelor's degree, and no children.

A thousand dollars bought you the illusion of being on a level playing field.

That night I asked Genevieve what else she wanted to tell me about herself. She said "Nothing." She was a private person. I was the same. We both smiled at that. For me that was good enough. Maybe even perfect. Over the last few years I'd dated women who were divorced and all they talked about was their bad marriages and what bastards their exes were. I'd dated women who had children and all they talked about was their kids.

It was just us. No families. Like Adam and Eve.

Kenya said, "Three minutes."

"Yup."

"Love at first sight?"

I smiled a weak smile. "Fools rush in."

Then I moved across the room, stood near her, close enough to smell her perfume. She moved closer to me in response.

She said, "So you don't have to belabor the point if it's not going your way."

"Belabor?"

"The three-minute thing."

"Yeah, guess so."

"Sounds very efficient," Kenya said with a twisted smile. "Like Sister."

"She is. Everything in her life is planned."

"You?"

"I'm the disorganized one. I throw darts at a board. She maps her life out."

Kenya raised a brow. "Don't tell me that she still writes everything on big cardboard."

"It's more sophisticated than cardboard."

"Good Lord."

"She will be the next Oprah."

Kenya shakes her head. "You don't want that."

"Why not?"

"If she becomes an Oprah, heaven

forbid, then you've got the slow Stedmanization of your manhood, which could be your worst nightmare."

"Stedmanization?"

"Eric Benet was Stedmanized by Halle Berry. Ben Affleck would've been Stedmanized by J. Lo. That was why he bailed. Now Marc Anthony is with J. Lo and about to be Stedmanized. No man should ever want to exist in a woman's shadow."

I said, "Well, there goes your invitation to *The Oprah Winfrey Show*."

She laughed a soft laugh, her voice again like the whispering of girls. "You're kind of funny, you know that? Cute and funny."

I asked, "How did you get to Stedmanization from three-minute dating?"

"Be honest. Was that three-minute dating thing . . . did you like that shit?"

"Yep. Much better than taking a woman to dinner then finding out she has three kids and an ex-husband, listening to her babble about a job she hates, delinquent child support, and an ongoing custody battle from appetizer to entrée to dessert."

"I have at least twenty-one questions that I always ask a man."

"Is that right? Like what?"

"Hmmm. Are you looking to be sexually involved exclusively, when was the last time you had sex, family plans, last time you had sex, have kids, want kids, have a baby momma, got baby momma drama, if you have a baby momma are you still having sex with her, ever been to prison, been fucked in the ass, do you fuck men in the ass, do you fantasize about fucking a man in the ass or letting a man fuck you in the ass, when was the last time you had sex, stuff like that."

"So you have a list. You make lists."

"Not like Sister."

"A list is a list."

"Deuce was . . . guess if he slept with that ugly *shit*, he was sleeping with everybody."

I didn't say anything. Her abrupt bitterness shut me down.

She shook her head. "Three-minute dating."

And just like that her bitterness went dry, its faucet turned off.

It surprised me that Kenya took all that in without any hard questions, just nodded in a way that said that what I'd told her didn't surprise her, that it sounded like the sister she knew, the one who was efficient, her life mapped out and posted on a wall

199

facing the rising sun.

Kenya asked, "You ever wonder about love?"

"What you mean?"

"Love. Why does it come? Why does it go away?"

I shrugged. "For some of us love comes into the room, kicks her shoes off, finds the most comfortable sofa, and lies down, rests, has no intention of going anywhere. For others love walks in smoking a cigarette, checking her watch every two seconds, jittery, with one hand on the doorknob, heart rate up, always in sprinter's position, ready to run."

"You sound like a professor."

"Is that a bad thing?"

"Not at all. Just sounds like you're a smart man."

"You came up with Stedmanization and now you're calling me smart?"

She laughed.

I said, "I'm trying to figure it all out. I have more questions than answers. Not smart."

"AIDS research?" Kenya smiled. "A smart man."

"What happened between you and your fiancé?"

That stalled her. Any happiness she had

drained away. "Don't know. Time, I guess."

"Time messes us all up. Forces us to change, to evolve. If you ask me, the problem is we evolve. We change. If only we could stay where we were. Inside that moment of bliss."

"Yeah, that would be cool." She sighed. "I've seen my friend's relationships crash and burn. They all start off so nice. Then everything seems to go bad. Mortgage. This. That."

"Normal things do us in. Maybe we don't evolve, maybe we digress."

"You're confusing me."

"I'm confused." I shrugged. "Trying to think it out. Trying to make sense of it all."

"Of all what?"

"Of life. Of the things I feel. Of my own desires. Of myself. Why I feel restless at times."

"So, that's it." She nodded like she understood. "The bottom line is that we change."

"Without a doubt. We get lost in a maze."

"Okay, since you're the smart one, how do we not get lost in the maze?"

"Shit, the question is if we get lost, how do we find our way back home?"

I saw it in her eyes. There was an undeniable energy between us the moment we met. I licked my lips and sighed. She parted her lips, made her tongue ring dance a sensual dance. Staring at her was like spending an idyllic vacation in the tropical South Pacific.

I told her, "Your skin is beautiful."

"Have Choctaw in my blood. Lot of us do. This used to be part of the Choctaw Nation. Creek and Cherokee were in this part of the country too. Until the government rounded up all the Native Americans and forced them to move west to Oklahoma."

"Didn't know that."

"Don't tell me that you don't know Sister is part Choctaw?"

"I know that. Just didn't know this was part of the Choctaw Nation."

"I see some Native American in your features. See it in your skin tone too."

I nodded. "My great-grandmother. My mother's grandmother. She was buried on Seminole sacred ground in Brackettville, Texas. I don't know a lot about her, just saw pictures. She didn't talk about her Indian heritage. She had bad experiences as a child."

"We're black, part Choctaw, part Cherokee, some Irish from what I hear. Part of our family is white. Pasty skin with red hair and green eyes. The South is a mixed bag of tricks."

I said, "Sounds like your relatives cross-pollinated more than flies in Mendel's lab."

She smiled. She had no idea what I meant, but she smiled. I stared into her gray eyes and science fluttered through my mind, theories on splitting and blending, chromosomes. When two plants bred, the variations of their traits were combined. I shifted, stopped studying her, ceased considering what was dominant and recessive, quickly shut that analytical part of my brain down.

She softened her voice and asked, "Can we stop bullshitting now?"

"Yes."

She said, "I really want to kiss you again."

"Do you?"

"That kiss was like a double shot of espresso."

"Was it?"

"Don't act like you don't know. Surprised me."

"Did I?"

"Had my clit doing the Harlem Shake."

"You had me at hello."

She paused. "In my room."

"Sure you want me to come down there?"

"Might show you my other piercing."

"Where is it?"

She winked. "Guess."

"Did that hurt?"

"Trust me. It was worth it. Every time I cross my legs I get closer to heaven."

"Sure you want me to come to your room?"

"Will you be a gentleman?"

"Depends on what kind of woman you are behind a closed door."

"This is getting crazy." She took a sharp breath, ran her hand over her braid, today her appearance so tame, regal, and bohemian. "Look, I don't want to hurt anybody, I really don't."

"It's all fun. Just talk."

"Yeah. It's just us shooting the breeze and bullshitting."

I nodded. "Yeah."

"Is it?"

"We can walk away."

"Can we?"

"What do you want to do?"

"Don't want you to think I'm . . . that this is easy for me." She paused, took another sharp breath. "Give me ten minutes. I'll think about it. You think about it. If you can get away for a few, come to my room. If you come and I don't answer the door, don't take it personal."

"If I don't knock on your door, don't take it personal."

"Actually, I don't want you to come. But I want you to, too."

She opened the door, walked away, head down like she was in conflict, didn't look back. I stepped out into the hallway, but didn't follow her. I watched. Watching her in high heels, the way her hips moved, was ecstasy. Her easygoing sway was like unwinding on the sandy white beaches and enjoying the glorious sunsets on Fiji. An island built for paradise.

I watched her get on the elevator, still not looking back.

A minute passed before I got on an elevator.

I licked my lips, shook my head, rubbed my eyes. Tingling rose, spread. I swallowed that feeling, a flaming desire to swim deep inside her, savor the clear and warm waters.

I wasn't going to her room. To her bed. I wasn't going to look for what was missing in mine. I closed my eyes. Reminded myself that nothing was missing in my world, that I was insane, that there was more to loving than sex. That I would not allow my frustration to cause me to chase the orgasm. I imagined Genevieve doing this to me, imagined myself going insane.

Love should be uncomplicated, uncompromising, and unconditional.

Love should not have room for distraction.

Headstones above the graves of many a failed marriage should be marked with that singular word, with those three syllables. *Distraction*. I would not be distracted. I would not lose my balance. Never. I loved my wife. Loved her mind and body. It was the brains behind the beauty that proved to be the most beneficial. I repeated that over as if it was my mantra.

I took to the hallway and hurried by Kenya's door, moved down three rooms, stood in front of the door to my room. Room key in my hand. Music was on the other side of my door.

Stedmanization.

That map that was on her west wall. Her list of accomplishments. I was on that list. I was a checkmark on a flowchart that told what and when she would be doing from now until she received her call to glory. If her life was flowcharted, that meant my life was flowcharted as well. That map told what I would be doing until that same moment. That I would not have children until she was ready. That nothing would be done until it fit her master plan.

The slow Stedmanization of your manhood, which could be your worst nightmare.

At first I thought the hallway was creeping by me, thought I was standing still while the world went by, floating like that famous shot in a Spike Lee movie. I looked down. My legs were betraying me, leading me closer to Kenya's room. I clenched my teeth, made my legs be still.

I despised Kenya as I inhaled, hated her interpretation of my life.

But I desired her as I exhaled.

I stopped moving, allowed my emotions to wrestle with my intelligence, what was felt debated with what was learned. In the end my intelligence told me that I didn't despise Kenya. Not her. *What she represented.* What Genevieve could not give me left me tormented. If I could cut that free-spirited part away from Kenya and give it to Genevieve as a gift, I would. What she has I had been denied for so long.

No, I would not give it to Genevieve in whole, but in measured doses, would give her just enough of what I felt was missing without being abusive to the woman she was now. Would mix it with honey, spoon-feed the Doctor Forbes who was so ambitious with the Genevieve who brought me smoothies, with the woman who taught children in our neighborhood how to swim.

I leaned against the wall, palms sweating, heart beating to its own drummer, while that battle between id and superego manifested itself. Id was violent by nature, the devil incarnate, more persuasive than the angelic part of me governed by morals and the principal of reality.

In Genevieve's battles between her id and superego, superego always won.

Genevieve was in one room waiting for me.

Kenya was in another.

I thought about *The Lover*. Those images. The young girl, devastated, sitting in that room on their bed, waiting for him to come after he was married, but he never went to her love.

The way my mother sat and waited for my daddy to come back, in vain.

And then at the end of that movie, her North China lover's chauffeured car just sitting there on the docks, in the shadows as her ship pulled away. He had married a woman who was not his first choice. His lover was heartbroken, destined to marry a man who was not her first choice.

First choice.

My wife was not my first choice. I was thirty when I met her. Had lived and loved more times than I chose to remember. And, with her being older, I knew I couldn't have been her first choice. That wasn't a bad thing; just a way of life, a way of finding love. I doubt if many people married their first choice. Because nine times out of ten, we weren't our first choice's first choice.

To someone we are all less than ideal.

That is not said to diminish love. It's said because that's the way life is.

That scene lives inside me. Unshakable because it was so palpable, so sad.

I raised my hand, stared at my wedding ring. My legs started to bend and I eased down on the carpet, my hand pulling at my hair. People got off the elevator, talking, walking by me.

I never raised my head.

My eyes were on my watch, the time, counting the minutes between heaven and hell.

I wipe my lips and look at my fingers, expect to see bloodred lipstick on my flesh. Nothing is there. I swallow and expect to taste her. Nothing is there. I inhale and expect to smell her. Nothing is there. I quiver, shake those wretched thoughts away, look over at my wife, expect her to be staring at me, reading my mind, her expression that of horror and disdain. She is like a child, so unaware. I look at Genevieve's black slacks and black jacket, gaze at her bronze lips with hints of gold, and force Kenya's bohemian vision out of my eyes. They are sisters. They are almost of opposite complexions and temperaments but of the same DNA. Melded together, in a controlled environment, in my mind, that Frankenstein-ian experiment would yield the perfect woman. I stare at my wife, holding her hand, and search for similar features, for family traits, find similarities to her sister in her forehead and nose.

She senses my uneasiness, asks, "What's wrong?"

"Just worried about you."

Guilt rises. She is a good wife. I should be on my knees until they are red with blood.

Bubba Smith interrupts my guilt trip, brings me back to this road trip when he says, "Got some cold water up here in a chest if y'all want some."

Genevieve shifts, runs her hand over her hair, says, "Please. Thank you."

Bubba Smith hands her two bottles. She thanks him and opens mine first, then hers, before she places both in the holders.

Bubba Smith says, "I have a copy of *St. Clair Times* up here. *Birmingham Times* too."

Genevieve mumbles, "No, thank you."

"Don't blame you, ma'am. Nothing in them papers but bad news. Woman was attacked with a chain saw then set on fire. Stalked her and her boyfriend, her ex-husband did. Paper said she had cuts and burns over ninety percent of her body. Bad enough that Bicycle Bob got killed by them two fools. Why they want to do a homeless man like that, only God knows. And that dang Eric Rudolph. I'm not for abortion, but I'm not for blowing up people about it either."

Genevieve tunes out his chatter, says nothing.

A moment later Bubba Smith says, "Radio control's on your arm rest if you want music. You might want to try 95.7 out of Birmingham. Lot of people I pick up like that station."

Genevieve's mind has taken her back to her own Neverland. She stares out the window as if she sees someone walking up the highway. I see no one. But we see our own ghosts.

Truckers' and the locals' noses come our way like dogs sniffing strange scents. Riding in a Town Car, we stand out from the dented pickup trucks and older cars that cruise the roads in this part of the world, a city that looks like a hardworking poster for Wal-Mart.

I pay attention, remember history and Jim Crow, try to hear the echo from long-dead sharecroppers and people who worked at the steel mills and coal mines. Listen to the black men who were shackled and given hard labor for petty crimes like vagrancy. Look to the branches on trees and look for the remains of ropes, reminders not to raise your eyes to a white man or woman, especially the latter. Listen for the sounds left behind by Genevieve's people.

A black woman being driven by a white man. Times have changed.

We come up on a real estate office that has a gravel easement leading into a paved parking lot big enough for six cars. A sign is out front, black lettering on a white bill-board.

LEEDS 1.5 STORY
3BR 2BA
OVER FULL BASEMENT
$179,000

Less than the cost of a one-bedroom condo in Culver City.

The scenery changes, becomes less city and more trees, populated with more trailer homes and dilapidated structures that could pass for *Blue Collar TV*'s Redneck Yard of the Week. Homes that are mobile and a yard filled with cars that aren't. Nowhere has a middle and this is it.

Bubba Smith says, "Don't mind my asking, what y'all do out there in California?"

Genevieve folds her arms and stares out the window, her foot bouncing ever so gently. Controlled angst. She wipes her palms on her pants. So uneasy with this trip that's taking us deeper into her history. I touch my wife; she licks her lips, but doesn't give me her eyes.

He says, "Told my wife about y'all. She was thinking y'all were in show business or something. Wanted me to ask 'cause she sings and would love to make a record one day."

I say, "Let me guess. She sings Loretta Lynn songs."

"Not no more. She'll cuss the Lord before she plays Loretta Lynn in our house."

Genevieve's body is here but her mind is on its own journey.

Bubba Smith said, "If you know anybody, would love to get the missus on one of them shows and get her an ambush makeover. Get her looking sophisticated. She would love that."

"We're not in show business."

"Too bad. She's going to the Super Soap Weekend at the MGM in Orlando and woulda been nice to get her all fancied up. She's gonna try'n meet Susan Lucci. The wife has started another one of them fan Web sites for that gal. That's Erica on *All My Children*, if you don't know."

I tell Bubba Smith I work at Nicolaou Laboratories. He perks up, keeps talking, and wants to know — if I don't mind answering — what I do there. I tell him that I work with a group of people who are working on a cure for a life-threatening disease that attacks the immune system.

He wants to know what I mean. I tell him that I am an AIDS researcher. It's not the type of occupation that yields a positive response. Not something you reveal and

214

others say they have always wanted to do the same thing. Curing diseases has no entertainment value.

He makes a noise, bobs his head, chews his lip, tells me, "God created AIDS."

"Is that right?"

"Yessir. That's why man can't find no cure."

"Why would God create something like that?"

"He wanted to kill off some *particular* creatures, same way he killed off the dinosaurs."

"I heard a rumor that an asteroid killed the dinosaurs."

"God sent the asteroid."

"Oh. Right."

Bubba Smith smiles a smile that says, "Checkmate."

Genevieve glances his way long enough to shake her head and sigh.

Welcome to the South, where God the Almighty is also the root of all evil.

I fight the urge to ask him to explain why God created the common cold, or polio, or syphilis, Parkinson's, Lupus, other ailments, but know that conversation would take us nowhere.

He shuns the Internet, would rather ride a donkey than fly in a plane, knows that he is smarter and wiser than I will ever be. His god has given him a level of understanding that surpasses educated men. And blessed him with a wife who gets kicked out of Loretta Lynn concerts for being too loud. I don't argue the acumen of his personal relationship with the God of his making against those things in science that he does not understand. This is his country. The parade of cars boasting pious bumper stickers reminds me where I am.

I've never read the Bible. I own a few versions. From time to time I tell myself that I'll read it cover to cover, will start on some distant New Year's and be done by the following Christmas, will become a scholar of the scripture and draw my own conclusions. And I will become fully aware of that part of history, of the relationship between the pagans and the Christians, of the Greek gods and the singular god that has risen and replaced all others.

Thoughts, images of my momma come and go. Remember her at South Union Baptist Church, singing and catching the spirit. She didn't go often, but when she did she rejoiced.

I lose that thought when I see a Confederate flag in the front window of one of the fourth-rate businesses. I want to curse. We pass pickup trucks and signs letting us know that not only were we heading into the heart of God's country, but toward St. Clair Correctional Facility as well.

In a low voice I ask Genevieve, "Is that where . . . your father . . . ?"

"Daddy's at Elmore. Just told you that last night."

That is my first time hearing her call him Daddy.

Her eyes glaze over and she lowers her head, wipes her palms on her pants.

She fades again.

Historic churches stand out like sentries watching sins. Each has its own marquee, some competition with the spiritual message. Ebenezer United wants people to know that God uses us not because we're perfect, but because we believe. Branchville Church declares, "God: Don't leave home without him." While at Calvary Baptist they offer "Free trip to Heaven. Details inside!"

Bubba Smith asks, "What street am I turning on to get to where we going, Ma'am?"

Genevieve inhales deeply, shifts as if she hates Bubba Smith. Or the smell of cigarettes that permeates his black suit and rises from his pale skin. Or his greasy hair. Or his ill-trimmed moustache. Maybe just hates his question. My wife has transitioned from this city spotted with trailer homes and dilapidated structures lining a two-lane highway, a route filled with old churches and immaculate American flags, to getting her PhD at a prestigious city that overlooks the Pacific Ocean. She has books in Spanish and French and Portuguese on her shelves, postcards of places where she has traveled and stayed at luxurious hotels. Places she went and made love before she met me. Our backyard is tropical. Our own paradise. Where Genevieve is the most comfortable.

Bubba Smith reminds Genevieve of all the things she wants to forget.

She sucks in some air. "Alabama Street. Toward the historic Bank of Odenville."

"Sounds like you know your way around."

She nods. "I know all about red link sausages and mountain oysters and going to the market and buying a half pound of hogshead cheese and a half pound of hook cheese and going down to Mississippi and seeing levees and standing in the dirt fields and watching crop dusters."

My eyes go to her, to her new openness.

I have never heard of those experiences.

Bubba Smith says, "I was born in Panther Burn, Mississippi."

"Panther Burn." Genevieve nods. "I'm familiar with Sharkey County."

"My daddy moved us from Panther Burn to Pell City when I was a boy, ma'am."

"Pell City. Springville. Acmar. Margaret. Leeds. Knew them all."

Bubba Smith laughs. "Get out of here. How long since you been this way?"

Genevieve mumbles, "Twenty years."

"If you ain't been here in twenty years things have changed. All these subdivisions, the way Moody is looking, and Jack's Restaurant. New post office. New fire station. They have a new fire truck. And two new police cars. And they are about to annex Peaceful Meadows. They get that subdivision and Odenville will have close to twelve, maybe thirteen hundred people. And they fixed up the park. Used prison labor to get that back in shape. Did a good job, you ask me."

Genevieve shakes her head, mumbles something, her tone thick and unfamiliar.

Bubba Smith rambles on, still excited, "You have to go down to Beaver Creek Shopping Center, that's at 411 and 174.

219

So much traffic they had to put in a stop light. And they turned Third Avenue into a one-way street. Ma'am, you said you was here twenty years ago?"

"It's changed a lot." Now her tone is clear again. Her eyes clear. Once again Doctor Genevieve Forbes. "There was nothing but churches and farms, haystacks and old barns, a few log cabins here and there. But yes, I do have memories of this area, of all these roads."

"Ain't that something? You have people from around here?"

"I was born here in Beaver Valley."

"We all came out of Beaver Valley. Little joke, ma'am. Don't mean nothing by it."

Genevieve doesn't hear him, is talking to herself, images and memories moving across her eyes like on a movie screen. "I grew up in what used to be called Hardin's Shop."

"Get out of Dodge. So you was born here."

"Inside a trailer home that always smelled like fried gizzard and liver."

"My wife makes the best fried gizzards. Lord knows that's what got me hooked."

Genevieve's face changes, become softer, innocent, as if she is becoming someone else. Surrendering. Melting. In her eyes, I see a thousand memories returning to her mind, as she stares at places that she forgot were real, and her every breath thickens like Southern air.

Bubba Smith continues to pry, asks, "What's your last name, ma'am?"

She pauses as if she has to think, looks at me, mouth open as if she can't remember.

I say, "Forbes."

She remembers, then nods. "Forbes."

"Forbes. Don't know any Forbes. You look familiar. Thought you might've been one of the Funderburgs. Not many people fly out here and come this way, not from Los Angeles. I reckon people out that way don't even know about Odenville or any town out this way."

My wife struggles to find herself, emphasizes, "Doctor Genevieve Forbes."

"I might know your people. I know most everybody 'round this way. Meant to say you looked familiar last night, but your last name, the name on my paperwork, it don't ring a bell with me. Asked the missus and she didn't know anybody last name Forbes out this way either."

Genevieve sits up straight. "I grew up across from St. Clair High School."

"Where exactly?"

"The trailer homes." Genevieve glances

at me, tries to read my surprise, then turns her eyes away and swallows. "Trailers behind the civic center. The Smith family."

"Fred Smith 'nem?"

"Yes."

"What you to Fred Smith 'nem?"

"I'm his granddaughter."

"His granddaughter?" Disbelief echoes. "Who your daddy, you don't mind me asking."

"Roger. He was a musician at the church."

"And he worked at a funeral home."

"Yes. He's incarcerated."

"Roger Smith? Roger?" Bubba gets excited. "They call him Gravedigger."

"Yes. Gravedigger is my father. He's my daddy."

Bubba Smith says, "Lord, good Lord. I'm a Smith. Bubba Smith. I'm your uncle."

Genevieve doesn't respond. I look at her. Her expression becomes void, a black curtain blocking out the heat and light of emotions, but heated tears are rolling down her face.

"We ain't never met because . . . good Lord, good Lord, good Lord. You're back to bury Willie Esther. Good Lord, good Lord. You . . . you're the one . . . your momma . . . and Gravedigger . . ."

"It was the talk of the town." Genevieve holds her left hand with her right hand, smiles a wooden smile, her voice cracks. "Daddy killing Momma. Black woman being killed by a white man who actually went to jail for it. White man killing a black whore. It was the talk of the town."

"Lord, have mercy."

We approach a road sign: ODENVILLE TOWN LIMIT.

A woeful moan escapes Genevieve. She diminishes right before my eyes.

I touch my wife. She moves my hand like I'm an electric shock, not to get away from me, but she's struggling for the controls, letting her window down, the damp air flooding the car.

She raises her voice, "Driver, pull over please."

Bubba Smith jerks, slows down, is rattled, voice shaky. "Ma'am?"

She rages, *"Stop the car."*

"Yes, ma'am. There's a Dodge truck riding a little too close behind me, have to —"

Genevieve is struggling to get her door open, her eyes filled with tears.

I pull her arm, yank her to me, shake her, snap her name, "Genevieve."

"Pull over." She gives up, puts her head between her legs. Her voice fades. She stops fighting, looks dizzy, lost. "I need . . . pull . . . stop . . . please stop . . . need to get out."

I snap, "Stop the damn car."

"Can't breathe. I can't breathe."

The car stops. Like time.

Like I should've as I walked toward Kenya's room a few hours ago.

twelve

Two hours ago.

Before Genevieve's memories overwhelmed her and sent her into a panic attack.

Two short hours ago.

I stand up and go to Kenya's room.

I get to her door, knock once, and prepare to call this insanity off before it starts.

She opens the door.

I expect her to have eyes filled with buyer's remorse, to look at me and shake her head, the better part of an hour being enough time for her to consider the consequences of her actions.

Her hair is down, wavy, no longer in a braid, no longer in the style of a schoolgirl.

She wears a smile, one more stunning than the one on her zed cards.

The air is on, room chilled, most of the lights turned off, and a candle is lit.

She has on high heels and black lacy boy shorts. Nothing else. Her skin is fresh, can

225

smell the brand-new scent from her quick shower. Her flesh shines, her lotion fruity, it glitters. The panther on her shoulder, the sun on her belly, her belly rings, everything about her glistens.

Her legs look so long, like forever in brown.

Her breasts, brown and free, soft and firm, nipples erect and as dark as my intentions.

One glance at her and I forget how my wife and I used to wake up drinking coffee, making plans to change the imperfect world into a diamond. I forget not to lust. My moral center moves away from me. I try to follow my own righteousness as it turns and races away from Kenya, from that woman who has the gray eyes of a cat, the smile of a witch, but centrifugal force throws me in a straight line of travel toward her.

Her scent comes to me, soft and gentle, lavender, so sensual. Her energy, so erotic, and that overwhelms me, floods me, almost capsizes me.

She says, "Close the door."

She walks away. With the eyes of a thief, I glance down the hallway, close the door.

Kenya moves across the room, slow steps, then she turns around, again smiling.

It's as if I'm lost and what I see in her eyes is the beacon to lead me home. What I feel in my belly, it's as if I'm still moving, going too fast on that unpaved, oil-slick road, and approaching a treacherous curve, afraid to look ahead at my destiny and unable to turn my head away. All I can do is hold on and hope for the best. I want to scream her name.

I look away only to be pulled toward her gray eyes again.

She smiles, sashays around the room, her movements subtle and sensuous, dreamlike with a little twitch in her step, her hips and breasts and backside moving like a song. Parts of her apple bottom hang below the border of her boy shorts. My eyes follow her rhythm. She stands still, surreal and dreamlike. I ride the glance beyond the border of decency, allow my gaze to become an unabashed stare. Mouth open, barely blinking, thoughts written all over my face, I ride this precarious road from curiosity into the land of obsession.

I ride and I ride.

I should run, but I ride.

What lives beyond obsession? Sheer madness. I'm on the border of that . . . that heated sensation that is both exhilarating and terrifying, when she glances my way, again, measuring, and she freezes. Small mouth, full lips that turn up into a never-ending expression of pleasantry.

I close my mouth. I blink. I swallow. I look away.

"Do you and Sister have sex a lot?"

"Not really."

"You know why married people stop having sex?"

"No, but I have a feeling you're going to tell me."

"Marriage legalizes sex. Anything legal is banal."

I think about my wife. I use to feel that way about her. How I lived to have her breath on my skin. How I wanted to be inside her every waking moment. How I loved to swim up her river and drink from between her thighs. Everything has changed. Things are not bad. Just different.

We love. We share. We grow. We are friends.

But with Genevieve the urgency for emotional eroticism is gone.

I close my eyes, wish this away.

When I open my eyes, her gray eyes are still on me.

Her glance meets my eyes and she rides her own expression.

228

Her face is unreadable, opaque.

She asks, "You and Sister still kiss?"

"Yes. Why?"

"Then there is hope."

"Based on what?"

"The first thing to go is the kissing. You kiss less and less. Even when you have sex the kissing becomes less and less. Soon it's just sex. You might suck a dick, he might eat you out, but there is no kissing. Even the sucking and eating becomes less. But the kissing is usually the first to go. Less and less until it's gone. Sex with no kissing. You become each other's whore."

"I love kissing."

She smiles. "The way you move your tongue, you love more than that."

What is this tingling, this fire I feel when I look at her? It's in my loins, but not only in my loins. It radiates, consumes me. A soft moan rises inside me. I clench my teeth and swallow my own madness. The fire stays. Spreads. Grows until it numbs me and awakens me all at once.

The power of a glance.

We stare.

Sinful thoughts rise like the sun on a Sunday morning.

I imagine her in ways that make my heart race, that embarrass me to no end.

She says, "You're afraid."

I don't answer, just stare as if I'm watching a provocative display at the Erotic Museum in Hollywood. She looks away first, takes small steps, moves in the opposite direction, her back to me. I remember to breathe. Making myself look away was a battle in itself.

My insides fall apart, tell me that I'm back to speeding on that oil-slick road, hydroplaning toward a brick wall. My stare is intense enough for her to cry foul, to tell my wife she is offended.

My fear rises.

She does something I don't expect.

She takes off her boy shorts.

Now she's only wearing her heels.

I blink a few times, then my smile rises.

She chuckles, raises her hand in a sensual motion.

I set free a soft laugh.

She walks to me.

Her lips part and she shows me the pinkness of her tongue and her tongue ring. I'm transfixed as that pinkness moves across her bottom lip, licking away her private thoughts.

She says, "We're supposed to kiss."

"Yeah."

She takes my fingers in her mouth, sucks

them one at a time, two at a time, three, then again one at a time, giving oral stimulation from tip to root. She licks my palm. I moan. She sucks. Sucks until I can't stand it. I pull away. Her hand grazes my face. I ache. Her touch kills me a thousand times, maddening. I pull her to me, cover her mouth with mine, begin kissing, first softly, then with voraciousness I've never experienced. I touch her vagina. She pulls away. I pull her back. We play that game until . . . moans and touches . . . until . . . she feels so good in my hands . . . until my explosion rises. We kiss. We kiss. And we kiss. Then we catch our breath, gaze into each other's eyes and see the inevitable, feel our wretched destiny approaching.

She whispers, "Come fuck me."

I stare, watch the leopard on her shoulder, hear it growling at me as she moves away.

"Fuck me or leave. Your choice."

She gets on the bed, dark skin on angelic sheets, legs apart. Her vagina is clean-shaven. Small lips, very tame, very beautiful. A five-star delicacy with excellent presentation.

I tell her, "Turn over."

She does, ass in the air, her face turned toward me, watching me.

I say, "On your knees."

She does. It's sheer beauty. A sea of black mystery resting on a white pearl.

I undress.

She shudders, holds me tight, lets out a wonderful sigh when I break her skin.

I love that sound. I have missed that sound.

I pull out, go in again.

Again she sighs, convulses in a way that hardens me more, melts my inhibition.

She curses, sings, "Oh god oh god oh god."

I pull out to the tip, ease part way in, do that over and over, too many times to count.

Her face tenses, back arches, ass rises up against me as her hands grab fistfuls of sheets.

I am naked, erect, deep inside her sanctuary, swimming inside her moist heaven.

That blessed place feels like home.

Kenya moans like she's on a tropical island, in warm waters, a place where you can see schools of fish and rainbow gardens of soft coral. She wipes the sweat on her brow like she is wiping ocean water away from her face. She looks back, whines, her face a wonderful ugliness as she anticipates my next thrust, and she stares deep into my eyes, moves her hand to where we are connected, and massages the ring on her clitoris as we dance the dance of illicit lovers.

She says, "Damn."

"What's wrong?"

"You kiss like a soap star . . . and . . . fuck like a porn star."

"Is that good?"

"Un-fucking-believable."

She moves against me and I hold her waist, make her sing like an angel, then she turns over, gets on top of me, rises and falls, moves like the devil, gives heaven and hell all at once.

Her dance is good. So good that I cannot stand the way she controls my pleasure.

I wrestle with her, get on top of her, put her legs up around my neck.

I thrust with urgency, as if I need to get this fire out of my body.

She moans, "Is this pussy good?"

I moan in return, "Yes."

"Is this pussy good?"

"Yes, your pussy is good."

"You're hurting me so damn good."

The sun is scorching my soul.

Madness.

Air leaves her lungs on the wings of a sensual sigh. Her legs fall and I crawl on top of her, my hands underneath her backside, pulling her into me over and over. Arms out at her side, pulling the sheets, she becomes my savior, my salvation, her body in the pose of a crucifix, all of her moans calling out for her god and his son, then her curses demanding me not to stop, not to slow down, to keep my pace, to go as deep as I can, to make her come over and over.

"Harder, fuck me harder, harder."

"I don't want to hurt you."

"I want to be hurt."

"Why?"

"So I can forget. Harder, please? Harder."

She pulls her knees to her chest, her feet on my shoulders. I give her deep penetration over and over. Then I'm on fire. Terrified and excited all at once. This is wrong. I cannot stop. Harder. She wants it harder. Flesh slapping. I groan. Her moans so provocative. I want to take her from so many positions, but this is not the time, this is raw, this is urgent. Alabama's humidity makes it hard to breathe. In no time, so much sweat covers our bodies that it feels like we're dipped in oils, slipping away from each other.

She growls. "Oh shit oh shit oh shit."

She is there, leg trembling then straining, grabbing sheets, eyes tight, biting her lips. Her vagina so wet, so hot, so alive. I kiss her humid skin, bite her, hold her backside, my own inner fire consuming me, taking me closer to nirvana. But I control my orgasm, make it slow, let it burn.

Her body tenses, jerks. Her whines tell me that she's coming again.

"Don't stop hurt me don't stop fuck me hurts so good so good harder fuck me."

Her moans and groans and guttural sounds are loud enough to wake the dead.

That excites me more. We are connected from the souls out to our skin.

Her back arches and tears river from her eyes.

She shudders and sings my accolades, makes more vocal sounds than I can count.

Another orgasm heats her skin, makes her chant for me to not stop.

I stroke her harder, struggle to catch my breath, but I don't stop, clamp my hand over her mouth to muffle the sounds, still the echoes of our sin refuse to let her stop coming.

She comes again.

My orgasm rolls through me in waves, so strong, feel the muscles move under my skin, so much heat, I stroke and float, strain, close my eyes and experience phantasmagoria.

My orgasm reverberates.

Then we are done.

Kenya takes one hard breath after another, wipes her eyes, clears her throat, finds the strength to shift me away from her. My skin slides across hers. We breathe out of sync.

I can't move. Out of breath. Legs are numb. Heart is fluttering. Brain is Jell-O.

Time stands in the corner, shaking its head before finally walking toward the future.

Kenya finally rises on one elbow. Her hair looks insane. Her expression, worn.

She drags away from me, her breathing as hot as the sun, as silent as sin. She gets up, legs wobbly, and runs into a wall. She shakes her head and staggers away. I hear her in the bathroom, water running, cleaning herself. She comes back with a towel, cleans me, then takes the towel back into the bathroom. She returns, sits on the bed. I want to go, but I do not know the etiquette for departing after a moment such as this. I want to leave, but I want to wait for the right moment. Leaving too soon could offend her. Offending her could be my demise.

So I stay.

Insanity evaporates with my drying sweat. Reality storms into the room.

I ask, "What now?"

"Feeling guilty?"

"Concerned."

"Because I have nothing to lose and you have everything to lose."

"Maybe. Because Genevieve deserves better than . . . than this."

She moves across the room, her steps still wobbly, opens her purse, puts a cigarette to her lips. Then her Zippo lights up her face as smoke plumes around her satiated expression.

I say, "It's a nonsmoking room."

"I know."

"This room is in your sister's name."

"Now you care about Sister. I see."

"Those things kill."

"So do crazy men."

"Not going to argue with you."

"Been smoking off and on since I was thirteen." She inhales and blows smoke out the side of her mouth. More wobbly steps across the room. "Stress relief, relaxes me, keeps me from stress eating. A model can't eat when she wants to. Have to smoke and imagine eating."

"Uh-huh."

"And not to mention my oral fixation."

Silence while she finishes her smoke. Her eyes come to me.

"You love Sister?"

"Yes."

She asks, "Why did you fuck me?"

Her severe tone stills my heart, puts cotton in my mouth.

She moves away from me.

She repeats, "Why did you fuck me?"

I shiver.

She is analyzing me. Analysis is condemnation. She judges me without judging herself, the kind of woman who looks out the window and never in the mirror. She gives herself an ambiguous victory while she gives me a vague defeat.

She repeats her question.

I refuse to defend my desires, what has been done can't be undone, would rather understand than judge. It is part of my own personal struggle, the struggle to become a person, to understand the injustice of life. I'm a carbon-based life-form made of mostly water, affected by the moon's gravitational pull, influenced by the energy of all other beings. I'm addicted to something, something beyond carnality, something I have to have to survive. I fear abandonment. That fear causes me to cling, but not in a suffocating way. I have to be loved in the physical and the spiritual. Not by many women, just one who can give and receive on the same level as I.

I say, "We're complicated creatures."

"More." Then she smiles. "Give me some more of that intellectual mumbo jumbo."

"Our emotions and needs are more than black and white."

Her smile widens; a vixen in control. "Uh-huh."

"So many shades of gray cover the human soul."

She comes back to me, her smile now gone. I am her defense mechanism, her way of avoiding something deep inside herself. She watches me consult my feelings. I want to be more than I am at this moment, but I have become less. As always the rainbow is more beautiful than the pot at the end. I feel like a failure. A rat in a laboratory experiment, its end predetermined.

I ask, "You think I'm a bad person?"

"You fucked me very well. Thought that you wouldn't be good in bed."

"It was nice."

"No, that was incredible. You fucked me like you were trying to claim this pussy. Haven't been fucked like that in a long time. I'm going to hate you for that. Fucking like that, the way you move, bet you could make me come if I were in a coma. I came *like that* and I was nervous."

"Couldn't tell, not the way you opened the door."

"You have the perfect dick. Nice girth. And long. You sure know how to use it."

"Thanks."

"It was a shock to my system to have that big dick inside of me. I wanted you very much. Didn't you feel how wet I was? Unbelievable. I came the *first time* with you. I've never come the first time with any man. We're in alignment, our bodies." She takes a breath, pulls at her wild hair. "Never been with a smart man. Not your kind of smart. Maybe that's what's been missing."

My weakness magnifies, the desire to touch her again grows.

She sees what I cannot deny.

She puts her cigarette down, comes over, mounts me, moves up and down.

She rides me, shakes her head, swallows. "God, you fill me up. And you hit my spot."

I rise and moan.

She tells me, "Don't come again."

I don't question her, just catch my breath and hold onto her. She moves up and down in slow motion, with smoothness, her vagina so tight around my penis, as gripping as a handshake between boardroom adversaries. She rises and falls in a slow motion. Her breasts come to my mouth. I suck her nipples. Breathing stutters. Toes curl. Eyes close tight. I drown in pleasure.

She moans. "Your body is so beautiful."

Her mouth covers mine. She gives me her tongue ring. I suck it over and over.

She says, "I'm really gonna hate you for making me feel like this."

She kisses me for a long time.

She tells me, "Open your eyes."

Even that simple act seems impossible, but I do. She is sweaty and beautiful.

She smiles, moves up and down as she whispers, "What's all that noise you're making?"

I struggle with my breathing, no longer in control of the orgasmic sounds I make. I take her breasts in my hands, clutch as if they are the preservers to keep me from going under.

She says, "That's it, squeeze my nipples . . . yes, yes . . . I'm about to . . . *ooooo*."

I watch her find her way through the gates of nirvana. Her legs tense, she strains, eyes tighten. I wonder if it's possible for her to come with her eyes open. The sensation hits her hard. She curses, jerks in waves. So remarkable and orgasmic that it astounds and intimidates me.

She catches her breath. "Did you?"

The fluid way she dances steals my breath, can only slap her butt twice and moan.

She reminds me, "Don't."

"Don't come?"

"No. Don't get me sprung."

She rides me, gives me agony to prove a point, that she refuses to be dominated.

She closes her eyes, bites her lips, flesh slapping as she rises and falls with enough passion to make the bed speak in tongues, then she whines and comes again, comes hard, then falls away from me. I catch my breath while she does the same. Again she wobbles across the room and lights a cigarette. She inhales and runs her free hand through her wild hair.

I inhale our scents, the combination of sin and satisfaction.

I stare at her. Right now I could love her with all her faults.

I have missed feeling a woman come while engaged in congress. I love that as much as I do my own orgasm. It's been too long since I have felt what I feel now, with this intensity. With Genevieve I had been feeling as if I had become part of the Peter Principle of sex — had risen to my level of sexual ineptitude, that no matter how I tried I would never be able to please her, not like this.

Kenya's cellular sings that song by Usher. It sings and glows. She stares at it until it stops its show, then shakes her head in a combination of anger and disappointment.

Kenya says, "I did sexy things for Deuce. Fed him mangos. Rubbed his body in oil. Gave him slippery sex in an incense-filled room. Oral sex at the movies. Sex on rose petals with candles all around. Sex in a black light with his hands tied and his eyes blindfolded. Me licking and kissing and sucking him, sucking and fucking him. Sucking him and making him come."

Her eyes stare down at me searching for the truth.

She asks, "Would you cheat on a woman like that?"

I close my eyes without answering, let her question become rhetorical. My body is numb, my penis still erect. Blood lives in all the wrong places.

Then the hotel phone rings. She leans, grabs the phone, and answers.

She thickens her voice, feigns a yawn, says a rugged, "Good morning, Sister."

I swallow. Stop breathing.

She grumbles. "I'm still in bed. Rough night for me too. Don't have anything for a headache. Maybe you should eat. It'll be okay. Everybody should be at the trailer in a couple of hours. I know, beef and pork, so you better eat before. Okay, I'll meet you in Odenville."

I watch her, a master at deception.

She hangs up and stares at me, almost grins at the uncertainty and terror in my face as it fades, but my dread does not vanish. Kenya lowers her head, her fingers pulling at her wild hair.

I say, "Genevieve doesn't orgasm. Not that often. She's a wonderful wife. I love her. But in bed . . . I need . . . what you gave me . . . I need that. It's selfish, but I need what you gave me."

It is not easy to articulate that, not easy to tell our most sacrosanct of secrets.

I want to continue to voice my frustration, announce other things about Genevieve.

She will give head but never craves oral sex the way I crave tasting her goodness. I think she can do without. Sometimes she hates the mess, doesn't want me to come inside her. She's kind in the way she says that *without* saying that, asking me to come on her skin, says that she loves it when I come on her skin. She asks me to pull out and come on her body — never on her face, she would have an aneurysm — just on her breasts or stomach, but never above the breasts.

I want to say that we rarely make love two days in a row. It's not flowcharted that way. I want to say that in public we are a wonderful couple, but behind closed doors, when the candles are lit and all inhibitions should be thrown to the wind, we are not equally yoked.

I want to say that she used to shower immediately after sex, but we had a talk and that came to a halt. She would wash me away like a whore does when she sleeps with a john. She didn't notice until I brought it to her attention. She cleaned after sex without a thought. Very ritualistic. Watching her hurry to shower while I rested in her scents made me feel tainted.

But I dare not say those things to Kenya, to my wife's sister, because as each word leaves my mouth, I will sink in my own putrid shallowness. I have spoken of Genevieve's sexual shortcomings without claiming my own faults, of which I own enough to fill a room. Still Genevieve accepts me as I am.

Kenya says, "Sister doesn't have orgasms?"

I pull my lips in.

Kenya knits her brow and glares at me, testing to see if I am lying. She sees I am not and her expression changes to that of a different type of disbelief. She regards me with pity, as if what I told her were a tragedy amongst tragedies, as if she can't envision life without orgasms.

What I have said, I should not have said. But once said, the damage is done.

Words written are erasable. Words spoken are irreversible.

I question myself, why I felt the need to confess something so personal.

My answer is that I seek a nullification of my crime. If not nullification, forgiveness.

What I have said does not leave me immune to moral responsibility.

She says, "Sister doesn't call me, not often. She ignores me. Chastises me when she sees me. No matter what I have accomplished, it's not good enough. That hurts. She ran away and left everybody . . . left me behind. I told her my father died . . . she didn't even respond."

"Not everybody is good at dealing with pain."

I think Kenya is going to cry. My insides feel her energy. She pushes her tears away and I do the same with my sadness. Our vulnerable moment evaporates, as if it never were.

"How do you promise anyone fidelity?" She asks me that without looking me in my eyes. "How do you promise someone forever? I mean, all you know is right now, that moment. How can you tell someone what your state of mind will be three years from now? How?"

I don't respond. I don't know if she is questioning her own life, or Deuce and their issues, or what I have said, or our transgression. If it is a question for me, it too shall become rhetorical. There is no answer, not from me, not for me. I don't pretend to know everything.

She says, "The love that's described in the Bible, I mean, people should love like that."

"What do you mean?"

"You can talk now."

I take a hard breath. "I can talk now. What love is described in the Bible?"

"The love Paul spoke of in Corinthians."

I laugh, uncomfortable with my ignorance. "What did this cat Paul say in the Bible?"

"Paul spoke of a love that always trusts, keeps no records of wrongs, isn't self-seeking."

I laugh. "Who loves that way?"

"You think that's a lie?"

"A woman not keeping a record of wrongs?"

She looks at me as if she exists on a spiritual plane that leaves her aware of things I will never be able to comprehend, shrugs away my ignorance, and glances at the clock. That's when I see it, the remorse crawling across her skin, frustration clouding her eyes, the love she had in her heart going cold and stealing her warmth.

She puts her back to me, her goddess-like figure in a sensual silhouette.

While I stare at her mystery, at her arrogance, at her pain, she glowers off into a world only she can see, whispers, "Wash your dick before you leave, before you go to Sister."

That is my permission to leave. I stand.

I ask, "Are we okay?"

"Make sure you make love to Sister so she will be none the wiser."

"Kenya. Stop it."

"Wash your dick before you go back to your wife."

"Don't trip, Kenya."

"That's how you do it, right?"

"Stop it, Kenya."

"Wash your dick and go back home as if nothing ever happened, right?"

I have become nothing to her.

I have become too small to see hear taste smell feel.

She is Medusa. She is Mephistophelian. Shrouded in darkness and mystery.

I move by her, head to her bathroom, my mind afire and legs unsteady.

On the way I see her laptop, Palm Pilot, I-pager, DVD player. And a U-Haul key.

I scrub our scent away, pull my clothes on, pass by her without saying anything else.

At the door I stop, this heaviness in my chest asking me to explain the unexplainable.

I leave her sitting in her dark and cool room, a new cigarette glowing in her hand.

Odenville stares.

I walk through my guilt, part my own sea of deception, and follow my wife up a two-lane highway. There is no sidewalk. Mud, gravel, and grass separate the road from the countryside, so she's keeping to the edges of the asphalt, moving in a straight line like she's on a tightrope.

Genevieve is calm. Her moment of insanity was brief. This is not new to us.

I say, "You haven't had a panic attack in a long time."

"In front of Bubba Smith, of all people."

"You remember him from when you were here?"

"He says he's one of Gravedigger's brothers. That's all that matters."

"You don't know all of your daddy's brothers?"

"The way I grew up, that's not unusual. Not for my family. We're a mixed bag."

Mixed bag. Same phrase that Kenya uses.

We walk until we are between Odenville Presbyterian Church and the town's fire department, in a parking lot for the Odenville Utility Company. A basketball court, tennis court, and a small park rest in the shadows of both modest structures.

I ask, "Why do all the businesses and churches start with Odenville?"

"Because we're in Odenville."

Stupid question. Aggravated answer.

I watch her and worry. She's not herself, not one hundred percent.

The one and only panic attack I ever saw her have happened over a year ago. It was a Saturday morning, kids were lining up to get in the pool for swimming lessons. Children were waiting and Genevieve was taking forever to come outside. No child was allowed in the pool until she gave them permission. Genevieve was never late with her classes, always started her class on time down to the minute. Late students weren't allowed in the pool, her way of training them for life in the real world, pulling them away from the concept of CP-time as being acceptable.

Lupe, our cleaning lady, came to the door and called me, did it in a discreet way. With her wide-eyed expression and her strong Spanish accent, she told me that something was wrong with Doctor Forbes, that she was angry and breaking things. I hurried upstairs, found Genevieve barefoot, a T-shirt over her two-piece swimming suit, eyes wide, throwing books and glasses and candles. I called her name over and over. Perfume flew into the wall. Boxes of tissue followed.

She looked different — lines in her forehead, eyes dark.

She was someone else.

Then whatever had possessed her went away while she held a picture frame in her hand. She lowered the frame, stood there breathing hard, looking at the destruction she had caused.

Whatever look she saw on my face frightened her as much as she had frightened me.

That was when she had to explain part of who she was. I knew her mother was dead and her father wasn't in her life, that she never talked about him, but the same applied so far as my absentee father was concerned, was the norm in the black community.

I didn't know her father was in prison and would die in prison.

She told me her mother was called the town whore and her father loved her despite her faults, her needs for variety when it came to carnal stimulation.

I asked, "What made you . . . what just happened?"

She whispered, "Othello."

The trigger, that day, was the television. HBO. *Othello* was on, the one with Laurence Fishburne as the Moor. She had walked into the bedroom when Othello killed Desdemona. In this version, a black man killing a white woman. Her brain made her a teenager again, gave her the five senses of that wretched moment, began processing too much of her past all at once.

She lost it, started yelling and throwing things at her never-ending memory.

That day, after the ghosts had fled, I held her until she told me she was okay.

She whispered, "He took a knife to her throat and killed her."

Her father didn't run outside naked and pretend he was crazy, didn't take her mother's body out on a boat and try to drown the evidence, just called the local police, lit up a cigarette, and waited. He was on the porch when the police came, no blood on his clothes because he had changed into a black suit, white shirt, and dark tie. Clothes he wore on Sunday mornings when he sat in the choir and played the piano for his pastor's congregation.

I asked her, "You saw it happen?"

"I saw it."

"You and who else?"

"No one was there but me."

Genevieve tells Bubba Smith to drive on, that she knows the way from here, that we will follow when we are ready.

"Ma'am, if there is anything I did to make you —"

I snap at him, "Can you please stop running your mouth and listen?"

"Yessir. But no need of you hollering at me like that."

The look in his face, the way he pulls at his crooked moustache in worry, shows his regret for talking so much. He gets back inside the Town Car, turns on his signal light, and after a few cars go by he pulls away. Not far up the U.S. 411 he turns right at an Exxon.

I ask, "How far?"

"Almost there. Can smell the gizzards from here."

Ford Escorts and F-350s whiz by. I wait for Genevieve to breathe again, to make a move. Another car filled with blond teenage girls goes by. They all turn, stop their incessant chattering, and crane their necks at the same moment, turn and stare at the strange people.

Another sign says we're on the Historical Stagecoach Route. Charlotte's Antiques, other small businesses surround us, this town breathing underneath a blanket of gray clouds, darker clouds in the distance letting let us know the storm of all storms will be back to torture us soon.

I catch a glimpse of a public park with colorful swings, a walking trail, and recreational area that rests between two churches. Genevieve stops moving. Her breathing is labored. But another panic attack doesn't rise. I touch her and she jerks like she's surprised she's not alone.

She says, "What if I begged you not to walk around that corner with me? To just go back to Birmingham, go see the Vulcan, go to the Civil Rights Museum, go to Five Points and eat at Surin West, go have fun and wait for me, or to just stay at the hotel, be supportive in that way?"

Her glass shield thickens. Moments like this, when I'm supposed to be her strength, she pushes me away. This validates my tryst with Kenya. And that angers me. It makes me want to scream. But I remain stubborn.

My words may ring as those of a hypocrite, so be it. Despite anything I have done, I love my wife. I desire her, crave her, but that is not always reciprocated, and that is both disheartening and deflating to the soul. Makes my love feel un-fulfilled, like a parasite still in search of a host. I have endless honeymoon fantasies, but our honeymoon is over.

It ended this morning when I went inside Kenya's room.

I play down my own anxiety, chuckle. "You expect me to walk back to Birmingham?"

"Wait at the gas station. I can send Bubba Smith back down when I get to the trailer."

"I'm here."

"Please?"

Her word is soft but that glass walls turns into brick.

"I'm going to meet your family," I tell her. "They're my family too."

She struggles with herself. "You're right. As my husband, this is your right."

"I'll turn around. But only if you turn around with me."

"I can't turn around."

"Why?"

"They know I'm here. I'm beyond the point of no return. For me it's inevitable."

"What's inevitable?"

"Plus, I have to know that Willie Esther is really dead."

"Closure."

She nods. "I have to know that I am free."

She starts walking. There is no sidewalk. I'm right there with her. We cross a small stream, Beaver Creek. The park is to our right. Picnic areas, colorful flower beds, plenty of swings.

Genevieve goes that way, into the park, up the newly resurfaced asphalt track. Her eyes tell me that all of this is new, that so much has changed. Her eyes also reveal her swelling angst.

Genevieve says, "Why are you so persistent? Who I am striving to be should be more important than who I was. You're always looking back and I'm always looking ahead."

"That's the Cancer in me. The Taurus in you."

"But you have questions."

"I want to untangle every snarl and see into every motive because your cryptic behavior leaves me in a constant state of vague uneasiness. Because I never really know what you're thinking. Most people have misplaced their memories, have left them in their heart's attic, and from time to time you're allowed a peek. You throw your memories away."

"Not all memories are good memories."

"I have no idea what your good memories are. You don't have pictures of family, of old boyfriends. No cards, no mementos. It's as if you were born the day I met you."

"In some ways I was."

"You had to have good memories before you met me."

"Meeting you. Marrying you. Waking up with you. Those are my good memories."

Her earnestness shatters me. She takes a deep breath and stops walking. First looking back up the road in the direction we have come, then toward where we are going.

She says, "When I met you, I loved you before you said a word. I thought, he's my Neo. He's the one. When I sat across from you at that table, I was nervous. I had a choice. I thought, tell him all, or tell him nothing. Tell him all, watch him walk away. Tell him nothing and maybe he'll stay. Tell nothing and he can't hurt me. Tell nothing and I remain perfect in his eyes."

Her words carry a depth I've never experienced. Continual intensity in her eyes.

My eyes tell her, no matter what she says, I'm not going back. I want to see the things that do not appear on her flowchart, on her wall that faces the rising of the sun.

She walks the trail. We are so close and

now she chooses to walk in circles, as if she has to move in the same counterclockwise direction her mind is spiraling.

Snails crawl by us as we stroll.

She stops walking and frowns at me. "You're pushy. So very pushy."

I don't respond.

It is *silent,* an anagram for *listen.*

That is what I do. Listen while she remains silent.

A few deep breaths later she nods, in a soft voice tells me that she is ready to talk.

thirteen

Genevieve says, "Willie Esther Savage was an evil woman. She was a smoker and an alcoholic who kept a dirty home and always called my mother a slut. Said that none of her children would ever amount to anything. Said that my mother messed up by being a slut. And that was the reason she was put on the other side of the fence."

"I don't understand."

"You will. Anyway, Willie Esther let everybody know that being a slut was why my momma got killed. She was mad because that forced her life to change when she had to raise seven children. She always threatened us, said she would send us to the other side of the fence if we didn't behave. She made us go to church at least three times a week. Anything to get away from her cigarettes and Wild Turkey. Three times a week I prayed that she would send me away, at least have the state come get me. I didn't care how bad a foster home was, didn't care how bad they abused you in the system, it had to be better than where I was."

"That bad?"

She pulls her lips in, starts walking again. "I ran away from here."

"Ran away? Where . . . how far did you go?"

She chuckles. "Made it to Atlanta. About one hundred miles. Had just turned thirteen."

"You ran away at thirteen."

"Willie Esther had beaten me so bad, so many times. One day I was on the way home from school and this car pulled up. It was a yellow car. Nothing fancy. Black man was lost, looking for the Interstate. I pointed. Was happy to see another black face in Odenville, even if he was just passing through. Asked him where he was going. Said he was going to Atlanta. Said he was going to Morehouse College. Think that's what made me want to run away to Atlanta. He told me about the black colleges. Told me about Spelman. I imagined all the black people, all complexions, the fraternities, sororities."

"And you ran away?"

"He was smoking a thin cigarette. He'd inhale and hold it a long time before he let

261

the smoke ease out of his mouth. It didn't reek like the stench from Willie Esther's cheap cigarettes. I asked him what he was smoking. He said it was something that took away sadness."

"You're telling me he was smoking a joint?"

"I told him I was sad a lot. Didn't know what depression was then, just said I was sad."

"He was lost, riding through here, lost, and smoking a joint."

"And he handed me one. Told me to sneak and smoke it when I needed to feel good."

"He gave you a joint?"

"Sure did. That was my first one. He smiled and told me I was too pretty to be in a place like this. Said a girl like me needed to grow up in the city, be around more black people."

I nod, suspend all judgmental thoughts, engage in active listening.

"Told me that I was too pretty, that I needed to get away from the karma of land that used to have segregated toilets, bomb threats, and sit-ins. He was the first person to tell me I was pretty, first that I remember, who said it and meant it. Think he was the first man I ever trusted."

"He . . . you and him . . . what happened after that?"

"Then he drove away. I wanted to chase his yellow car. Wanted to run as fast as I could and catch that yellow car. My car to freedom. I remember thinking, if I could only get to Atlanta."

"What did you do?"

"Stood there with my eyes closed, clicking my heels."

She says that as if she were telling me about her first true love. I look out at the calmness in Odenville. I say, "Hard to imagine."

"No, it's hard to forget. Memory is my tormentor. Memory keeps us in its own prison. You have no idea how she embarrassed us in public, called us *niggers* in front of white people."

"Genevieve, you don't have to —"

"I have to."

I say, "You don't have to be afraid. She's dead now."

"Memories don't die. Did you know that memories are what do us in, the inability to forget? You ever wonder why people with Alzheimer's look so calm and peaceful, so childlike? Because they forget everything bad." She takes a deep breath, lets it out with a frown. "I can feel her energy. I can still see her. That filthy, amoral bottom-feeder was the size of a double-wide trailer and she . . . she . . . God, she wore more makeup than a carnival freak."

Her sharp tone is new to my ears, disturbs me to no end, but I maintain my composure.

I touch her hand and say, "Genevieve . . . okay."

"Hated the way she said . . . the way that evil bitch *yelled* my name. She was loud and crazy. Beat us like we were runaway slaves. Not a strong hand out of love. It was hate. Everybody said that she did that because of the drinking and the nerve pills, but it was hate."

I lean forward, interested again. "Nerve pills?"

"She always had to go away for *treatments* at the state hospital when, and I quote, 'My nerves get bad from all these *leftover* niggers in my home. Need to send these mutts to a shelter.' When she was gone it all fell on me. I had to work like a mule and keep up the house. Cook, clean, everything. No matter what I did it wasn't good enough. There were so many trifling men around . . ." She shudders and shakes her head, frowns, rubs her eyes, trapped in her own mind. "Anyway, everybody talked about how crazy she was. And the crazy stuff she would do."

"Like what?"

"Like the year she thought that God was talking to her through the TV."

"You're lying."

"But only if it was on Channel 11, so no one could change the channel. That black-and-white television stayed on Channel 11 a whole year, I kid you not. Grandpa Fred took her for some treatments when she thought God told her to collect dirty undergarments from the neighbors and wash them by hand in order to clean their souls and save them from hell."

"Get out."

"She was nasty. She smoked over food while she was cooking on the stove. All the counters had cigarette burns where she put them down for a minute to prepare the food."

"Can't even imagine."

"We all grew up in a crazy house."

"I understand."

"*No you don't.* She was really tough on me. If I did something she saw as wrong, something as simple as not running fast enough when she called my name, even if I didn't hear her, she beat me. She beat me if my grades weren't good enough. I'd get beat for having an A-minus. If I cried because of the pain, she beat me for crying. Maybe because I was older or something, I don't know, but she did things to me that she didn't do to the others."

"What . . . what did she do?"

"She . . . I don't want to say that. Not that."

Silence descends from the sky with the weight of a feather.

She says, "I'd broken one of her favorite glasses. An ugly antique thing. I knew a beating was coming that would make them put me on the other side of the fence. I imagined her sitting there with the television on her soap operas, all the windows up, cigarette in the corner of her mouth, looking over that fence and yelling my name every day. Talking about me like I was nothing. So I stuffed clothes in a Piggly Wiggly bag and left. No money. Just ran away and . . ."

After her voice fades I say, "You ran away?"

"I was missing for six months."

"Six months? At thirteen?"

"Yes."

"You came back or they found you?"

"I came back. Never should have. But I came back. And the abuse got worse."

I'm trying not to shake my head, trying to not frown or show any body language that implies judgment. I digest her words then ask, "How did you get to Atlanta?"

"All I knew was I had to get to the Interstate."

"That's at least ten miles."

"Thirteen. From my momma's tombstone to the Interstate, thirteen miles on the dot. One mile for each year I'd been on this earth."

"Prophetic."

"No, pathetic."

"Still, long way for a little girl to walk."

"It didn't matter. I would've walked barefoot from Selma to Montgomery to get away from here. Nobody could stop me. My belief was strong and my purpose just, so no obstacle was going to stand in my way. And I was sweating, trying to get my nappy head, ashy elbows, and boney knees out of this hell. Made it down there and put my thumb out."

"Somebody picked you up when you were a little girl?"

"Truckers don't care how old you are. As long as you can walk, you're legal."

"You could've been killed."

"Like my mother. Or I would've killed myself. Or killed Willie Esther."

"How did you . . . what did you do for six months?"

"I. Survived."

Her husky voice splinters, tells me that I'm asking her to take me down an unpaved road that I may not want to travel. Asking me if I want to go that deep into the rabbit hole.

Silence falls between us.

Then she laughs. Husky voice gone. No flame in her eyes. Genevieve again.

I ask, "You okay?"

"Remembering something I had forgotten."

"What?"

"There was a huge water mill along the road on the stretch of highway I-65. Between Birmingham and Montgomery. It had a giant wooden Satan holding a pitchfork, bending up and down. There was a sign next to it that said 'Go to Church or the Devil Will Get You.' "

"That's funny?"

"I used to see that Satan and . . . it scared me because it looked like *her*. The shape of its head. The smile. You would think a sign like that would make you laugh, but it terrified me."

I rub my hands together and wait. Too many thoughts are going through my mind, imagination in overdrive, imagining what a thirteen-year-old girl could do to survive in Atlanta.

Then Genevieve stops walking. "I feel sad. Have to do something."

She reaches into her purse and takes out a round Altoids can.

I sigh and grit my teeth. This is one reason she wants to be alone.

But I am here. She can't make me go away.

Genevieve opens the lid. No Altoids are inside. Two slim cigarettes rolled in dark brown paper are in her possession. Underneath flags that honor each branch of the military, she takes out a lighter and fires up her salvation, takes a hard pull, and ecstasy makes her sigh. The glow on her face is the one that I want to give her. I want to be her pleasure. I want to have the power to steal her sadness.

I struggle with this moment, at how prepared she is. I tell her, "You lied."

"Wish the swings were clean."

"Can't believe you smuggled drugs on the plane."

"Would love to swing."

I bite my bottom lip. Genevieve is a master at small deceptions, the kind that aggravate.

She shakes her head, and looks at me dead on. "Kenya is such a liar."

"Kenya?" That disrupts my anger. I open and close my hands. "What lie?"

"I went down to her room." She takes a pull. "She was fucking somebody."

I want to swallow, but I don't. "You walked in on her?"

"Didn't have to. Could hear her out in the hallway."

She takes her final pull, holds it a while, then sets the smoke from the magical herb free, exhaling slowly. She puts what's left back in the Altoids can, stuffs the can in her purse.

"You feel better, Doc?" I ask with sarcasm. "Keep doing that until we get arrested."

"Kenya is addicted to drama, always in the middle of some drama."

"What are you addicted to?"

"I could ask you the same."

"Just keep your demons on a chain."

"You do the same."

We cross a small stream, Beaver Creek. We're moving at a decent pace, approaching Odenville Methodist Church. The marquee has made an acronym using the word Bible. "Basic Instructions Before

Leaving Earth." Then we come up on the Bank of Odenville. Its windows are dirty. That institution long abandoned. Across the street wait Odenville Town Hall and the Jim Bailey Civic Center; both buildings combined are only about the size of our home in L.A.

Genevieve stops in front of the Odenville Library, a building the size of our garage. A blue sign on the side of the building announces that Mary Banks is the librarian.

Genevieve smiles. "They have a new library. The old library was inside the old bank building. And Mrs. Banks is still here. I bet they have computers and everything."

"Look at that smile. See, you do have good memories."

"The library was my escape from madness. I loved Mrs. Banks. Wonderful woman."

I hear a dog barking and I look to my right, down Third Avenue, a narrow one-way street with more old houses, maybe a few more trailer homes. Down that way a rottweiler is chained to a pole in the ground. In front of his home I see what he's barking at. A U-Haul truck. It's parked as if it were meant to be hidden from the rest of the world.

Kenya is nearby. That means we are here. On the other side of the railroad tracks are two rows of trailer homes with rusted aluminum siding. Spaced out over the uneven land. There are two rows of those rectangular-shaped habitats; one row has eight, the other seven. All are in various states of disrepair. At least one looks as abandoned as the Bank of Odenville.

We cross Alabama and turn on Ware, then head toward a DEAD END sign. We turn on Wellington Park Lane, I taste her in my mouth. Feel her skin on my fingers. Hear her sighs.

Now as Genevieve takes another breath, I find it hard to breathe, hard to walk forward.

Mental anguish shortens my breath. I need to burn a shrub.

I ask, "Which trailer?"

She motions with her head. "Last one. The purple trailer on the orange bricks."

We pass by neighbors riding bicycles. Across the way there is a man holding his daughter, both of them sharing a strawberry Yoo-hoo, looking over at us. Young boys with Skoal faces and 305 baseball caps stop working on a dirt bike and stare. Pasty-faced teenage girls stop smoking and gawk at us as they drive out of the cul-de-sac.

I ask Genevieve, "The trailer next to the graveyard?"

"Put your hand down. Bad luck to point at a graveyard."

Cars and pickup trucks are parked in that section. People are outside. Adults. Children. All look this way. Bubba Smith is there, hands in pockets, cigarette at the corner of his mouth.

Kenya sashays into sight.

She stands on that land like a Valkyrie; her gray eyes a blazing pyre. Fear and mythology intertwine, sailing around my skull like phantoms. A lone word clings to me: Götterdämmerung. A dusk of the gods. Collapse of civilization as I know it.

My breathing roughens, consciousness disturbed by Kenya's power. She is my Götterdämmerung, and with just a few words, my marriage, and my life, will forever be changed.

Genevieve nods. "My mother's grave is no more than five yards from the front door."

"You grew up with a graveyard right outside the front door?"

"My mother was killed one Saturday night, that next Wednesday she was put in the ground right outside my bedroom window. From the front door to her tombstone, twenty steps."

"That's horrible."

"Right on the other side of the wooden fence, if you can call that a fence."

I repeat, "Other side of the fence."

"Yes. Death lives on the other side of the fence."

fourteen

Grandpa Fred waits for us on the blacktop road leading to this section of trailer homes. I know it is him because as we approach, he coughs. The rattle in his lungs resounds from thirty yards away, the emphysema trying to get a good grip on him to engage in its final battle.

Genevieve's paternal grandfather. A man whose son sits in prison as the outcome of a love gone bad. What he endures psychologically, I can only imagine. He waits underneath gray skies and the threat of rain. He sits on the edge of an unmarked road, cigarette in hand.

I had imagined that old man with his back bent, his skin leathery and wrinkled, the etchings in his face a road map to days gone by, sitting in a worn and frayed chair, cane at his side, thick glasses on, his free hand dragging back and forth over the stubbles and rough texture in his pockmarked face, maybe shifting his stained false teeth side to side.

Grandpa Fred is a portly man, double-chinned, a round face and a body that looks like one huge round ball resting on top of a larger round ball. He has gray sideburns that remind me of Elvis Presley. He has a thick gray handlebar moustache, wider than his face and curled up at its ends. He wears oversized tan pants and a red, white, and blue plaid shirt that he can barely button up, the right sleeve rolled up to his elbow, and a thin black tie, loose around his neck.

He sits like a general monitoring his troops, an army cap resting on his head.

I keep an eye on Genevieve as we get closer. She seems okay. Easy steps, breathing under control, back straight, purse hanging from her right hand, eyes are on her destination.

Moments ago, when Genevieve told me about her past, about Willie Esther, part of me wondered why she didn't go live with her paternal grandparents, why they did not intervene.

As we pass by an abandoned trailer home and get closer, I think I understand why.

Grandpa Fred does not come down the gentle slope to meet Genevieve, does not get up from his seat as she approaches. He sits because he cannot stand. His wheelchair is his home.

His pants are rolled up and pinned. His legs are gone up above his knees. Nothing left but nubs. The army hat he wears announces that he has given this country part of his body as a testament of his loyalty to the red, white, and blue. In the end he lives in an old trailer home and rests in an antiquated wheel chair. God bless Uncle Sam. Now I see why his right sleeve is rolled up as well, nothing there but a nub extending from his shoulder to where his biceps used to be.

The closer I get, the less of him I see. There are no false teeth for him to shift side-to-side as I have imagined. He has four teeth in his mouth. Four long teeth. There is not much left of the man, only a head of dyed black hair and round torso resting in an old-fashioned wheelchair, a military head and bloated torso with a left arm that holds a cigarette. The sight of him almost scares me back the other way. *Come one, come all, step right up, hurry, hurry before the sideshow begins.* He waves his only hand and it surprises me that it is a perfect hand, all fingers present. Then he coughs hard and long, as if raising his hand upset the delicate balance in his body, coughs away parts of what is left of his decaying insides. He catches his breath and spits on the ground, wipes his mouth with the back of his hand, and puts the cigarette back up to his thin lips. The move is done in a way that says he has done that thousands of times. He smiles his four-tooth smile, then inhales as if he is turning his nose up at both death and dentistry.

He puts the cigarette at the corner of his thin lips, leaves it there for safekeeping, and extends his pasty hand to mine, the same pasty hand he just used to wipe his mouth.

A man with one hand does not have a lot of options.

I have no choice. I extend my right hand to his left, and we do an awkward handshake.

Grandpa Fred says, "You must be that research man from Fresno."

"Yes. I'm that research man from Fresno."

"The one Jenny Vee done married."

"Yes. I am the man Jenny Vee done married."

His grip is strong and clinging, that sun-deprived hand coarse as sandpaper, fingernails uneven and stained from years of holding cigarettes. In the back of my mind I wonder how a one-handed man cleans his only hand after he uses the bathroom. After he urinates. Or takes a shit.

He evaluates me with his eyes, as if he were reading my mind, trying to see what I know about this world, if I am friend or foe, before he nods and grumbles, "Pleasure to meet you."

"Thank you."

"You got soft hands. Like a thinking man."

My lips rise to hide my offense. I answer him, "Yessir. I'm a thinking man."

He lets my hand go, then scratches an itch on the other side of his face with his nub. The tobacco stench he left on my hand seeps inside my flesh. I keep my hand and its unpleasant smell away from my body, afraid of soiling my clothes.

Grandpa Fred's eyes go to Genevieve; his pot-smuggling, weed-smoking granddaughter.

My adulterous eyes go up the road. Toward Kenya. She leans against that wretched fence as if she has done no wrong. As if she were the master of this game we're in. Seeing her makes me feel as if a blood vessel is about to rupture and cause me to suffer a stroke.

Genevieve puts her hand on top of Grandpa Fred's hand, says, "Hello, Grandpa."

"My, my, my." He pulls his lips in and nods his head. I expect the tears to come, but there are none, just internal grief. "Last time I saw you . . . last time I saw you . . . look at you now."

"I was a skinny little girl with long, unruly hair last time you saw me."

"All that gray in your hair."

"I know. Yes."

"Ain't you beautiful. Like a movie star."

"Why, thank you, Grandpa Fred. Last time you saw me I was a brown-eyed ugly duckling in hand-me-downs. That's what you told me I looked like the last time I saw you."

"My Lord. If I did say something like that, I'm sorry."

"No, it was true. I didn't have clear skin. I was never mistaken for a prom queen."

"You wasn't an ugly duckling."

"I was only given Willie Esther's old clothes. She'd half-kill me if I altered those clothes. She said that if they fit they would attract boys and attracting boys would make me a slut."

"I know, I know."

"It's okay. It was the truth. I wore what I

280

could. What she allowed me to wear."

Her pain escalates. With each word I understand the depth of her animosity.

Grandpa Fred has a coughing spell, then shifts his four teeth the best he can. "Never meant to add to what Willie Esther did. Wish I had known I had caused you pain."

Genevieve pushes her lips up, but her eyes can't lie.

She says, "Water under the bridge. It was all for the best."

"And you done married now."

"I'm married to this wonderful man. Yes."

"Chirren?"

Her lips come halfway down. "Willie Esther used to tell me that I was going to grow up and be a whore and have a litter of leftover niggers just like Delphinie did."

"I'm sorry. I don't know what to say to you."

Her smile returns. "We don't have any children."

He nods. "If you ain't your momma all growed up and citified, I don't know who is."

The mention of her mother and Genevieve withers, her eyes go toward the graveyard.

She stands tall, asks, "What should I expect? I mean will they —"

"Nobody gon' bring up no old things. Kenya here. She done told people you was here."

He moves his four teeth back and forth. A coughing fit comes and goes. I hold his wheelchair, afraid it might start rolling backward. He inhales his cigarette, gets settled.

Genevieve asks, "Who is that Bubba Smith? He's irritating me to no end."

Grandpa Fred inhales again, still pondering. "He's your daddy's stepbrother."

"One of your other illegitimate sons."

"From back when I was sowing my oats."

"How many other kids did you have?"

"Guess around nine, maybe more. Bubba from my other family in Miss'sippi." He scratches himself with that nub. Coughs. Inhales. "Now I'm reaping what I done sowed."

"I had a fit in front of him, Grandpa. Almost jumped out of the car."

She does not give me that raw emotion, that trust, gives it to a man with fewer limbs than Mr. Potato Head. I'm right here and she refuses to peel back the layers. I am her husband.

Grandpa Fred shifts the best he can.

"He ain't gonna say nothing to nobody."

She nods, her expression as dark as a gypsy's skin. "How long will this take?"

He says, "We gon' head over to First Baptist for the wake in an hour or so."

She asks, "Funeral home driving the family over?"

He nods toward a brick church beyond the graveyard. "No need having 'em come all the way out here just to drive us right there. No need wasting money on foolishness. We can do like we always do and all of y'all drive or walk across the cemetery to First Baptist."

The wake. I had forgotten about that Southern tradition, a ceremony left over from days gone by, when family and friends sit in a room with the dead and pray that they will wake up.

Grandpa Fred asks, "Given any thought about going out to Elmore to see Gravedigger?"

"Not really."

"Gravedigger would love to lay his eyes on you."

"Twenty years." Genevieve speaks with reluctance. "Seems like it was this morning."

"Time for healing. We not long for this world. Time for healing."

To them I am not here. I am a six-foot-one-inch fixture with the value of a shade tree on a cloudy day.

Genevieve just said her father has been incarcerated twenty years. If that was twenty years ago, then she was seventeen, maybe sixteen. She ran away at thirteen, came back and endured three more years of suffering, only to witness her mother killed.

Kenya says she was there too. My brain tries to reverse engineer the situation, to come to conclusions without asking about what is sensitive, but too much is heavy on my mind.

Kenya escapes between family members with the ease of a ballet dancer. So limber to be so tall. The tallest in the lot. Her colorful skirt swings and my heart moves with her rhythm. In my mind, we're back at the Tutwiler, on her bed, her legs open for me, her sighs echoing.

I become to them what Bubba Smith was to us; I push the bloated man in his carriage. The damp wind blows his stench directly into my nostrils. His Jenny Vee walks at his side, silent, eyes back on our destination. Grandpa Fred has a NASCAR sticker on the back of his wheelchair.

Grandpa Fred says, "The neighbors

brought cakes and pies. Plenty food for er'body."

Genevieve swallows, then nods as she lies, "We already ate."

He says, "If you don't mind my saying this, I will. It's not nice, but I have to speak my mind. Jenny Vee, I'm glad I didn't go before Willie Esther. Never woulda got to see you again."

Genevieve grunts. "Thought that cantankerous bitch was gonna live forever."

In that moment, she sounds as Southern as Grandpa Fred. That new voice stuns me.

Grandpa Fred inhales. "We all thought that cantankerous bitch was gonna live forever."

Then Genevieve does something I've never seen her do.

She turns her head to the side, clears her throat, and spits.

Esther. Nazareth. Ruth. I meet them and several others first. They are the slow-moving elders. Then there are the hyper teenagers. Champagne. Tanisha. Shaquetta. I meet at least ten of them as I cross the yard. Neither the teenagers nor the younger children have any idea who Genevieve is. They stare at her, a woman in black with perfect hair. They stare at us. The perfect-looking couple in tailored Italian clothing and Swiss watches.

Jimmy Lee is one of Genevieve's brothers, has the same grade of wavy hair, only he possesses a receding hairline, about five-foot-five, not much taller than Genevieve. He has golden eyeteeth. He is twenty-five years old and wears a banana-yellow suit and a black-and-white polka-dot tie.

He says, "Good to see you . . . how you say your name again?"

My wife says, "Genevieve."

"I kinda remember you."

"You don't look nothing like I thought you would look."

Unfamiliarity and discomfort rests between them. It's sad. He looks at me, at my suit, evaluates me head to toe, yields a judgmental pause, then comes to some conclusion about us.

Genevieve pulls away, says, "Good to see you. You're looking nice."

"That's my wife over there. Velma, come meet my big sister."

"Tired of you hollering at me like I'm a child, Jimmy Lee."

"Come here, Velma. Don't show out in front of my big sister."

His wife is at least five-foot-nine. Velma. Works at Wal-Mart in Wildwood. I doubt if she is twenty. She wears leather jeans with vertical suede patches. She has a moustache. Not thin hair on her lips. A moustache. Her chin is dark, has bumps from shaving with a razor.

Jimmy Lee says, "These our chirren. Y'all come meet y'all auntie from California."

They have six children, four of them his from other relationships. Little Jimmy Lee. Shaquanda. Bonquita. Lexus. Three of those four are between seven and eight. Mercedes is three and the baby — Sean John — is one, both of the latter the fruit of their labor.

The children address us with epithets, yes sir and no ma'am, something California children would never do. Growing up in this land of vintage automobiles has its pluses.

I step back from that reunion, but Genevieve takes my hand, not wanting to be alone.

Jimmy Lee has bad skin, weathered with a bad diet, will not look under forty in the best Hollywood lighting, walks with a one-sided spring to his stride, as if his right leg were part of an anxious pogo stick. Velma laughs and chews gum nonstop, blows big pink bubbles; her rear end jiggles and she swings her arms when she walks. Her hips sway like she was born to breed. Velma keeps asking if we have any children; it pains me to say I have none. Their little Brady Bunch is testament that propagation of the species seems to be their favorite pastime. They ask what are we waiting for and I manufacture a laugh, or manage to change the subject.

I meet elder men with names like J.B. and J.R. and J.D. and J.P and J.T. Their wives have names like Queen and Big Momma and Esther and Little Ruby and Josephine.

At some point they all ask Genevieve, "How you say your name again?"

"Genevieve." My wife says that, remaining close to me. "Genevieve Forbes."

"And you Gravedigger and Delphinie's oldest girl-child."

They come to see Genevieve, they judge, they shuffle away mumbling.

Genevieve moves away, seems as if part of her family wants to talk to her in private.

She tells me, "I have to represent my mother's interest in this affair."

"I'll be okay," I tell her. "If you need me,

send me a text message."

They travel to the other side of the fence, stop feet away at her mother's grave. I watch Genevieve. She seems so small, as if being here deflates her soul. She knows I am watching her. We have that connection. She glances my way and smiles at me, thumbs up. She's okay. I stare off to the right, and see St. Clair High School no more than a peaceful hundred yards away. A banner runs across the back announcing that Piggly Wiggly sponsors its sporting events.

I look the other way, toward Route 411.

I imagine Genevieve as a child, running up that road, grocery bag underneath her arm.

Bubba Smith and a rotund man with a thick moustache and greasy blond hair come up and stop near me. Bubba Smith is talking with his hands, excited. The blond man with the greasy hair wears a black suit and a preacher's collar. And he carries a worn Bible.

Bubba Smith says, "On the Internet. On that eBay. I kid you not."

"Virgin M-M-Mary in ten-year-old grilled cheese."

Bubba Smith grins big and wide. "Can

you imagine the mold?"

"M-m-maybe it was government cheese."

"Reverend, that is the *exact* same thing I said when the missus told me that non-sense. Said it had to be government cheese. Ain't no other kinna cheese good after ten years."

The reverend winks at me, let's me know he's humoring Bubba Smith.

I interrupt their conversation long enough to ask for directions to the bath-room. Bubba Smith points toward the trailer. It's open to everyone. Tells me I can't miss the john. Four wooden steps that look like they were constructed in a middle-school shop class lead up to a screen door. I test each one, not sure if the weather-beaten and time-worn steps will support my weight. They creak but don't give under my heaviness. That aluminum door is bent, feels as if it's about to fall off the hinges. So many unpleasant odors greet me as I step inside a dark place that, with the exception of the small kitchen, has no overhead lighting, just huge lamps on worn-out end tables. I breathe through my mouth, wipe the soles of my shoes on a ragged towel being used as a mat, say hello to a few people and take in this claustrophobic space as I do so.

Paneled walls. Wooden ceiling fan. Worn blue carpet bejeweled with cigarette holes.

A blue-haired woman with varicose veins and a bad hip asks, "Who child you?"

She is standing near a worn-out mahogany table filled with flowers and sympathy cards.

I say, "I'm Genevieve Forbes's husband."

"You Johnny who husband?"

"Delphinie and Gravedigger's oldest daughter. Genevieve."

She thinks for a moment. "The girl that ran away from here?"

"Yes ma'am."

"Lord, have mercy. Where that child at? Thought she had passed on."

"She's outside. Very much alive."

"You know her momma was killed just about right where you standing."

She says that as calmly as she would tell a friend the sun is shining.

I swallow, shift away from that conversation. "Where is the bathroom?"

"Delphinie buried right there. Third or fourth grave, right over there."

A younger man helps her get out the door. People who are leaving the trailer point down the hallway, tell me that someone just went inside the bathroom.

I wait, looking around. Smell a combination of cigarette smoke, Pine-Sol, and stale odors that remind me of a resting home, unidentifiable fried stenches that are melded into everything. Pictures of Jesus, Martha Stewart, and Ronald Reagan show who she held on high.

Those images are on the wall facing the rising of the sun.

Ronald Reagan's picture is up the highest. Then Jesus has an inch over Martha.

In the kitchen area, water spots are on the warped floor. Rust-colored, circular spots are on the ceiling over that damage. Deep-fried foods. Okra. Pies. Butter beans. Peach cobbler. Nehi and Grapico sodas. Milo's Sweet Tea. Strawberry Yoo-hoos. Grapey grape Bug Juice. Beer. I skip the macaroni and cheese, pork chops, and meatloaf, find some meatballs, put two on a paper plate, grab a plastic fork, and eat most of one. I eat with the hand that doesn't stink of Grandpa Fred. I look at the small television and I'm glad it's not on Channel 11. I try to imagine Genevieve and all of her siblings confined in this cramped space. It would be maddening.

In this dark and dreary room

Genevieve's mother died a horrible death. But death's spot is not what I came to see.

Kenya comes out of the bathroom. She is why I came inside this trailer home.

If there will be more words, perhaps a confrontation between us, so be it.

fifteen

There is a dark moment of uncertainty between us, its depth immeasurable.

Kenya takes slow steps into the room, her wild hair moving with her sashay, her colorful skirt swaying side-to-side with her uneasy and uncertain rhythm, and she pauses before me.

I chew slow and easy.

She asks, "You like those?"

I swallow before I speak. "Pretty tasty."

"Those are mountain oysters."

"What are mountain oysters?"

"Bull's nuts. You're eating testicles."

My eyes widen. Her hand covers her mouth, muffling her laugh. I spit into a napkin over and over, then hurry into the bathroom gagging. Kenya's laughter spirals, follows me.

She yells, "You might want to chase those nuts with some red Kool-Aid."

I wipe my mouth on a paper towel and laugh a disgusted laugh. When I look at the back of the bathroom door I see a worn razor strap. The slave master's whip. I peep inside the medicine cabinet. Medications for hemorrhoids and manic depression. I feel for Genevieve.

When I make it back to the front room, Kenya is alone. Everyone is outside, some are lining up. Kenya stands in the front window, arms folded. Her perfume caresses me. She takes my plate from me, empties the food into a container before she trashes the paper plate.

Her face fills with concern. "Heard your wife had a conniption fit on the way out here."

That derails me. "Bubba Smith told . . . ?"

"That peckerwood was about to have a fit himself. You scared him pretty good. He ran and told everybody that you started holding Sister, yelling at her, and you cursed him. Said she went crazy, was scratching and hitting on you, kicking the seats, trying to jump out the car."

I curse him and his moustache. "It wasn't like that. She . . . it wasn't like that."

Kenya says, "Told Grandpa Fred 'nem you had him so upset he almost had a wreck."

"Grandpa Fred 'nem?" I take a sharp

breath. "Everybody knows about her attacks?"

She nods. "If they didn't, they do now. That's why everybody went outside to see y'all walk up. That's why everybody still outside. They're all interested in LaKeisha."

I'm about to head back outside, go straight to Bubba Smith and have a few words, but I see a stack of obituaries are on a table. Willie Esther Savage.

Curiosity stops me.

I pick one up. Surprise replaces anger. I had expected her to have long, wild hair like the ghost in *The Ring*. Or have a long nose and be as green as the Wicked Witch of the West.

I motion at this embodiment of veiled evil and say, "She looks like Elizabeth Taylor."

"With all that big red hair? Hair so red she looked like *I Love Lucy*."

She is beautiful, as was my mother. Owns a beauty that would be hard to control.

I say, "She does have a lot of hair."

"You could hike up one side of her hair, ski down the other."

"Guess there is no vertical limit on hairstyles out here."

"Not at all. Would have to ride a gondola to get to the top of that do."

"What is she?"

"Her momma was mulatto and Choctaw. They think her father might've been Irish because of the red hair. Either way, that one-drop rule kept her in her place. She black."

"She looks like a white woman."

"She tried to pass."

"Did she?"

"Yup. Some of the old folks used to get drunk and whisper that her first husband left her down in Lower Alabama, abandoned her and her two babies when he found out she wasn't as pure as the driven snow. She didn't like white people and she was always calling dark-skinned blacks out of their name, always yelled and screamed and talked with a lot of anger."

I ask, "Where were the men?"

"What do you mean?"

"Did Willie Esther ever have another husband, a boyfriend or anything?"

"Time to time, some men who looked like they worked at a coal mine or in construction came by. Men who were exposed to chemicals or asbestos or coal or something that damaged their lungs. They'd sit outside and drink scotch and smoke and swat mosquitoes. But none that stayed the night or she went to spend the night with."

"So you never saw her with a man."

"From what I hear, none of the men around here were good enough for her. She thought she was still who she used to be before she was run out of Lower Alabama, thought she was special, above everybody else. And ended up scrubbing toilets to make a dime."

Willie Esther. Tried to pass. Tried to re-invent herself, be someone else, and failed.

Kenya says, "She ended up cleaning white folks' houses. Bet that had to fuck with her."

"I suppose so."

I put the picture down, pick up a red book. *Odenville: A History of Our Town, 1821–1992.*

Kenya says, "One-fifty-one and one-sixty-nine."

"What?"

"If you want to see any black people in that history book, page one-fifty-one and page one-sixty-nine. We show up in the seventies." She chuckles. "On the men and women high-school basketball teams. Two brothers on page one-fifty-one. A sister on page one-sixty-nine."

"Damn. This close to the Civil Rights

movement and . . . two pages?"

"Not two *pages*, two *pictures*. That's it. Look at that and you think we showed up in the seventies. Group pictures at that. Showed up as hood ornaments for the basketball team."

I say, "Better than seeing photographs of brothers hanging from a tree."

"This ain't where you come to get enlightened and have in-depth discussions about slavery, the Middle Passage, and Dr. Martin Luther King, Jr. They ain't heard of the Middle Passage and think MLK — well, it's not like Odenville shuts down to celebrate King's birthday. You write about what you care about. What you want to remember. History should be inclusive and honest. Even if it's ugly. If not, it's one-sided and half-truths are propaganda. My daddy told me that's why we have to keep our own records, write our own history. Their history is not our history."

I spy as Kenya rambles in her neo-soul political tone.

Nothing about this family in that document. Nothing about Genevieve.

Kenya says, "I really feel for the sister on the basketball team."

"Because she was the only black?"

"Had to be horrible playing sports in

this humidity with a press-and-curl in the seventies."

I put the book down, go toward the window and stare out at a peaceful territory that might see Darwin's *The Origin of Species* as a frontal assault on the dogma of God's creation of mankind. The window is single pane; its curtains are thin, sun-beaten, hues ranging from their original red to a faded pink, frayed and thin where they have been victim of the most heat. The single-pane windows are smudged, fingerprints inside, dirt on the outside.

I ask, "Why did Willie Esther have so much hate?"

"Racial purity is a big deal to some people. Not just white people. Black people want black people to be with black people. Sexual segregation. That's what America teaches us to do the best, hate others because they are different and in the meantime learn to hate ourselves."

"You're harsh."

"You see the cute little Confederate flags in the businesses on 411? This is 'Bama, Boo. We learned from the best of the worst."

"I don't get it. Why would Willie Esther hate her offspring like that?"

"You're not listening."

"Okay, I'm listening."

"The South is a bitch to its colored children. You have to develop thick skin or the South can be a motherfucker. Maybe she couldn't handle it, got treated bad and that was all she knew. She just passed her anger on down the family tree. Horrible things happened to her mother."

"Like what?"

"The kind of horrible things that happen to women."

I wait without asking, hoping she will say, and at the same time hoping she won't.

She speaks very matter of fact, "First off, Willie Esther's mother was raped when she was a virgin. Got knocked up with Willie Esther."

"Willie Esther . . ."

She whispers, "Was a rape baby."

"Damn."

"And there was a rumor that Willie Esther was raped too. That's when she was hiding out in Lower Alabama. After her husband left, after they found out she was a lying-ass colored girl, she was raped. Some people think that grief-stricken motherfucker sent the men over to do it. Southern-fried justice. After they ran her out of town, she came up here."

It takes me a moment to regroup. "This is getting to be a bit much to digest."

"Especially with bull's nuts on your stomach."

"Especially."

"Guess you don't want a plate of chit'lins."

"Now I know what I smell. Thought the plumbing was backed up."

"Willie Esther. Rejected by white people and scared to be a black woman. Yep, she tried to run away from who she was, tried to be somebody else, failed like you wouldn't believe."

Astonished, I blink a few times, shake my head and tug at my goatee.

She goes on. "A lot of foul things happened, especially in 'Bama. Man or woman, there was a time, with all the open racial hostility, that it was dangerous for anybody black to be black."

My lips move but no words escape.

She clears her throat and rocks, tells me, "So you can see why Willie Esther wasn't too fond of the situation between Delphinie and Gravedigger. She was an outcast. Then Delphinie went off and had all those half-breed babies and ended up killed on the living room floor."

I take a breath.

"Add this to the historical buffet," she says. "One of those rapes produced Delphinie."

My breathing ceases for a moment.

Shakespearian thoughts rise. Shows I have seen flash before my eyes. Oedipus kills his father, fornicates with his mother. Medea butchers her children and feeds them to their faithless, philandering father. At the end of *Hamlet* there are nine corpses onstage, some poisoned, some run through on swords. Richard III slays his nephews, boys ages nine and eleven.

The evil things that Kenya has told me are worse than any theatrical performance.

My heart swells with empathy for Genevieve. I own the same compassion for Kenya.

I ask, "Any pictures of Delphinie around here?"

Kenya walks across the room, opens and closes a few drawers, heads down the hallway into a bedroom, moves things around, comes back with Polaroid pictures, hands them to me.

She says, "Strange going through dead folks' things. Never know what you might find."

In one photo their mother is a teenager, kind and gentle with long, wavy hair. Very

Choctaw. Same compact and sensual body as Genevieve. Others show the volcanic fire in her eyes, the growing desires that she could not hide. In another Delphinie wears a tight dress on a fuller figure. She has had many children between the two pictures. The faded Polaroid shows the weariness in her eyes, but her smile sings that the fire inside her remains unquenched.

Kenya says, "She always kept her hair long. That was her pride and joy."

I ask, "Any photos of Genevieve?"

"No photos of LaKeisha Shauna Smith here. Think Willie Esther got mad and burned them up or something. Grandpa Fred might have a few over at his house. You should go see them."

"What about pictures of you?"

"I'll never show anybody old pictures of me. Bone thin, black, and flat-chested with all that acne, no way. Thank God I put on some weight and grew some hips and a little ass."

"And the breasts."

"Gift from Deuce. Upgraded for him. That fool loves breasts. Used to . . . never mind."

My eyes meet hers. I imagine things illicit. Envy broils my adulterous flesh.

I hand the pictures back to Kenya; she slams the pictures on the kitchen table, her face filled with lines, her thoughts on Deuce. Heat rises inside of me. My jealousy startles me.

Again I should leave. But I find reason to stay and compromise what is left of my soul.

I say, "Genevieve looks like her mother. Jimmy Lee does too."

"Jimmy Lee, Jabari, J-Bo, Darius, they all look alike. I take after my daddy's side."

"You're the tallest woman here."

She says, "Tallest in the family. A Jolly Black Giant in a family of Lilliputians."

The one-armed and legless old man is out there by the graveyard, his eyes on the freshest of the graves, cigarette smoke pluming around his head. Daring death plain and clear.

I tell Kenya, "Grandpa Fred is an interesting character."

"We call him Tree Stump."

"That's cold-blooded."

"Not to his face."

"Guess that makes it better."

"Funerals are excitement for him. Gives old people like him a reason to get out and roll around. All he does is drink Miller Lite and watch Vietnam War movies from sunup to sundown."

"Is that so?"

"He's still fighting a war." Kenya motions at Grandpa Fred. "He's one of the lucky ones."

"What do you mean?"

"The government is wrong for the way veterans are treated. Men and women serve this country, come back, and are basically homeless. Or invalids with no way to support their family."

She fidgets, moves away, soft stroll taking her across the room. She toys with her wild hair, straightens up things that need no straightening, gives attention to everything but me.

She asks, "What did you come in here for besides the testicle tasting?"

"To see you."

"You don't have to come in here to test the temperature. I know you love your wife. I know you're scared that I might trip out. No matter how I feel about them, this is my family, remember that. We both know what we did was wrong. The terrified look on your face when you had busted your nut said it all. I know it wasn't shit to you. It wasn't shit to me."

"Kenya —"

"You've seen me. Now go back to your wife."

I stand there, nervous. She ignores me.

I tell her, "Genevieve was outside your room. She heard you."

"Everybody in the Tut heard me." Kenya shrugs. "Hard to be quiet when you getting dicked down like that. Dick like that and she can't have an orgasm? I find that hard to believe."

"You're calling me a liar?"

"Let me tell you this, Daddy Long Stroke. Game recognizes game."

She continues cleaning, now jittery. She cares what Genevieve knows.

Hands in pockets, I rock side-to-side, change the subject. "You're going to the wake?"

"I'll go to the funeral tomorrow. Today my job is to stay and watch the house, as if there were anything worth watching. Always thinks somebody will steal their mason jars or that picture of those dogs playing poker." She moves back to the window. "I get to play Donna Reed and meet anybody who comes by with food. Make sure food is heated up when they all come back."

I drift and stand next to Kenya, close enough to inhale her aroma, but not close enough to touch, not so close that if anyone comes in eyebrows will rise. We spy on Odenville. Genevieve does not come toward the trailer. Either her memories, or the essence of Willie Esther, causes her to avoid what's inside. At our home in Los Angeles, outside my bedroom window, we have a view of the sun rising over downtown. At night we go to bed with the city's skyline within reach. What I see, in my eyes, is morbid. Not to mention atrocious urban planning. I cannot imagine this being my view at sunrise, then watching the tombstones turn into haunting shadows at sunset.

My eyes go to Grandpa Fred. I think a moment then say, "I'm confused."

"Most of us are."

"No, I mean. Grandpa Fred. Willie Esther. They both lived here?"

"Hell no. Grandpa Fred used to live in the trailer home next door, but now he lives right there. Small two-bedroom house across the street. He's moving on up like George and Weezy."

With sarcasm, she motions at a simple white home facing the same cemetery. A wheelchair ramp runs from the driveway to its porch. An American flag waves out front.

I say, "His son and Genevieve's mother . . . were next-door neighbors?"

"Small community. When the hormones are raging, not a lot of options. Grandpa Fred and Willie Esther never cared for each other. They'd spit in the wind before they spoke."

"Why the unfriendliness?"

Kenya rubs her hand across her dark and sensual skin, telling me of their issues.

She says, "So, the story goes that when Gravedigger Smith had caught a case of Jungle Fever with Delphinie Savage, it was like the Hatfields versus the McCoys meets Romeo and Juliet. As far as everybody was concerned, from what I heard, that made them both tainted."

"Tainted?"

"Tainted. She had a white magic stick inside her, so that was all she wrote so far as black men. Doubt if she had anything to pick from worth talking about. He was probably looked at as a race traitor. Doubt if a white woman wanted him after he'd been into the heart of Africa."

It takes me back to Pasadena. It was the same way. The things we forget as we ride the wings of Affirmative Action into our own clouds. I digest this history. "Almost forty years ago."

"Forty years, not that long ago. If Grave-digger was a black man and Delphinie was a Miss Daisy, no telling what would've happened to him. Brothers used to get lynched for whistling at Miss Ann or not stepping off the sidewalk fast enough. Sleeping with? Scary thought, huh?"

I rub my goatee. "Times have changed."

"Not as much as you think. There are people here who are still fighting the Civil War. They're set in their ways and holding onto things that are long since past. Don't matter about right or wrong. They wave that Confederate flag like it's a religion. Shit, they need to pull the troops out of Iraq and send them to 'Bama, Mississippi, and Georgia."

"Okay, where did Gravedigger and Delphinie move to after they got married?"

"Moved? They lived right here."

"In this trailer?"

"Gravedigger married Delphinie and they moved their broke asses right in here."

I nod. Those few words explain a lot. I didn't understand how their mother was married to Gravedigger but ended up getting killed in this trailer. Now I do. This was everybody's home.

Kenya goes on, "But, from what I've

heard, Delphinie would go away, just walk out the front door with her purse, leave and not come back for a long time, sometimes weeks."

"She'd just . . . take the children and leave?"

"She didn't take anybody. Delphinie would say that she was going to the store for cigarettes and it might be weeks, maybe months before they saw her again."

"Why?"

"Because Gravedigger couldn't give her what she wanted. He couldn't get her out of Odenville. Guess he was happy being here, digging graves and playing the piano at church."

"So, she'd run away and leave all of you here?"

"She left everybody with Willie Esther. Lots of mothers in the South do that. Have children young. Realize we're not toys and we cost money. Realize that children can be the inhibitors of dreams and fantasies. So they leave their children with their grandparents. Got so bad that Willie Esther used to make Delphinie take somebody with her when she went to the store. Preferably the youngest. Delphinie would have to come back if she took the youngest."

I swallow and blink a few times. "She left everybody with Gravedigger."

"Please. When Delphinie went away, a couple of days later, after Gravedigger had screamed and cursed and damn near went love crazy, he would vanish too. Leave everybody with Willie Esther. Sometimes he would go stay with Grandpa Fred. A few times he went into Birmingham, went bar to bar looking for Delphinie. Sometimes he'd just wait for her to come back. He wasn't gonna keep those children. Let Grandpa Fred tell it, not a man's job to work all day and look after children, not when the woman he married ain't doing nothing."

I nod. "So everybody stayed here and with Grandpa Fred."

"Oh, hell no. Just Gravedigger. We *didn't* and still *don't* go to his crib."

"Why not?"

She almost laughs. "Tree Stump didn't want no halfbreed colored children over there messing up his funky little trailer. Compared to this dump, his shack was a castle. He had an air conditioner. Willie Esther didn't. He'd let us sweat like pigs while he sat up in that tin can, air conditioner on high, sipping sweet tea, and watching his color television."

"How was it for you growing up here?"

"I was in Dunwoody with my daddy most of the time."

"Dunwoody?"

"Over in Georgia. After Delphinie died, things were crazy, so they sent me to go live with my daddy. Actually he came here to see me, saw our welfare lifestyle, went to Grandpa Fred's trailer, and he took me with him. So I was with him most of the time. I came back after I was a teenager. Went to school out here one year. Got in trouble. Well, was having problems at school and with Daddy's wife. Of course that bitch thought it would be best to send me away."

"How was Willie Esther to you?" No answer. I ask, "How did Willie Esther treat you?"

When I turn around, Kenya is across the room, crying, wiping her eyes with her hands.

She says, "Great. Messing up my eyeliner."

Her sudden tears unnerve me the same way Genevieve's attack did.

Kenya says, "I'm okay. Thinking about Daddy. Sadness and anger, it comes and goes."

"What anger?"

She shakes her head, pulls her lips in, doesn't say. "Cancer is a bitch."

"Pancreatic?"

"Prostate." She nods. "Typical black man. *Hated* going to the doctor. Anyway, I went to Stone Mountain to take care of him. Was already too late. I fed him, changed his linen, cleaned his bedpan. Everything was in reverse, me doing for him what he did for me when I was a baby."

"They say 'once a man, twice a child.' "

"When a man is dying, all he wants to do is bare his soul. To make things right."

I nod.

"I was talking to Daddy, then he asked me to go get him some breakfast, came back and he wasn't breathing. He was gone. All the pain was gone from his face. I wanted to try to revive him, but I let him be. He knew he was about to die and sent me away. He knew I would've tried to revive him. He always told me that he didn't want that. Had his DNR order written up. He was already talking about how tired he was. I didn't try. I sat there next to him for hours. Crying."

The door opens and a group of children come inside. Kenya gets them all plates of food.

She tells them, "Make sure you bring the

leftovers back in here. Jimmy Lee and Velma want to take the leftovers back to their mutts. They have more mangy mutts than children."

She rubs their heads, laughs with them, then sends them back outside. Doesn't want to get food all over the trailer. She puts on yellow gloves, cleans off the chipped counter, puts trash in a big green bag, does chores without thought.

One glance at my wedding ring tells me to run away from here.

But I stay.

She says, "Let's stop doing this circle dance and talk."

"Yeah. There is this . . . I'm uncomfortable."

"You have nothing to worry about. I wouldn't do anything to damage your marriage. I'm as much to blame as you are. All I had to do was not open my door. I did what I wanted to do."

The skies turn a deeper gray. Rain will be here soon.

Kenya's cellular sings again. She frowns and ignores Usher's song.

More children come inside the trailer home. I step outside.

Minutes pass before Genevieve and the others come out of Grandpa Fred's home. The war veteran coughs like he's not long for this world, struggles, but gets his breathing back on track, and lifts his hand so he can smoke. Raises that nub and scratches his face again. I cringe.

Bubba Smith is at the Town Car, cleaning the windows. He spies toward Genevieve. Peeps back toward me and toys with his Dale Earnhardt moustache. I'm frowning. He gets nervous. One phone call to his employer and Bubba Smith will be at the unemployment office.

Genevieve feels my anger, my discomfort, and her eyes come this way. I wave. She waves back, still on the other side of the fence having a meeting with older members of her family. She makes no motion that tells me to come toward her, so I stay where I am, in the company of strangers. Looks like some neighbors have come by, all of them gravitating toward Genevieve, all amazed at her survival and transformation into culture and wealth. Genevieve seems accepting of them all, but I know her; she's ready to run down the road screaming.

The children leave the trailer home. I step back inside, search for something edible.

Kenya asks, "Want me to fix you a plate?"

"No."

"A man shouldn't have to fix his own plate, not when his wife is around."

I linger, watch her do other things. I say, "It surprises me. You're very uxorial."

"Uxorial?" She eases a hand on her hip. "What the hell does that mean?"

"It's a compliment. The way you said you took care of your dad . . . caring . . . wonderful. You're not boilerplate. You have style of your own. And you have the characteristics of a wife."

"Characteristics of a wife?" She rolls her eyes and laughs. "You calling me domestic? And if you are why don't you say domestic instead of using that complicated word?"

"Raise the bar. People get comfortable swimming in the warmth of their own ignorance."

"Whatever. You need to stop trying to impress me by sounding academic."

"Impress you?"

"You've been trying to impress me since I met you in the hallway at the Tutwiler."

Kenya smiles and I do the same. She says that if she were my wife, my world would be perfect. She touches a passionate part of me long suppressed by the need of another. If I had met her first, I could have loved her first. Then I would've still marveled at Genevieve's intelligence and viewed her as the optimum choice, the woman to propagate the species with.

Married to Kenya, I wonder if I would have committed adultery with Genevieve.

More cars pull up outside. More of the elderly have arrived.

I ask Kenya, "Tell me some more about your family."

"Already did. Poor white trash meets Negroid in the countrified hood. That sums it up."

"I want to know about my wife. Tell me about Genevieve before she ran away to Atlanta."

Kenya tenses. "I'm talking too much. What LaKeisha wants you to know about LaKeisha, she'll tell. But don't expect much more than what I've said. This is the South. Secrets born here die here."

"What other things are people hush about?"

"Only reason I'm talking this much is . . . is . . . you know why."

"Tell me."

"Because of this morning. You did me righteous, hurt me so damn good, did something to me I didn't expect and I'm not comfortable with what I'm feeling right now, not at all."

At times her voice changes, sometimes hip, sometimes shunning any Southern influence.

I let her words settle before I whisper, "Tell me."

She whispers in return, her tone the merging of pain and confusion, "Don't. Do. That."

"Don't do what?"

She snaps, "Don't. Use. Me."

"Okay, then tell . . . just help me out on one thing. You told me that you were there when your mother was killed by Genevieve's father. But Genevieve told me she was there by herself."

Her eyes go to the floor, to a specific spot, as if she can hear the screams, see the madness in a man's eyes as he kills the thing he loves, see all the blood that was shed.

I say, "I'm not trying to use you."

"Bullshit. Don't use me to find out what your wife is ashamed of."

"I'm family. Maybe I'll ask around."

"Being married to one of us does not make you one of us. Grandpa Fred has this place under control. People might whisper, but nobody's gonna talk, not to you. The neighbors don't know you and I doubt if they'd talk even if you had a warrant signed by Jesus. I asked questions for years and got no answers. Damn shame. Only one way to get *enlightened* in this family."

"How?"

"Find somebody on their deathbed. That's the only time people around here will talk, when they are trying to lighten their loads in hopes of floating up to the pearly gates. The scent of the Grim Reaper is like a truth serum. Makes them talk so much you wish they would shut up."

"You were just talking about Willie Esther. You're not on your deathbed."

"Maybe because since my daddy died . . . I feel like part of me is dying on the inside."

That shuts me down.

She snaps, "Look, fix your plate and get out of here before people start gossiping."

Kenya hates me.

I take an extra crispy leg from a bucket of KFC and leave her alone, the door slamming behind me. I loathe her as I draw in each adulterous breath. She has stolen my righteousness. I blame her because I find that easier than accepting the blame for my own actions.

I stand near the fence, head aching, rubbing my goatee, staring at that marker for my mother-in-law. I would go over there, but I cannot lie to the dead. Delphinie knows my truth.

My cellular rings once, then vibrates. I have a text message.

From: Doctor Genevieve Forbes ARE YOU DOING OK?

I look up but I don't see her. I reply that I am fine. Lies come so easily.

Bubba Smith smokes and watches me. I catch him and he turns away, makes himself busy. I go confront Bubba Smith, let him know that I am beyond pissed with the way he ran up here and spread the word about Genevieve's panic attack. I tell him that was unprofessional.

He strokes his NASCAR moustache and says, "Yessir. But since we all family —"

"That's my *wife."*

"Yessir, I know, but I think that my daddy and the rest of the family —"

"What happens in the car stays in the car," I snap. "What happens while you're with us, nobody's business. I'm tempted to call your employer and let them know how unethical you are."

"But, please don't. Just ain't nothing like that ever happened while I —"

I walk away, letting his desperate words evaporate in the wind.

I'm not as angry as I pretend, not with him. I just need him to be afraid of me.

Genevieve. Thirteen-year-old runaway. Gone for six months. It disturbs me to no end.

Disgusting images roll through my mind, a montage of things I don't want to imagine.

Then I see a family of cockroaches moving through the grass. I lose my appetite.

I take my plate back inside. Kenya snatches the plate from my hand, stuffs it in the trash, makes sure everything in this space remains in order. Type A. Like Genevieve.

I tell Kenya, "On a side note, I saw a U-Haul by the Bank of Odenville. Easy to see from that street over there. If they were trying to hide it, they really should move it down a little bit."

She gives me her gray eyes, wipes her hands, chews her bottom lip, and nods.

I say, "Doubt if Bin Laden would attack Odenville, but that truck does stand out."

My eyes are on Genevieve as I slip by Kenya, my fingers tracing the rise and curve of her backside. The way she jerks, the coldness that settles between us, it leaves me uncomfortable.

I am in pain because I want to touch her. I want to hold her. I want to place staccato kisses on her mouth. I want to hold her ass and tongue her while I ease inside her over and over.

I want to hear her sigh, that sound that resounds like a sweet poem.

As the metal door creaks open, I look back at my Götterdämmerung. She does not react.

Again I feel the coldness of trepidation moving up my spine to my neck.

I want her to not despise me for being less than a man.

I want her to not ruin the world I have.

But I cannot lie about my own needs.

I can only try to understand this heinous and destructive crime of passion I have done.

I say, "The only thing I regret about this morning is that I couldn't give you the kind of love you deserved. I wanted to caress you without rushing, explore all of your erogenous zones. If that angers you, I apologize. I did not want to leave you feeling like you were a whore. Or with the impression that I'm some sort of a nymphomaniac. Or that I had those thoughts of you."

Her expression remains void, unmoved by my confession, impossible to interpret.

I ask, "What are you thinking?"

She plays with her tongue ring, takes a slow breath before she sighs.

I say, "Tell me."

Without looking at me she whispers, "I still feel you inside me, stretching my walls."

She is across the small living room, the low voice of a sensual girl, her dark and full lips barely moving. I close my eyes. Imagine I am slipping inside her, can feel her velvet-lined vagina pulsating around my desire. I close my eyes tighter; envision and feel the tip of my penis moving inside her. Can see her vagina, those three uneven vertical lines, feel those uneven folds parting.

She whispers, "I really should suck your dick then show you how good I can fuck you."

My words are flowers and in return she gives me language as crass as Marlon Brando in *Last Tango in Paris*. She bestializes what we have done, her way of destroying romantic illusions and offering reality, of saying she is not naïve, reminding me not to make this what it cannot be.

I study her. I look beyond the facade she

shows, beyond her body, beyond the tattoos, beyond the tongue ring, beyond the things she has done to herself to reinvent and redefine herself and make herself unique, separate herself from her own past, as Genevieve as done.

I search for the Kenya behind the mask.

The gaze she returns is more than gasoline searching for a fire. It is a look I recognize. I saw it as a child. And when I was thirteen, a thirty-year-old Ecuadorian woman who had just lost her husband owned the same expression. It is the receptive stare of a woman in search of love.

She grabs her skirt, pulls it up, and reveals smooth legs up to her thighs.

She says, "You can have this right now, if you like."

That disarms me.

She touches the wrong parts of me in the right way. She knows she does.

She sighs and desire shifts the topography of my inner landscape.

Who knows what might have happened right then, at this moment in a dilapidated trailer that faces the grounds of the dead, with my wife and her family right outside that door, if we had not heard a scream, followed by what sounded like a crack, followed by many screams.

sixteen

"Woman, last time telling you," Jimmy Lee snaps. "You better respect me."

Velma shrieks, "What is your damn problem, Jimmy Lee?"

"Bad enough you keep disrespecting me in front of my kids, Velma, but I ain't gonna have you stand over my momma's grave *telling lies* and down-talking to me any kinna way."

The Reverend steps in, tries to calm the masses to no avail. Old people stare, shaking their heads, letting fools be fools. Bubba Smith keeps to himself, as people do when domestic issues rise. I head out not knowing what to do, knowing that I am only an observer.

Velma holds her mouth. "You hit me in front of everybody . . . how could you?"

"Watch your mouth. Done had enough of you back-talking me in front of my kids."

Genevieve heads toward them, then

stops. She is out of place, no longer of this world. I stand by her, my fingers on her shoulder. She raises her hand to mine, her grip tight and strong.

I ask, "Should I help . . . something?"

"No. Leave them alone."

Jimmy Lee and Velma stand on the other side of the fence, yelling at each other. Velma is holding her mouth. Six children cry like a choir of pain.

So many people are yelling their names, but there is too much crying from the distraught symphony of traumatized children for anyone to hear anything but ear-piercing pandemonium.

Velma pulls off a three-inch heel and hurls it at Jimmy Lee. It misses. Then she takes off her other shoe and slings it hard. Misses again. Hits a tombstone. Jimmy Lee adjusts his polka-dot tie and stands his ground like he wishes one of those shoes had dirtied his yellow suit.

Reverend tries to intervene, Bible raised. It does not help. He does not get too close. He is a pacifist. Grandpa Fred tries to talk, but his cough is never-ending. Everyone backs away, like firefighters in the hills of California allowing a raging brushfire to burn out in its own time.

Velma stands barefoot on soggy ground,

hand holding her injury, yelling at the top of her lungs, "Look at this blood on my brand-new blouse. Can't take this back to Wal-Mart with blood on it. Now I'mma have to keep it."

"How many times I tell you to shut your trap with that fabrication?"

"Jimmy Lee, how am I s'pose to sang at Willie Esther funeral with my mouth looking like this? You hit me too hard that time. You coulda kilt me, hitting me like that. Tired of this mess."

"You know what you said. Told you about going on and on with that lie."

"And I'mma tell er'body you're beating on me over some stupid stuff."

"Last time warning you to close your trap before you make me shut —"

"You reap what you sow, Jimmy Lee. Let's see how well you act when it's your turn to reap."

He says, "I'm not gonna let a damn stripper from Miss'sippi talk to me any kinda way."

"For your information, dumb-butt, I used to be an *exotic dancer,* not a *stripper.*"

"And your flabby titties all out in front of everybody."

"My titties ain't as flabby as your butt. You met me at my job. And all these kids you got and you calling me out? You got mo' baby mommas than Bobby Brown. You done gave me the claps three times in the last three years and you calling me out? Why are you tripping?"

"Dumb-ass stripper from Miss'ippi try'n to act like she smarter than me."

"You're the dumb-ass. *The Matrix* was invented by a black woman."

Jimmy Lee stands and grits his teeth. "Stop. Spreading. Lies."

The source of their argument. *The Matrix*. A movie. Everyone gasps in confusion.

He snaps, "Say that again and I'll knock your damn teeth out."

"What you gonna do this time? You already beat me up at a gas station. Dragged me out of the car like I was . . . like I was nothing. And you did that in front of my kids."

"Ain't no pussy better than my dick. Last time telling you that. I told you to either shut up talking crazy or get the hell out my Cadillac and *you chose* to get your butt whipped."

She snaps, "*The Matrix* was invented by a black woman and Hollywood stole it."

Jimmy Lee lights a cigarette, talking to himself, then turns and limps toward the church.

Velma barks, "It was, it was, it was, it was. A black woman is the true Oracle."

Jimmie Lee marches on. It feels like the drama is over.

Then Velma yells, "Your Papa-Smurf-looking butt better get back here."

Jimmy Lee turns around and tries to run after Velma. She runs between tombstones. He hobbles after her, chases her around grave after grave. He can't catch her, not with that bad leg.

The screaming escalates.

He yells, "I'm tired of you doing thangs to irritate me. Putting my medicine and thangs on a high shelf so I can't reach 'em. You think it's funny when I have to get a chair to get thangs."

"I'm tired of your short butt jumping up in my face and hitting me. I need to be with a tall man anyway. A man who can reach thangs both standing up *and* laying down."

"Keep insulting me."

"Shorty. Tiny Tim. Troll."

Jimmy Lee looks toward us, makes eye contact with Genevieve, his big sister.

Velma keeps on insulting him, yelling, "What you gonna do about it, Mini-Me?"

He pulls his lips in, looks down across his yellow suit to his pointed-toe shoes.

330

He throws his cigarette at Velma, then hobbles across the graves toward the church.

Velma calls after him, "And like I said, *a black woman* created *The Matrix. A black woman* created *The Matrix.* I'll say that from sundown to sunup. *A black woman* created *The Matrix.*"

Jimmy Lee keeps his disconcerted pace, lighting another cigarette as he hobbles away.

Velma yells, "You better come get some of these damn kids."

He raises his middle finger.

"I did *that* and see where it got me. With two of your damn chirren. Butthole. You better turn your Hop-Along-Cassidy-looking ass around and come get these damn chirren. These ain't even my chirren. I'm tired of you leaving all these bad-ass chirren with me all the damn time."

His one-legged pogo hop-walk makes him look more cartoon than real.

"Jimmy Lee, I ain't playing with you. Come get these damn kids of yours. *Jimmy Lee.*"

Velma leans against a tombstone, breaking down, that marker the only thing to keep her from crashing to the earth. The tears fall and the screams to come get the kids rise. Blood runs from her nose through her moustache, courses across her chin to her razor bumps.

Grandpa Fred's wheelchair loses control, starts rolling backward as he continues his coughing fit. Bubba Smith runs and catches what's left of his old man before he tilts over.

In the meantime, six children continue screaming.

Velma spits out her bloody chewing gum and yells, "Little Jimmy Lee be quiet. Shaquanda let momma leg go. Let momma go. Bonquita, you better stop wiping your nose on your clothes before you get buggars all over your good dress and . . . one of y'all go get Lexus and y'all take Mercedes and Sean John — do something. Will y'all please stop hollering, dammit?"

Family members and the Reverend approach her, slow steps toward a wild horse.

The blood that flows from her nose into her moustache makes my flesh crawl.

Then Velma smiles, tells people she is okay, that it was nothing, says, "Sorry about holding y'all up. I'll be ready in a minute, Reverend. Little Jimmy Lee, stop crying and get my shoes for me. Take 'em inside and wipe 'em off real good. Shaquanda get momma pocketbook."

The traumatized children cry louder.

Velma coughs, loses it for a moment, adjusts her sagging breasts, then chokes on her blood and saliva. Mud has spattered up and down her clothing, left her speckled in filth.

She recovers, becomes defiantly still and tight-jawed, her expression vacant and cold.

She looks strange, like a photo scanned on cheap equipment, not quite right.

She nods as if she's come to a cold-hearted conclusion.

She walks away, her smile now sardonic, confirming the answer in her head.

Her hips have no sway, her arms no swing as she lumbers toward the trailer, six children following her, six children crying, six children with runny noses. Velma lowers her head and holds her swollen lip, manufactures a trembling laugh, one that reeks of contempt and embarrassment.

Ancient people. Young people. All are standing. All are mumbling and watching.

This drama is not new; it's in their eyes, in their non-action. For the Savages, for the Smiths, this is nothing new. My mind shifts, as it does at moments I wish it would leave things be. Shifts and Mendel's famous principles of hereditary transmission take over my thoughts.

Genevieve is next to me now, teeth clenched, my wife holding my hand.

Family and friends rush Velma toward Willie Esther's trailer home to get her cleaned up. She spits and reassures everyone, "A black woman did invent *The Matrix*. I'm not lying."

Genevieve looks at me, sorrow and embarrassment in her eyes. She lowers her head as if she didn't want me to see all these defective people — people with kickstands — in her past.

She wants to get away. She wants to light up a shrub and find that blissful feeling.

She says, "This is why. I should have. Come alone. Or not. Have come. At all."

I suck my bottom lip and nod, admitting that in some ways Genevieve is right.

She says, "What you're looking at, that's my parents when we were growing up. Those snotty-nosed kids screaming their lungs out, that was us. Watching them fight like cats and dogs. Velma and my brother, tonight they'll be in the same bed. In the morning she'll wake up and cook breakfast, busted lip and all."

I don't say that that reminds me of my grandparents, just say, "That's scary."

"What could there be more terrifying

than a husband and wife who hate each other?"

Genevieve looks at me after she says that, her thoughts deep, expression unreadable.

I give her direct eye contact, search for a hidden message behind her tense eyes.

I say, "Maybe, for them, enemies sleeping in the same bed, nothing is more exciting."

She looks away, defeat swimming in her eyes. Genevieve probably believes, in her heart, no matter how much she plans, flowcharts, and swims upstream, she still might end up like this. Like a snail being embarrassed of that slime trail its ancestors leave in their path, so it suddenly decides it's going to jump species, become a clam, or a swan, and deny its past.

She asks, "Knowing these will be their relatives, sure you would want to have children?"

I squeeze her hand tight. "Not now, Genevieve."

Genevieve runs her hand through her hair, her expression that of irritation at full throttle.

Grandpa Fred's rugged cough has lasted from the alpha to the omega of the domestic brawl, that cough so persistent that he hasn't been able to utter a word since the fiasco erupted.

I look at him and can almost see the tumors riddling his lungs and brain. I can see a skeleton with a scythe standing behind him, his crooked finger extended for that contact, his finger teasing the edges of Grandpa Fred's face, deciding to let him suffer before he gives him that gentle touch. Then the old man's face morphs into fear. Grandpa Fred sees him too.

Then her scent invades my senses. Kenya, my sweet weakness, stands near me.

I move closer to my wife the way the unrighteous need to move closer to Jesus.

In the background I hear a motorcycle approaching. The hum of a Fat Boy. Harley-Davidson. I recognize the sound of its engine as it punctuates the screams of children.

I pull away from the sound of freedom, my five senses wafting back to this scene.

Kenya stands on the other side of Genevieve, arms folded, head shaking.

Standing next to Kenya's height, my petite wife seems smaller. As if she was dwindling.

Kenya speaks to no one and everyone all at once: "I was born in a manger surrounded by liquid crackheads and chain-smoking alcoholics who had been displaced from their motherland; physically and mentally abused to the point that we devour ourselves with self-hatred; prayers go up and come back unanswered because He is not accepting our I-pages."

When Kenya finishes her poetic tirade, I look at her. She looks away, arms folded, gray eyes turning red, lips tight. If not for these screams there might have been our moans.

Now, like the rest of the world, I have angered her.

Genevieve says, "Kenya, we should talk."

I try to swallow my own fear; my heart breaks into a dangerous, unbridled gallop.

Kenya shifts. "Sure, Sister. You're the oldest. Whatever you say goes."

Genevieve takes a sharp breath. "Call me by my name, please."

"LaKeisha Shauna Smith."

"That is not my name, Kenya."

Kenya chuckles. "You're insane."

"Excuse me?"

"Not my words. Everybody here thinks you're flying over the cuckoo's nest."

"Is that right?"

"That name you have, that way you say it, like you're French, it's so pretentious, and that's what makes it so insane. I refuse to say it because it's stupid. Like in the movie *Breakfast at Tiffany's*, where Audrey Hepburn's character Holly Golightly invents this glamorous New York persona that lives like a well-heeled socialite, but she comes from the same kind of countrified background. That's you, Genevieve. You're no Audrey Hepburn, but you are a friggin' Holly Golightly. You might come back all dressed up like Oprah, wearing expensive jewels, but all these snaggletooth folks who suck down white lightning and shoot at the moon, this is you."

The world stops rotating. And I do not own the power to make it spin again.

Genevieve folds her anger, tucks it inside her jaw, lets her rage move through the lines in her forehead, course through the veins in her neck before she pauses, struggles to keep her tone civil and tuned to kindness, and in a difficult voice she asks, "Why do you hate me so much?"

"I'm not the one who hates. I'm not the one who ran away and left everybody."

Genevieve takes a breath. "Tomorrow, after Willie Esther's funeral, let's talk."

"Sure. We'll talk about the heartache I've gone through, watching my father shit all over himself and die a slow death, listening to him ramble like he had dementia, about my whole life, about how I'm a slacker and I don't live up to your expectations, we can talk about all that."

Kenya storms away from Genevieve, anger in her trembling lips, tears in her eyes.

Genevieve calls Kenya. She does not answer, just heads toward the trailer, her wild hair dancing with her insolent stroll. Genevieve becomes rigid. She will not go toward that trailer. Kenya stops at the steps, but does not go inside. They call her, older members in her family, they need her help. She puts on a respectful smile and hurries, becomes the uxorial woman, maybe the kind and subservient child, tries to assist the Reverend in getting people organized.

Genevieve stares. She mumbles, "Holly Golightly. Flying over the cuckoo's nest."

I say, "I love your name, Genevieve. Love the rich way it sounds."

"Thanks. I really needed to hear that right now."

"You're beautiful, poignant, and poetic. You're a rare and wonderful language."

"A rare and wonderful language no one understands."

"I do."

"Do you? Honestly, do you even understand me?"

"I love everything about you. I love the way you move. I love your arms. You have grace. I love the way you look at me. I love your toes. I love the shoes you wear."

"Do you love me? Now that you've seen this, do you still see me with the same eyes?"

"You're still my Genevieve." Again I squeeze her hand. "That's all that matters."

I allow her name to roll off my tongue, its correct pronunciation drenched in warm butter.

She smiles a moment, then that glimpse of joy vanishes. "Have I been a good wife?"

"You're a wonderful woman."

"But have I been a good wife? Have I lived up to your expectations or am I a disappointment? Things you said last night . . . your tone . . . I've been troubled all day."

"You said some pretty damaging things to me as well. On the plane you told me that you wished that we never . . ." Hurt halts my words. "Never mind. Not now. We're here for a funeral."

"You pushed me. You know you push me. You push me until I snap. And I say

340

things that I know I shouldn't say. About your . . . *that* relationship . . . I'd been holding that in for a while."

Her face overflows with distress. She takes a few breaths, centers herself.

Once again I ask, "You okay?"

She shakes her head. "Tell Bubba Smith that I'm ready to leave."

"What about the wake?"

"I'm ready to leave. There is too much mental static here. I'll . . . I'll have another attack if I stay here, I feel it. I have to get away from here, from all of this madness. And these memories."

Kenya's gravitational pull, it slows me, misdirects me.

Obsession rises.

I don't want to be here with her, yet I do not want to go away. If I leave her, I know that we will part and I'll never see her again, not in the unrighteous way I've selfishly enjoyed her.

I tell Genevieve, "You flew a long way not to go the last few feet with your family."

"If I go with them where will you be?"

"Bubba Smith can drive you over. I can wait in the trailer."

Her eyes go toward her sister. She clears uneasiness from her throat.

Kenya is the gun I hold to my head, finger on trigger.

"No," Genevieve says and scowls. "I only need to see Willie Esther's dead face once."

"We're already here, wherever here is, we're here."

She tells me, "Stop transmitting. Receive what I'm telling you."

"You're right. I'm listening."

"I can't handle this. Maybe I'll do better with the funeral tomorrow."

She wobbles where she stands. My heart splinters as I take her arm.

I ask, "You okay?"

"Migraine. Can't take much more of this noise. I need . . . I need some space."

I nod, knowing what she needs. "I'll tell Bubba Smith we have changed the plans."

"Let me say a polite good-bye to a few of the elders and go back to Birmingham."

"Want me to go with you?"

Genevieve shakes her head. "Old people are so depressing."

"Why do you say that?"

"All they talk about is who's sick, who might be sick, who died, how long it took them to die. All they talk about is bad news and death. 'Your uncle just died, Bae Bae got cirrhosis, 'member Sonny

342

Boy? Yeah you do — you met him when you was two. Anyway, he just had a stroke.' I want to scream, 'Can't you at least start the conversation off with something happy?' "

As she walks away, Velma and her still-crying children come out of the trailer.

Velma yells, "I cain't go in church with my mouth all messed up like this. And these chirren . . . Lord give me my strength. I'mma stay here and y'all tell Jimmy Lee to come get his chirren."

The trailer door creaks and slams hard behind her and her wailing tribe.

The sound of that Harley-Davidson draws closer. Then it idles, can hear the one-of-a-kind *pop-pop* sound followed by a pause. Nothing sings like the unique song of a Harley. This one is louder than most, very distinctive. It's been customized, mufflers removed.

Driven by the abrupt sound, Kenya looks to her left, sees the Harley approaching, moving slow, the rider searching the faces of everyone he passes, looking for someone in particular.

The rider sees Kenya and speeds up, Harley-Davidson resounding like a god's thunder.

She curses, then her eyes go toward

Odenville Library, toward a barely visible U-Haul.

She doesn't have to say that the rider in the black leather jacket, the white man with the frown plastered on his face, is Deuce. She has been found.

seventeen

Deuce possesses a chiseled body, a gift from the God of Steroids.

But he owns a face that makes Ernest Borgnine look like Brad Pitt.

Many colorful tattoos cover his neck. My first thought is that hopefully he has a nice personality. But the hard-core expression he has as he shuts his bike down speaks otherwise.

He unsnaps his cruiser helmet, takes off his goggles, dusts down his leather jacket.

Kenya says, "How did you know I was up here?"

"Is that any kind of way to tell your husband-to-be hello?"

"You're not my husband-to-be."

"Guessed you might hide out here."

"Good guess. Now what do you want?"

"Look, no time to mess around. I'm in trouble."

Kenya says, "I want my charge cards re-activated."

He nods. "Those breasts are looking pretty good."

"Don't start."

"I paid for them but I can't compliment them?"

"Deuce, I told you, soon as I'm able I'll reimburse you."

"Drives me crazy imagining another man holding onto my breasts."

"These are not your breasts."

"I'll repossess them if I have to."

"Quit talking crazy."

"Six thousand of my hard-earned money says those tits belong to me. Unless some man is going to give me my money back, all my money plus interest, those tits are mine."

"Possession is nine-tenths the law."

"Oh, I can fix that real fast with a steak knife. I'll leave you the way I found you."

He looks at me. Reads me. Sizes me up. His eyes daring me.

Kenya says, "He's family. LaKeisha's husband. My sister that lives in California."

"Didn't know you had a sister, let alone one in California."

"Well now you do. This is her husband."

He ignores me, asks Kenya, "How did

you get out here?"

"I flew."

"Now that's funny. I called the airport. Hartsfield was shut down last night."

"Obviously not."

Her lies are served warm with the texture of heated butter.

I interrupt, say, "Nice Fat Boy. One down, four up?"

His eyes cut me up and down. "You ride?"

"A Ducati. Liter."

He huffs. He rides a cruiser. I ride high-end Italian. We're in two different classes.

I want him to see me as Rambo but he stares at me like I'm Seinfeld's sidekick.

With that he is no longer concerned with me. A few of the veins in his neck subside, but not many. He walks by me like I don't exist. I'm a speck of snow in a blizzard.

He walks toward Kenya. She moves away. Then they freeze and stare at each other. Tension flares. He's shorter than me, taller than Kenya. His mass looks to be twice mine.

"It seems as if I've lost a U-Haul."

She acts like she's looking in her pockets. "Sorry."

He's not amused. "Don't play with me, Kenya. Seems like I packed up my home and my business in this U-Haul. Seems like I had a falling out with you over the phone. Since then crazy things have been happening. Slashed tires on both my cars. Windows broken in the house."

"Damn, Boo. Somebody done put a mojo on you."

"Two nights ago I went to bed and when I woke up everything I owned was gone."

"Damn shame. Guess somebody took a Slim Jim and hotwired your truck."

"The key is missing too."

"How did that happen?"

"First I was thinking that whoever did it came in through my garage while I was sleeping."

"Did you ask that ugly shit I caught you sleeping with?"

"But the house alarm was on. I think I must've left the key in the truck."

"Well, that was smart. Anybody could have your truck. Instead of blowing up my phone and riding out here to harass me, maybe you should've been looking around College Park. Two days ago? That truck could be in Canada or California by now. Maybe down in Mexico."

Deuce sucks on his teeth, nods his head, thinks for a moment.

He says, "Right now I need to find that

U-Haul and get it back out to Bankhead."

"Call the police."

"Call the police?"

"Yeah. If somebody stole it, report it stolen. And while you're on the phone, get my charge cards reactivated."

Kenya walks away, dress swaying as she heads away from the trailer.

Deuce hesitates, grits his teeth, and follows. He's confused, not sure if she's lying. If I wasn't acquainted with the truth, I'd believe her. This is her lover. I imagine them together.

Seeing him angers me. Again heat rises.

Then I look toward the beauty and brilliance of my pot-smoking and enigmatic wife.

I go inside the trailer. On the counter is a brown purse, the designer kind with golden Ls and Vs overlapping each other. The bag feels heavy. I open it up and look inside. Makeup. Other womanly effects. Condoms. I find what I'm looking for, the keys to the U-Haul.

And I find what is giving her purse its weight. A snub-nose revolver, Smith & Wesson.

I swallow. I own fear for Kenya.

Then I go to Bubba Smith. I tell him that I'm taking a short walk to the

349

highway, going to clear my head with a stroll to the gas station, might get something to drink.

He says, "Rain coming. I can run you up there."

"Wait on my wife."

"It won't be a problem. Daddy asked me to run up there anyway. Wanted to fill up those three gas cans." He motions at three big red canisters on the side of Grandpa Fred's home. "Daddy likes to keep extra gas around in case he needs it for his truck or his boat."

"Bubba Smith, just wait on my wife. When she's done, come pick me up at the gas station. I know this is your family, but you're on the clock. We're paying you, understand?"

"Yessir."

"Do that on your own time."

"Yessir."

Rain starts to fall as I hurry down the road and stop at Alabama Street. Under the darkening skies I pause between the library and the defunct bank, sky crying a little harder, as I stare over the civic center toward the row of trailer homes. No one is looking my way. I spy toward St. Clair High School. Then I notice an elementary school nestled in what looks like a cul-de-sac, almost concealed from the rest of the community. I continue up the street, my pace quick and steady. The fourteen-foot U-Haul rests on a narrow street in front of a trailer home.

A dog barks. I jump, break into a run. A rottweiler is charging at me. But he is chained to a pole in the ground. Over and over he tests his chain, wishing I'd come toward him.

I rush to the truck.

I'm no longer an educated man. I'm a fourteen-year-old boy in Fresno about to steal the battery out of a car. My old life crawls over my mind as I get inside, looking around for trouble.

I am unraveling. The moral part of me spiraling and dissipating into nothingness.

I drive Kenya's crime toward the elementary school.

That is where I leave the truck.

The sky cries harder by the time the Town Car pulls up in front of the Exxon. I come out, Gatorade and Fig Newtons in hand. Customers in pickup trucks stare as Bubba Smith hops out to let me in the backseat. He opens the door. Genevieve is in the backseat. So is Kenya.

The *pop-pop-pop* of the Harley comes

right behind them.

Genevieve gets out, once again elegant, looking soigné and sophisticated. She is a beautiful swan. Getting away from the trailer homes, only a few feet, has changed her.

She smiles at me. I smile in return. She owns the gravity of my emotions.

Then Kenya gets out, heads inside the mini-mart, wild hair dancing.

Her lips are turned down, gray eyes tight, pace that of annoyance.

Deuce turns off his Harley.

Before I can ask what's going on, Genevieve tells me, "Kenya needed a ride back."

I nod. I figured she would. Her options are few. I ask, "How did she get here?"

"Probably rode one of her lies."

I ask, "What's up with her friend? You meet him?"

"Said hi. Outside of that, they're not saying."

"He heading back to Atlanta or staying with her?"

Her eyes frown and her lips smile.

Genevieve says, "You were inside the trailer a long time."

I wonder why she is saying that now. She smiles but now I see that her smile is illusory, insincere and baiting. I shrug and re-

352

spond, "Didn't seem like you wanted me with you."

"I take it that you spoke with Kenya?"

"Is that what she told you?"

"That's what I'm asking you."

"Some. She was cleaning up. Other people were in and out."

Genevieve pulls her lips in. "What's going on, Sweetie?"

"What do you mean?"

She takes a sharp breath. "What did you and Kenya talk about?"

"She talked about her dad. His cancer. She broke down crying."

Silence.

I say, "She told me that Willie Esther was raped. And her mother before her."

Genevieve pulls her lips in, nods.

Then I speak the obvious. "Looks like it's about to storm."

"Yes, it is about to storm on us." Her tone is slick and metaphorical. She looks to me, reads my eyes, then looks away, tense and sad. "Willie Esther is trying to run us out of town."

She stares at the highway. Her road to emancipation. In that instant she looks thirteen. I can't shake what she has told me. I can't say it does not matter. I can't erase this memory.

Genevieve says, "You probably have more questions."

I nod. "Probably."

Kenya comes back, pack of cigarettes in one hand, bag of pork rinds and a bottled Coca-Cola in the other. Nicotine, swine, and caffeine. She gets in the backseat, the passenger side.

Genevieve asks, "Have I not been a good wife?"

"Why do you keep asking me something like that?"

"Because." Genevieve nods. "I am very uneasy with something myself."

"Since when?"

"Since this morning." She pauses. "I pray and hope that I'm imagining things."

"What things?"

"That Willie Esther's evil is reaching up from hell and giving me hallucinations."

Bubba Smith hurries and opens the door on our side. Genevieve doesn't want to sit next to Kenya. Despite my height, I take the middle seat, my right leg up against Kenya. My left leg rests against Genevieve. My guilt squirms between love and lust.

Quietly, deep inside myself, in the corner of a distant nether region, I almost smile.

Kenya moves the softness of her leg

against mine, sighs like a soft poem.

Genevieve holds my hand, holds me tight, her palm as wet as a river.

I don't ask any more questions, but I can figure out what has happened, how we all ended up in this car together. This is our momentary prison. Thanks to Jimmy Lee, *The Matrix*, and a strong backhand, Velma isn't going to the wake, so she and her wailing kids will be at the trailer, wiping blood from her moustache as she keeps all burglars away. With Deuce in Odenville, Kenya is rattled, now ready to flee. He is a hawk, watching her, following her wherever she goes, so she has to make her lies seem true, she has to leave with Genevieve.

The radio is on. News. They talk about the storm that's coming back this way. In between that they give sound bites: Inmate was struck and killed while picking up trash on I-65.

Bubba Smith repeats, "Inmate got hit and killed while picking up trash on 65."

I say, "Guess that was God's will."

"No sir. It was an accident."

I want to ask how he categorizes a tsunami that sweeps babies from the arms of their mothers and kills enough to populate a large city, or a five-hundred-pound GPS-guided bomb that hits the wrong target and kills seven innocent children. I want to ask because I do not know.

I want to ask because if things are predetermined, then I can rationalize Kenya.

I can say what we have done was meant to be, it was written.

I can say that I have no accountability for my actions.

I can be absolved.

Genevieve leans forward, her expression trenchant and doughty, her eyes on Kenya, says, "Deuce, heard him say he was just getting here from Atlanta."

Kenya does not respond. Genevieve sits back, shaking her head. She knows that Deuce was not on the other side of Kenya's bedroom door inducing screams of passion.

Deuce stalks twenty yards behind the Town Car, his Fat Boy idling at another pump. He has gone into his dual saddlebags and taken out yellow rain gear, put it on. He is prepared. He is intense but he is patient. Rain falls on him and he wipes away that useless water. He revs up his Harley. Makes it sing. He will not waver. He is determined to go wherever she leads.

I want to know what secrets and lies are concealed in that U-Haul.

And at the same time part of me tells me

that I don't want to know.

Not all knowledge is good knowledge.

The insatiable desire to know is what brought me to Odenville.

Genevieve's ghosts are doing pirouettes inside my head. The things Kenya revealed haunt me as well. This insufferable world is part of my mind now, an indelible part of my memory.

Mile after mile I see the same thing over and over. I keep seeing a young girl hurrying up the highway, undeterred by the rain, grocery bag under her arm, her thumb out. Mile after mile I see her again. Like in *The Twilight Zone*, where the driver keeps passing by the same hitchhiker, Death, we pass the same girl a hundred times. Sometimes she is walking fast; sometimes she is running, never looking back. Always a face painted with fear, always with her thumb extended.

Genevieve squeezes my hand. The illusion of the girl dissolves like sugar in water.

But I think about Willie Esther. She tried to reinvent herself, failed miserably.

All of these apples are from the same tree, one that wants to discard its branches.

Deuce shadows us up the two-lane Interstate, a slow and easy drive from Odenville back into the city of Branchville and all of its churches and American flags. The windshield wipers are working overtime. Kenya spies back every few seconds, the sky sobbing harder.

Genevieve says, "Kenya, explain to me why you need a ride if you drove to Odenville."

No reply from the woman with six-thousand-dollar breasts.

Genevieve's tone is stiff; she asks, "What does Deuce do for a living?"

Kenya folds her arms, crosses and un-crosses her legs. "He's a writer."

"Last night you said he was an actor."

"Same difference."

"And the moon is blue."

Halfway through the city of Moody the skies open up, visibility is bad. Kenya smiles, hopes that Deuce will stop his pur-suit because of the weather. But the condi-tions force Bubba Smith to slow down as well. I look back and Deuce is no longer there. Kenya relaxes.

Genevieve asks Kenya, "When did you graduate from Sarah Lawrence?"

"Why?"

"That's a simple question. When did you get your degree in literature?"

Thunder and lightning are in the distance, the wind becoming a howling wolf.

Genevieve says, "Grandpa Fred told me you dropped out two years ago. Told me he had to send you money to get out of New York. Says you've been in Atlanta ever since."

"Whatever."

"Did he lie?"

"Well, I'm modeling now."

"And the moon is blue."

"Holly Golightly."

"Last time, Kenya. Last time I'll allow you to call me out of my name."

"Or what, LaKeisha Shauna Smith? Or what?"

Animosity rises between them.

Genevieve says, "Look at the way you've mutilated yourself. The way you mutilate your body. Crying out for attention the only way you know how. Acting out your pain."

"I have pain." Kenya glares out the window. "I sure do. At least I can feel."

My chest tightens, but I sit on that anxiety. Refuse to go back to Pasadena.

Blood. I see my mother's blood. Feel its warmth dripping on my cold skin. I see her face. First young and beautiful, her smile

359

withers away until nothing is left but gray ashes.

Genevieve touches my hand. "You okay?"

I jerk back to this reality. I nod. My breathing is short. Heartbeat fast.

Kenya's eyes are on me. I'm embarrassed.

Genevieve says, "Uncle Bubba, could you slow down, maybe pull over."

He asks, "Need me to pull over again? I promise I can do it quicker this time."

I straighten up and tap the back of his seat, say, "I'm okay. Keep driving."

Genevieve returns to her own thoughts, staring out at the road she is familiar with.

I look at the truckers. My mind moves from Pasadena to a foul and dark place.

Then Bubba Smith says, "Ain't that something? He done caught up with us again."

Kenya looks back and curses, crosses and uncrosses her legs again.

Bubba Smith says, "I'm surprised he can see, the way it's raining. Ain't like he's got no windshield wipers on his helmet. It's coming down. Yessir, gonna be some more flooding tonight. He's riding the heck out of that motorcycle. Hope he pulls over up here at the Interstate."

Now Kenya's body is tight, I feel her muscles knot up against my leg, as if she were praying for him to cross the overpass and head back toward Atlanta. Her hopes and prayers go unanswered as he trails us back to Birmingham, continues to follow Kenya in pouring rain.

Bubba Smith says, "Bet it don't rain like this in Los Angeles."

"Not since Noah," I say. "Not since Noah."

"Ain't that something. We all family."

I say, "I suppose we are."

"Can't wait 'til I tell the missus. Yessir. We family."

I glare at the truck stops. Frown on the eighteen-wheelers sporting Confederate flags. Scowl at the burly men getting out of those trucks, bellies hanging over their pathetic waistlines.

Again Genevieve squeezes my hand, stares out the window, the rain her tears.

My other hand touches Kenya, slips her the key I had stolen.

As she takes the key, she sighs again, her finger tracing my palm.

I ache.

eighteen

I ache.

She breathes through her nose as she gives me congress with her mouth, deep-throats my lingam, her head moving with smoothness as my coarse moans sound my splendid agony. She uses her right hand to stroke me at the same time, in rhythm with the rise and fall of her mouth, her grip as firm as a virgin's vagina. She sucks me like I am candy. Works me toward the oblivion of orgasm. But she will not let me get there. I harden and strain and she slows, lets my orgasm subside. She is Tantric. I get hard, then go soft, get hard again, a highly desirable sensation, like riding a wave, bobbing up and down. Hardness and softness are two ends of the pleasure spectrum. Over and over, with her every movement, I surrender mammoth-sized moans and I die a thousand little deaths.

Thunder and lightning stand sentry outside my hotel window, but I cannot hear the noise because of the thunder and lightning in this room, can only feel the heat from her mouth, can only hear the wet and succulent sounds from her greedily gobbling up my heavy-veined erection.

She stops. I moan and cry for her to not stop. But she stops. She backs away. Leaves me writhing at the door of Nirvana. My every nerve is alive. She sits back, skin glistening with humidity, her mouth glistening with traces of me, hands on her breasts, squeezing.

She watches me.

She tells me, "Get a lubricant. I want to try anal."

"What?"

She turns around, on her knees, her delicate ass rising in the air.

"What's gotten into you, Genevieve?"

"Fuck me in my ass."

An empty bottle of Riesling sits on the table, next to it a single glass, lipstick on its rim. A damp towel is across the threshold of the door to our room. The DO NOT DISTURB sign is on the door. Air is on. A window is cracked. Still the room reeks of ganja. Genevieve is in rare form.

She repeats, "Fuck me in my ass."

"My penis would annihilate you."

"Then annihilate me."

"You okay?"

"Anything you want. I'm game. What's your fantasy?"

I push her down, turn her over.

"Too bad we didn't get the flight attendant's number. We could've had fun."

I tell her, "You're loaded."

"Not loaded enough."

"We need to get some food."

"I have your food right here."

My kisses travel from her neck, linger on her breasts, the right one first, then the left, then I squeeze her nipples and kiss her stomach. Her legs float apart. I pinch her clit between my thumb and forefinger. My tongue licks where I pinch. Two fingers move inside her hollow.

She moans, "Get a lubricant. Fuck me however you want to fuck me. You want to transmogrify me into your personal whore. Here's your chance. Make me your whore."

I lick her until wave after wave rolls through her body, until her legs tense, until she comes, then my tongue dances, makes small circles and figure eights until she begs me to stop.

I do not remember the last time I made her come like that.

I do not remember the last time she came.

We fall away from each other.

I am still erect, throbbing, soft moans my only language.

She trembles, rides her orgasm to its end.

In between the flashes of lightning, as the room changes from darkness to light, I stare at her and what I see startles me. Her breasts are but dots on her chest. She is young. With pimples all over her skin. I see her with crooked teeth and in pigtails and hot-combed hair and skinny legs decorated with dark spots that come from being bit by a thousand mosquitoes.

I move away from her, catching my breath, my lingam softening, diminishing.

She does not see my panic, thinks the subtle choking sound I make is a prelude to my own Nirvana. The darkness hides the madness in my eyes.

She asks, "Do you want children?"

It takes me a moment and a thousand blinks to calm down.

She repeats her question.

I answer, "You know I do."

"What if they hate me? What if I hate them? What if I birth what I loathe the most?"

"That's a chance we all take."

"What if I hate them and beat them and . . . what if what if . . . what if they drive me mad?"

Naked, sweat covering our bodies, we both stare at the ceiling.

She says, "Can't believe they left the smoke detector hanging from the ceiling by wires."

She crawls over me, drags herself to her wine. Sips an empty glass. Shakes the empty bottle. Then she goes to her tin can, opens it, fires up what's left of her herbal remedy.

She puts the back of her head on my leg, inhales twice, says, "Blow me a shotgun."

I take her medicine, put it in my mouth backward, and blow a steady stream of paradise.

She coughs, shakes it off.

Then she takes it from me, inhales. "For every beating the others took, I was beaten as well. My siblings were my responsibility. When I was in school trying to study, Willie Esther would take my books and tell me that I had six kids to keep up with and I couldn't spend my time being lazy hanging around the library and reading all day."

"So you hung out at the library."

"If I could. The library was my escape. I read about places far away, places I wanted to go. France, Spain, Corsica, Malta, China, Norway, Sweden, Denmark, Belgium, and Germany."

"Places you've gone."

"Yes. I'd educate myself after Willie Esther had her scotch and passed out."

Again I ask, "Do you want children?"

"No. I did before I came back here. Before I saw this family again. No."

"So, now you don't want children."

"Now, at this very moment, I'm totally uninterested in having children."

"Because . . . what would they have to do with our children?"

"I have already raised six and they didn't turn out that well."

I ask, "Why did you come back?"

"To spit on Willie Esther's grave. I'd pull up my dress and shit on it if I could."

"You're joking, right?"

Genevieve looks toward me. She comes to me, takes my penis in her mouth, her other hand still holding her medicinal salvation, licks me, sucks me, soothes me. She pretends she wants to stop. So I beg her to keep going. She licks the sides, base of the tip.

She sucks a good dick. Sucks a damn

good dick. Right now that bothers me.

She moves away, inhales. Her mouth is still damp, the remains of semen, my jism.

She says, "I didn't come back for the funeral. I came to see my mother's grave. And if I have the strength, to go to jail and visit my father. Most of all, I had to come back for my own sanity. Came back so they could see that even with all they did, they didn't break me."

"You make it sound like you were run out of town with torches."

"I was. But I came back in the backseat of a Town Car. I'm educated. I make more money than all of them put together. I've come back with an intelligent and handsome husband. A man who understands science and cares about quantum physics. A wonderful man who reads *The Odyssey*. *The Iliad*. Books on the Greek gods. I've been sailing, snorkeling, Jet Skiing, scuba diving, surfing. I have danced at night clubs in Fiji. I'm coming back with my head held high."

The woman I am staring at, I do not recognize.

She asks, "If you could change anything about this marriage, what would you change?"

"My hunger for affection isn't satisfied. I'm starving."

"We have everything. A nice home. We have everything."

"I need reciprocity in other ways. I need more intimacy. More sex."

She reaches to the nightstand, puts down her joint, and picks up her purple friend. It's barely larger than the double-A battery that fits inside. Her wonderful clit stimulator. My nemesis.

She says, "Sex. Is that your primary concern?"

"A starving man always thinks of food."

"You're not starving."

"I should know if my own stomach is growling."

She lays back and I take my archrival from her, turn her stimulator on, stare down on Genevieve's anticipation as the purple man hums. Genevieve guides my hand, shows me where to touch her with that perpetual vibration, where to hold that miserable hum so she can quiver in response. I suck her breasts, pinch her nipples. Her muscles tighten and she makes subtle sounds like she's ascending into high heaven.

I whisper in her ear, "Lovemaking is worship. Am I wrong to want to worship you as much as I can? Am I wrong to want to explore sexuality with my wife as much as I can before the sun rises on my Viagra years? Am I wrong to want my tongue to twirl on your clitoris every day?"

I talk to her, say sweet things, say dirty things. Genevieve's breathing speeds up as she releases involuntary wails, has orgasm after orgasm, four back-to-back, two small, two devastating. She jerks and sighs, but never sings like this under the power of my loving.

I move away from her and watch her, the ego part of me feeling unfulfilled.

Time eases by while she catches her breath, while I exhale my envy.

Genevieve crawls over me, gets what's left of her shrub, sets it on fire again, inhales.

I say, "You're hitting it hard today."

"I know. I'm sorry. Doing what I have to in order to cope. If I had done this before we left the hotel, if I had got my head right, then maybe I never would've broken down in Odenville."

Again she puts her hand on my erection, strokes, keeps it from fading to flaccidity.

She asks, "What were you saying?"

"I'm more concerned with emotional security and you're interested in financial security."

Her mouth covers my lingam; her warmth nurtures me close to orgasm, then backs away. The electrical sensation leaves me in a sweet pain, heart racing, gripping the sheets, toes curling.

She inhales her joint, asks, "What is sex to you, honestly?"

"What is . . . what is it to you?"

"Don't answer a question with a question."

"Make me come, Genevieve."

"No."

"Yes."

"Not yet."

"Please?"

"Do like you tell me to do, ride it."

I reach for her and she backs away. I go after her and she moves away more.

I settle where I am, on my back, penis pointing toward a heaven I may never see. I take deep breaths. Feel the tingles moving up my spine. I breathe. I breathe.

I ask, "What's on your mind? What are you thinking about right now?"

"When we met. What I know. What you know. Those thoughts."

"What?"

"Your mother was killed. Mine was murdered. Your father was gone. My father was gone in his own way. You'd been abused as a child. A pedophile had had his way with me."

"Is this what happened when you ran away? When you . . . with the truckers?"

"Use your imagination."

"Why don't you just tell me so we'll both know?"

"Is that what you want to hear? About my exploits as a wayward child? Would that arouse you? Hearing about a girl-child and a pedophile? Would you romanticize that?"

"I just want to know who I've married."

"What if . . . tell me, which would you rather believe? That when I made it to the highway I sold myself to get to Atlanta? That I sold myself for food and shelter for six months?"

"Is that what happened?"

"A lot of child prostitution goes on in Atlanta. All up and down Stewart Avenue."

I repeat, "Is that what happened?"

"A lot of little girls are running from graveyards, evil grandmas, and truck-stop tricking."

She said *grandmas*. Not *grandmothers*. Her Southern inflection perfect and on point. I don't push, just wait for her to speak again. Allow the wine and ganja to loosen her tongue.

"I choose to believe that the day the young brother came through Odenville in that yellow car, I choose to believe that I got in that car. That the brother drove me away from there, that he gave me something to take away my unhappiness, and I got high from Odenville to Morehouse."

Rain falls hard. My erection dwindles.

"Maybe I'd pretend he was someone I wanted to be with. Prince. Michael Jackson."

I listen to our silence.

"Genevieve?"

"Yes, my love?"

"If you had left in that yellow car, would he have had sex with you?"

"Ass, gas, or cash. Nobody rides for free."

A wave of thunder and lightning creates a light show in our room, on our moist faces.

I ask, "What is sex to you?"

"When I was younger it was stress. Weight gain. Vaginal issues."

"What kind of vaginal issues?"

She shuts down and asks, "What is it for you?"

"Question with a question. That's a no-no."

"I'm modifying the rules to fit my needs. Answer."

"It can be a drug. It can be intoxicating and addictive. Wonderful with the right person."

More thunder. Lightning. She says, "Gravedigger wasn't a good provider. He spent his money on God knows what. My mother used sex as her commodity. You need something, a man has it, sex gets you a temporary reprieve. When a woman is poor, sometimes sex is all she has to barter with."

"Is that what your mother did? Bartered?"

"Just like her mother before her."

"But you're not like them."

"No, I am not like them. Everything I have I achieved on my own."

I ask, "What if you're a woman who has everything? What is sex to you then?"

"Then sex is just . . . sex."

She licks my erection, the head, around its edges, breathes hot breath on my flesh.

My desire to pursue that line of conversation dissipates, ambushed by the possibility of falling into the abyss of dissatisfaction. Her moves are so poetic,

374

my moans becoming haikus.

Her cellular rings. She keeps her hand on me, stroking me. She puts her burning shrub on the nightstand, uses her other hand to flip open her phone. Strokes me while she talks.

"Yes. Real estate funds have had a fantastic run, not only in California. I'd advise a core holding that has sector funds. Yes, government bonds are good. The government never defaults on a bond because they just tax us to get their money back. Uh-huh. Well, now you know."

I muffle my groan. My wife. So striking and mystifying all at once.

She leans and takes me in her mouth again, the phone up to her ear.

"I'm in the middle of something. We'll talk soon."

She finishes her call and inhales. I become her ganja. She puffs the magic dragon and colors swirl in my head, makes this room my psychedelic shack.

My legs strain, my toes curl, all the while I am thinking, don't chase what used to work.

My orgasm rises to the point of no return.

Her tone deepens. "You want my mouth on you, don't you, my love?"

I moan.

I beg her to not stop.

"You like the way I suck on your wee-wee?"

Her voice has become Southern and juvenile. I strain to look at her.

Herbal smoke flows from her nostrils. *"You wanna come in my mouf?"*

Again her greasy hair is in pigtails, breasts no more than little bumps, skin filled with pimples, teeth crooked. She is tiny and naked. Nothing more than a naked child.

I try to get away, but I can't.

My release will be explosive.

I fight it.

I lose.

I'm coming.

She covers my erection with her mouth.

Feeds on me until I have to beg her to stop.

Beg her to stop.

Beg her.

Stop.

nineteen

The telephone rings over and over.

I wake up in the darkness of our hotel room, disoriented. I'm sweating, yet I'm shivering as clouds dissipate around me, the residual from Genevieve getting blown.

The phone continues to ring.

I call Genevieve. There is no answer. She is gone.

She left me senseless.

Movement is impossible. I am but a shapeless blob of tallow in need of hydration.

I stare at the phone. It stops ringing.

Then it rings again.

I answer.

"This the research man?"

"Grandpa Fred?"

"Yessir. I catch you sleeping?"

"Yeah."

His voice has an echo, sounds hollow. He is on a speakerphone.

I look at the nightstand. Ashes from my

wife's herbal bush. An empty bottle of wine.

She is gone. No message. No note. Just gone.

"You looking for Genevieve?"

"No, sir. Looking for you, not Jenny Vee."

"For me?"

"I called to apologize."

"Apologize?"

"For the way Jimmy Lee and Velma carried on today. It sho' 'nuff upset me the way they carried on today. They get like that time to time, usually on a Friday night when one of them been dranking too much, but I ain't never seen them get that bad with no liquor, not in front of folks."

"That wasn't your fault."

"Not all Jimmy Lee fault. Velma forgets that God created man first. Not woman."

"Well, still no need to apologize for them."

"And since I done reflected on it, I need to apologize to you for what I said 'bout your hands being soft. I apologize. Would rather issue you this apology man-to-man, face-to-face, and I will again when I see you again, but I had to say this before I closed my eyes tonight."

"No offense taken."

"Then we coulda shook hands on it."

"That's not necessary."

"Just that, if you don't mind me speaking my mind —"

"Go right ahead."

"You people from California, hard for us folks from Alabama to take you serious."

"Why?"

" 'Cause you're from California."

That sums it up.

People in the land of Winn-Dixie, tent revivals, and river rats see my world as nothing. Amazed and unimpressed by the image we have delivered to their doorsteps. I can only imagine, through their eyes, what we looked like walking toward those trailers. We are the circus. We are wheat grass, tofu, and Botox. We are freeway congestion at sunrise and road rage at sunset.

We are spawns of Beelzebub riding Rodeo Drive in cars that cost more than a house.

We are excess.

We are waste.

We are shit.

And this call is his way of flushing the system clean.

He coughs. He finally coughs. It lasts thirty seconds or more. In between his hacking I hear the sounds of guns and planes, a commentator saying stay tuned to the History Channel.

Sounds like Grandpa Fred lights a cigarette and inhales.

He says, "Down here we talk without cussing, at least we try to. Most of us. Jimmy Lee, he spent too much time up in North Memphis. And if we have to cuss, we try to be original about the way we do that. We have a way of cussing without cussing. Good manners don't cost nothing."

I nod. "I understand. I'll apologize to Bubba Smith."

"He worried about his job. All he does outside of that is the volunteer fire department, but he loves driving people around. Loves meeting people and talking to strangers. He harmless."

"He has nothing to worry about. Tell Uncle Bubba Smith I said that."

That settles the main reason for his call. Looking out for his son's welfare. Family. Something about him reminds me of a fearsome general whose mere word could subdue his own troops. At the same time, he has a gentle way about him, is a vulnerable man.

He asks, "How Jenny Vee doing?"

"She was upset, but she's okay."

380

"We didn't run y'all away, did we? She coming tomorrow?"

"I think so. She said she was."

"She done had it rough. But His eye was on the sparrow."

"Yes. She done had it rough."

"Willie Esther gone now, so she don't have to fret over those things no more."

"Genevieve told me that she ran away when she was a teenager."

Just like Kenya did before, with the mention of Genevieve running away from here, Grandpa Fred falls silent. I can hear it, a wall made of concrete being constructed between us.

He asks, "Can we have honest words between us?"

"Sure."

"I don't like talking about certain thangs over the phone." He whispers. *The gub'ment.*

"I understand."

"And I likes to be careful what I say. Just like one snowflake can shut down Alabama, one wrong word or mistaken phrase can shut down what we're trying to build between us."

"Speak your mind."

"Would've liked to have talked to you today, but so much was going on."

"Well, if you want to talk face-to-face, I'll be with Genevieve tomorrow."

"Hurt my heart today, things she reminded me I said. All in jest, mind you. Yessir, that sho' nuff got me to thanking and wondering. Don't want her to remember me as one of the people who did her wrong."

He coughs. A minute goes by this time before I hear him inhale his cigarette.

He asks, "What you know about cancer?"

"What you need to know?"

"Been coughing up blood from time to time."

"You need to get to a doctor."

"And one of my testicles, it done swoll up."

"How big?"

"Size of . . . size of . . ."

"A mountain oyster."

"I reckon."

"You need to get to the doctor, Grandpa Fred."

He coughs.

"They cain't do nothing for me. When it's your time, it's your time. Death don't give a rat's ass about —"

He coughs.

He says, "Jimmy Lee was over at the

church, upset and crying when we got over there."

"And Velma? She okay?"

"She always had a mouth on her. No real home training. That wild horse don't like the reins Jimmy Lee puts around her neck. Yessir, he went out and got the wildest one he could."

He coughs. I wait.

"He sho' hate he lost his dignity in front of Jenny Vee like that. But Velma didn't make it no better. She go up to Jimmy Lee job at Birmingham Steel acting like that. Now he was messing with some other gal down there, but that ain't the way a woman should act. Now, I ain't saying Jimmy Lee was right, but Velma came between Jimmy Lee and his last wife, so she knew how he was. And she ain't no better, done had her share of men from what I hear."

I rub my hands together in impatience. He goes on, "Him seeing Jenny Vee didn't help him much."

"Because . . . what?"

"She done done well for herself. He probably looks at her and thanks less of himself. He always done had a temper, never could pay attention in school, repeated a couple of grades."

"Maybe he needs some help."

"He talked to some folks but that didn't turn out too good."

Again, that cough.

When he gets back in control he asks, "Personal question for you son, if it's okay."

I suck my lips in and massage my goatee. I resist releasing a sound of irritation.

I say, "Sure. We're family. Might have a few questions of my own."

"About Jenny Vee."

"Yessir. About Jenny Vee."

He coughs and pauses, measures whether or not what he wants to ask for is worth what he wants to give in exchange. I suck my jaw anticipating a Herculean task as a favor.

He asks, "Can you get ahold of some of that Viagra?"

"Viagra?"

"Bubba asked me to find out. He's scared to talk to you, being he's working for you. Said you get upset too quick for his taste. He wanted me to ask. I said I would. Jenny Vee being a doctor and you being into all kinds of medicine. He says him and his wife, well certain thangs a man has to do to keep his stallions from breaking out the gate and roaming in other pastures."

We pause.

I say, "Grandpa Fred."

"Yessir."

"The Viagra is for you, isn't it?"

He pauses.

"Reckon so. Would be nice to feel like . . . like my old self. Might not do nothing, but I hear tell from a fellow over at this place I go to play bingo on Sunday nights . . . well, they say it helps with your blood circulation. Might be mighty nice to . . . to . . . get my blood circulating like it used to and be a man once again before all is said and done. Been ten years since I plowed a field."

I smile but I don't laugh.

He says, "Get something like that around here, er'body will know."

"Small town. People talk. I understand."

Grandpa Fred. Viagra. Some toothless woman with equal handicaps. Coughing his way into Nirvana. His four long teeth. Those nubs waggling.

There are some things I do not want to imagine.

I say, "Grandpa Fred."

"Yessir."

I whisper, *"The gub'ment."*

He whispers back, *"Right, right."*

I sit back and again I almost smile.

Again I whisper, "When I get back to California, I'll see what I can do."

That is a kind lie from my mouth to his ears.

We hang up.

Before I can stand, the phone rings again.

She says, "May I speak with Sister?"

"I'm alone, Kenya."

She takes a breath. I imagine her posture changing. Close my eyes and see her hips. Her tongue ring. Her wild hair. My wife's scent covers me but it is her sister I taste.

She asks, "Where is the truck?"

"Kenya, you okay?"

"Where is the truck?"

"Where is your friend?"

"He's in my room. Where did you move the truck?"

In her room. The man she did sexy things for. The man she fed mangos and gave slippery sex in an incense-filled room. Kissing. Sucking. Fucking. Coming. He's in her room.

Silence. Jealousy. And relief that she's okay.

I tell her.

She says, "Thanks for looking out."

Then there is a pause, both of us measuring, unsure.

I am the first to speak. "Where are you?"

"In the lobby."

I ask, "You haven't seen Genevieve?"

"Not my day to watch LaKeisha."

Again my eyes go to the ashes. The empty wine glass. I walk to the front of our suite. The damp towel is still across the front, but moved back from the opening of the door. Forty-five-degree angle.

Worry moves up my spine.

Kenya asks, "What do you want to do?"

"What do you mean?"

"This evening isn't turning out the way I had hoped it would. Was hoping you could get away. I wanted to be sexy for you. Dance for you. Sexy and sweet or naughty and sexy."

I close my eyes and groan, insides rolling like a ball of confusion.

She asks, "Could you get another room on a different floor? We could sneak away."

"Don't know." I make excuses. "Deuce is here. Genevieve, I don't know where she is."

She sighs. She knows what that sweet sound does to me. That sound is my Viagra. I don't want to but I start to tingle. I am drained yet the sun starts to rise on my desire.

She says, "I'm horny for you. If I don't see you again, think I'll always be horny for you."

I say, "Better stop doing that."

"Why?"

I joke, "What you have might make me want to leave my wife."

"And what you have makes me want to be your wife."

Silence.

I stare up at the ceiling, at the smoke detector that hangs by its wire. Then at wallpaper. Pristine on the outside. Soul in need of wide-ranging renovation. That is how I feel inside.

She says, "Relax, I know that can't happen."

"No, it can't."

"Maybe I'll change my name and get all pretentious like Holly Golightly."

"Don't call her that."

"LaKeisha. That sound better? It should. That's who she is. Maybe one day I'll look into three-minute dating. Or even better, maybe I'll lose my Southern accent and get a degree in Stedmanization. Fly out to California and come back with an educated man on a leash."

"Fuck you."

"Bastard. You ain't about shit. Motherfucker. I should tell LaKeisha right now."

"You don't want to do that."

"You threatening me?"

"Don't threaten me."

"You fucked me and now you're threatening me?"

Silence.

She says, "I'm out. Need to get the truck."

"How are you getting to Odenville?"

Silence.

She backs down, clears her throat. "Haven't figured that out yet."

"You have money?"

"You don't have to pay me off."

"Kenya, a lot of your family is in jail for everything from murder to . . . stealing frogs."

"As if you care."

"I do. About you, I do. You have a gun in your purse. A truck with God knows what's inside. Deuce chasing you in a thunderstorm. If it's money, then I'll give you what you need."

Silence.

"No, I don't have any money. Deuce . . . my cards . . . you know my situation."

"And you know mine."

Silence as I think.

She says, "Don't believe you're trying to pay me off."

"Helping you out. Not paying you off. Just trying to keep you out of jail."

Then she makes that sound.

I ask, "Are you crying?"

"What if I was?"

I say, "I'm coming down."

She pauses. "That might not be a good idea."

"You're right."

"We see each other and . . . might not be a good idea."

We hold the phone.

She says, "Come have your way with me."

"Lord knows I would love to get inside you and stay until you gave me an eviction notice."

"Well, I'm the landlord. I say you can move in and out and in and out . . ."

My wedding ring whispers my wife's name.

Still I hear her voice, imagine her smell, her tongue ring, her vagina, and I rise.

The gates are open and I see the Trojan horse, the undoer of a nation.

The destroyer of a civilization.

My fucking Götterdämmerung in three-inch heels and six-thousand-dollar breasts.

I wonder if hell will be like this room.

Bleak, a smoke detector dangling over my head.

She says, "They have at least seven conference rooms. All of them can't be occupied."

I need Genevieve to walk in that door right now. Need her to kick the door down and save me. If she cannot come through that door then I want to hear her voice in the background, want to hear her walking up behind Kenya, want her voice to break this witchspell. But Genevieve does not. I close my eyes and I pray that she does. My prayer goes unanswered.

My voice is but a whisper, "I need to shower."

And hers the whisper of girls. "Hurry."

She hangs up.

I take out Kenya's zed card. Stare at her gray eyes.

Hurry.

I imagine being with Kenya again. I close my eyes and see her naked, her head on my chest, her skin hot, set afire by too many orgasms to count. I imagine my tongue tasting like her secrets.

I scrub away the scent of my wife. Put on jeans and a long-sleeve retro shirt. My reflection is overdressed. My reflection is too obvious. I take the shirt off, put on a T-shirt.

As soon as I step outside my door, three rooms down, Kenya's door opens. I prepare to see her face, her hand reaching out for me, long brown legs in high heels and lace.

Deuce steps into the hallway. Black leather pants. Biker boots. Jean jacket.

He sees me and walks on. I am nothing. We both end up at the elevator, waiting.

Deuce grunts. "Kenya says you do AIDS research."

"I do."

"You experiment on people."

"No. Mice and rats."

"Really? How do rats and mice get the virus?

"We inject them."

"Inject? Oh, so you fuck them in the ass?"

I don't smile. Neither does he.

"Sounds horrible, doing Mickey Mouse like that."

The elevator refuses to come.

He asks, "What made you go into AIDS research?"

"Personal reasons."

"How personal is personal?"

"Personal enough."

He motions at my T-shirt. It's blue with white letters. **PV=nRT**.

He says, "Thought that spelled pervert at first."

"Not too good at spelling, are you?"

He nods. "You got me that time."

"It's an equation. Thermodynamics. Ideal Gas Law."

"Gas? Like a nice fart?"

He laughs a little. I don't. My palms, damp as rivers.

I say, "Kenya says you're a writer and an actor."

He chuckles.

I say, "You're not?"

"I'm an investor."

"What kind of investments?"

"Movies."

"Movies?"

"Adult films. Porn."

My blood coagulates. My head aches.

I ask, "What made you get into porn?"

"Pussy." He smirks. "Sweet pussy."

I open and close my hands.

"While I'm fucking amazons you're probably jacking off to something on Amazon.com."

He laughs at me and looks away.

In his mind he is Thor. And Harley-

Davidson is his iron horse. He is a man women revere, a creature with more athletic prowess than intellectual proficiency. And I am nothing more than a court jester. He is right. He seduces amazons while I spend my nights surfing Amazon.com, waiting for my wife to feel wifely.

Something inside me goes wrong. Terribly wrong.

The elevator door opens.

Only there is no elevator.

Only an open shaft descending down into seven stories of blackness.

Without hesitation I push Deuce.

His arms make huge grasping circles as he spins and turns and tries to get his balance, wobbles in his biker boots, reaches for the door frame, grabs its edge, still wobbling.

He grabs my T-shirt, the intelligent one he ridicules.

He grabs it by its sleeve.

The sleeve rips.

His eyes meet mine. He is no longer smirking. No longer mocking.

But I am smirking. I am mocking.

If I save him, he will kill me. That truth is in his eyes.

Without hesitation I kick him in his gut, leave him without air, unable to scream.

He falls to his death.

The elevator doors close like the period at the end of a sentence.

I stand there in shock, my mind telling me to hurry and take the stairs. My mind telling me to go back to my room before anyone else comes out in the hallway. My mind telling me to just start walking, to get away from this spot, to walk and find a way to make each step calmer than the one before. I don't move. I stand there and burn three hundred thousand brain cells.

I blink out of my trance when the elevator opens.

Back to reality.

Deuce gets on first, his biker boots thumping the marble floor.

I look down at my T-shirt. It is perfect. I get on the elevator.

The elevator door closes. We descend.

We stand on opposite sides of that mirrored coffin, my envy aimed at the marble floor.

I ask, "What did you say made you get into adult movies?"

"Pussy. Just said that."

The elevator door opens.

Kenya stands before us.

Her lewd smile becoming a glare of disdain.

Kenya turns and walks away, heads down the hallway toward the bar.

Deuce takes his time and follows her toward the Grill.

I follow Deuce.

Only I do not see Deuce going after Kenya. Gravedigger and Delphinie, that is who I see, them in their final moments. Deuce's pace tells the world that, despite his easy stride, his patience is wearing thin. He calls her name twice. Kenya doesn't slow down or yield to his size or temperament. She walks, but does not run. Her purse shows the weight of her courage.

"How much?" I ask Deuce. "You hear me? How much?"

"For what?"

"How much for you to go away and leave Kenya alone?"

"You trying to buy yourself some six-thousand-dollar tits, Fart Man?"

The bar is empty. Restaurant still closed for renovation. Deuce gets close and Kenya puts her hand in her purse. Then she takes her hand out and sits down.

"I was nothing but good to you, Deuce."

"I think I was pretty good to you too, Kenya."

"You slept with that ugly shit."

"Well, that ugly shit just happens to be my wife."

"Your ex-wife."

"Okay, my ex-wife."

"You said it was over."

"I'm sorry, Kenya. She came by. We got to talking. Had a couple of beers. Shit happens. What more can I say? I'm here to apologize. I'm here because I care about you."

"You're here because you think I have that stupid U-Haul."

"I care about you."

"You care about what's in the U-Haul."

I stand there, no place to go.

I say, "Kenya, I'll buy the tapes from him."

"What tapes?"

I look at her, then look at Deuce. He smiles.

"Kenya, he said he was into porn."

She says, "He's an actor. He ain't worth shit, but he's an actor."

"Pornography?" He gives me a look of mock outrage. "What kind of man do you think I am?"

I feel so gullible.

Then Kenya tells Deuce, "He's a man with a dick better than yours."

That pauses us all. Outside, the winds blow in all directions.

Kenya wipes her eyes. "I fucked him, Deuce. Fucked him good."

Deuce stops smiling.

"Bet that hurt, didn't it, Deuce?"

He frowns.

"I fucked him and he made me come like I never came before."

"Thought this was . . . you said he was a relative."

"I fucked him. And if you hadn't gotten off that elevator, I was about to fuck him again."

He stands up. "Bitch."

"Bet you wish you had never turned off my charge cards now, huh?"

"You ungrateful bitch."

Kenya stands up. "Call me out my name again."

He does, over and over.

In the same room I witnessed four lovers engage in passion, almost the same spot I watched the European and Italian men give pleasure to the Indian and Spanish women, once again I become a voyeur. But things have changed. Then I saw pleasure, now I stand on the shores of pain, wave after wave of vulgarity crashing into me, washing away any foolish notions I had of me and Kenya.

I should go. But I stay.

Kenya and Deuce, I remain the voyeur, watch them argue, listen to them talk to each other in a disrespectful way that appalls me. Kenya. This is who she is, mask removed. Her anger so great, soul so vindictive, as if she reacts to what is given, then returns it tenfold. There is beauty, but that beauty is devoid of emotional maturity.

Kenya snaps, "That ugly shit you fucked me over for."

"You fucked this pervert?"

"What, you deaf and stupid?"

"Bitch, that's why I never stopped fucking my ex-wife."

"What?"

"Now who's looking stupid, huh?"

"Motherfucker."

I look at Deuce and I no longer see him; I see me years from now, across the kitchen table from Kenya, her speaking to me in such a way that makes my blood boil, that causes rationality to flee, that causes me to say and possibly do things I will regret before the next sunrise. I see the type of person I do not want to become.

I do not see lattes, warm conversations, and jazz.

I see frustration. Perpetual pain. A wounded heart that will not heal.

Kenya struggles to get the gun out of her purse, struggles with her own irrationality, with intent. Anger dances in her eyes. They are Gravedigger and Delphinie in reverse.

I will be the witness to this crime.

Something simple saves Deuce from getting shot. The U-Haul key. As Kenya yanks the gun out of her purse, the U-Haul key flies out, lands on the table with the sound of a brick hitting a marble floor. Her lie echoes so very loud.

Silence.

We all stare at the key.

Kenya holds the gun by the handle, tight at her side.

She puts the gun down on the table.

Stares at the gun.

At the U-Haul key.

"Lying bitch. I can't believe you stole my furniture."

"Half of that shit should be mine. I've been putting up with your ass all this time."

"Give me my goddamn key."

"Here's your fucking key." She snaps.

"Your shit is in Odenville."

"Nothing but a lying bitch."

"One more 'bitch' and a bullet will fly up your ass."

"Where's my damn U-Haul? Where in Odenville?"

"Parked in front of the elementary school."

He nods. "We still have that other matter."

"We're finished, Deuce. You can go back to that ugly shit you were fucking."

"Well, somebody owes me for two tits. And if we are through, I intend to collect my due one way or another. So, either you or the pervert come up with my money, or you better be ready to use that gun, Kenya. That pussy might be yours, but those tits belong to Deuce."

Silence.

"Come get your tits, Deuce. Bring your bad ass on over here and get these tits."

She holds the gun, its barrel pointing at the ground, now her finger on the trigger.

"C'mon, Deuce."

A sudden vibration causes me to jump, makes all of us blink.

It's my cellular phone. A text message. From Genevieve. She needs me.

Deuce says, "Me and my ex are getting back together."

"That ugly shit can have your shriveled-up nuts."

Deuce bobs his head and clenches the key in his hand.

He looks at me like he wants to hit me, then shakes his head and walks away.

A few people come into the bar, unaware.

From here we can hear Deuce's Harley start up and head away.

Kenya puts her hand on mine. "Why are you looking at me like that?"

Logic rises above emotionality. Sanity above insanity. I play what if and ponder how long happiness would reside with us. Not true happiness, but that illusion that shields the light of the truth by covering our eyes with the blackness of our own carnality, blinds us with our own desires. How long will it take for me to wake up and wish she were Genevieve? How many orgasms will rise and subside before I realize that orgasms are all she has to offer? How soon before I shed this selfish shell and ease back into my intellectual clothes and attempt to have a meaningful conversation, one not rooted in either race or anger, one that is not of the loins, and see that blank look, or even worse, that impatient expression that rings of irritation in her eyes, or hear her tell me to simplify my language, to dumb down my world in order to make her feel at ease?

A model who doesn't model. A writer who doesn't write. A poet with half a poem.

Tattoos. Body piercings. Hair that moves like a stallion, wild and free. Everything about her is wrong. Terribly wrong.

I move my hand away.

I shake my head.

Her eyes widen.

I say, "Genevieve might be a Holly Golightly, but you're not close to being Genevieve."

I expect her to react, to sling curses and say many unkind things about my character.

She does not give in to her jealousy.

Her eyes tear up.

I pat her hand like she is a child.

I say, "I have to go."

"I won't be here when you and Sister get back. But I'll be in touch. One day soon. I'll get the number from Grandpa Fred. We can have that talk."

"Where are you going?"

She shrugs. "Maybe I'll get a taxi and

catch a Greyhound and go back to New York. I have friends here. Was going to drive that U-Haul up there and sell off Deuce's shit. But, hey. Could just go somewhere new. Make some new friends. Get another tattoo. Another piercing."

"More pain to cover the pain."

She gives me a rugged smile. Again I expect her to curse me, talk to me the same way she talked to Deuce. She turns her eyes away from me, arms folded beneath her breasts, her back straight, militant, and in a stiff tone she says, "I can take care of myself. Been doing it all my life."

"What about the funeral?"

She reaches into her purse. Takes out an obituary. Her father's. Everything about her softens. She stares at the obituary for a moment, then she finally says, "I've been to the only funeral that's going to matter. Would tell you to give this to your wife, but it's the only one I have. Tell Sister . . . tell her . . . we'll resolve what's wrong between us some other time. We're not ready yet. I'm not ready for that yet. I thought I was. Really thought I was. Daddy would be ashamed of me for some of the things I've done."

"Why did you . . ." My thoughts jumble. "Why me?"

She says, "Why did I fuck you?"

I nod. "Why did you fuck me?"

"We have our issues." She's talking about her and Genevieve. Hurt rises as she plays with her tongue ring and yields a vindictive smile. "To prove that she's not any better than any of us. To prove that I can get anything she has."

"To take what she has."

"Maybe."

"But you can't. Nobody can."

Her hands go to her wild hair; her head lowers in sadness. She wipes her eyes. Cries without making a sound.

My cellular rings again. Another text message from Genevieve.

I get ready to leave Kenya, then pause and ask, "You need money?"

She shakes her head.

I have four hundred-dollar bills in my wallet. I give her three.

I say, "New York?"

"Someplace. New place. New tattoo."

I nod.

She waves good-bye, dismissing me once again.

Then I walk away.

twenty

Sweat makes my T-shirt stick to my back as I get out of a taxi.

I'm back in Odenville on Route 411 and Alabama Street. At the Exxon.

The taxi pulls away and I begin my stroll up the dark road toward the Methodist church.

I dial her cellular number.

She says, "You got here quick. Keep walking. I'll see you."

We hang up.

The moonlight takes away enough of the darkness for me to find my way.

The heels on my dress shoes betray me as I stroll across Beaver Creek.

Genevieve waits on the corner at Alabama Street. In front the town library. Not the new one that has been built on the foundation of a historic hotel. Directly across the street from where the library used to be when she lived here as a child. She faces the defunct Bank of Odenville,

406

its windows dingy and opaque. She sits in the darkness and stares at the abandoned place that was her escape, if only in her mind, her legs folded underneath her, once again a little girl.

This is where she vanished to. She rode a yellow cab back to sit in front of the library.

"Where do we go when we die?" she asks. "Where does the soul go?"

"In the ground until Judgment Day," I tell her, then sit next to her. "That's in the Bible."

"When did you ever read the Bible?"

"We will all be dead and in the ground."

"Willie Esther is not in the ground, not yet."

"But Willie Esther is dead."

"For real?"

"Yes, my Genevieve, yes."

"Just like my mother."

"And just like my mother."

She looks at me with an emotional stare. Words try to rise but she holds them down, shakes her head as if to say not now, not in this order. Things must be given in sequence.

The sky grumbles over our heads.

Genevieve says, "When I came back, Willie Esther started putting things inside me."

"What are you saying?"

"Willie Esther. She put things inside me if I was bad. I don't mean actually bad, I mean bad inside her mind. She would look at me and I knew she was about to come after me. She'd do that and say that if she had done that to my mother, then my mother would not have been a whore leaving all of these leftover niggers running around her house driving her crazy. Then she'd walk across that graveyard and go to church on Sunday morning, stay all day long."

I reach to touch her. She moves my hand away.

"The library, Willie Esther didn't come here. This was a post office before it was the library. She might've come in here then. But she never went inside this building when it was a library. It was safe. I could go inside and get away from all of this, escape inside my mind."

"God bless the libraries."

"And the librarians who dare us to dream. You have no idea how many people the libraries have inspired. You have no idea. A library is more than a building made of bricks."

"Of course."

It is so quiet here. So peaceful. I cannot

imagine anything bad happening in this town.

Genevieve speaks again, responding to the memories and thoughts in her mind, tells me, "Willie Esther put things inside me."

"Inside you . . ."

"So I conditioned myself to not react when she put something inside me. Like a . . . like a slave who wouldn't give the master the satisfaction of screaming when he was beat with a whip."

A moment passes. I ask, "Anybody know?"

She mumbles. "Now I can't uncondition myself."

"Did anybody know?"

"I've never told anybody that. I've never said that out loud."

I reach for Genevieve. She shakes her head. Does not want to be touched.

She takes a deep breath. "She said that would keep me from being a whore with a litter of leftover niggers. What she was doing, she'd pray while she did it, like she was some sort of a healer. She'd wash the sins out of the neighbor's clothes. Had the television on Channel 11. And she'd put things inside of me. To keep me in line and keep me from being a whore."

I grieve and listen.

"If I reacted, she wouldn't stop. That reaction, that told her that the devil was inside me trying to get out. She wouldn't stop. So I taught myself to *not* react. To *not* feel. To *not* give in. She whipped me. Oh, yes. That bitch beat me. And she put things inside me."

"Why didn't you tell anybody?"

"I was ashamed. Thought it was my fault. Thought if I told somebody they wouldn't do anything. They didn't do anything about the beatings. Thought she would . . . put me on the other side of that fence. She always threatened to do that. Put me right there with my momma."

She puts her hand on mine, ready to feel my energy.

She asks, "Should I have told you that? When I met you, in those first three minutes, should I have told you that? Should I have put this on my résumé, what I am telling you now?"

"Not in the first three minutes, but you should have told me. You should have trusted me. Then I would have understood you. I would've known what you were sensitive to. I would've known why. You shut me out one minute, then you almost let me on the other side of that glass wall, then

410

you're gone again, behind a thicker glass shield, and I have no idea who you are."

She cries. Her glass wall shatters and she gives me her emotions and she cries.

"I've been carrying this cross for so long. Carried it from Odenville to California. Now I will put this cross down. It may not make my life easier, but at least it'll be easier to walk straight."

I rub her shoulders, kiss her eyes.

She wipes her eyes and sighs. "I wonder who I would've been if I had stayed here. If I would've had a nice home. Or if I would've still lived in one of those trailers. If I would have had seven kids by the time I reached thirty. Wonder if I would be wearing a long flowered dress and have cabinets filled with plum preserves, mango chutney, strawberry jam, orange marmalade. I could be a grandmother by now. Sitting on a porch with a big stainless steel bowl between my legs shelling peas and watching the grass grow. Chewing Skoal and spitting in a tin cup."

"You would've become the town librarian."

"Yeah. I would have liked that."

"Maybe the mayor."

"Doubt that. Not with my family history."

"You hate this place."

"Just that trailer. The devil's den."

"You love the library."

"Yes." Her smile comes back. Wide and strong. "This library is my good memory."

"I understand."

"Part of me has always wanted to come back here and just drive around, smell the earth, look at faces. Have one of those red hot dogs that are linked together with string."

Silence.

She says, "I have put most of my cross down. Put down some of yours."

"Not that easy."

"Fire is the devil's only friend. I remember the preacher saying that in a sermon."

"What does that mean at this moment?"

She doesn't answer, just asks, "Will you ever tell people the truth about Pasadena?"

"What about Pasadena?"

"Don't back away. Your mother. How she died."

"That car accident in Pasadena killed her, you know that."

We pause. "Your mother didn't die in that car accident."

My voice cracks. "She did."

"She died two years after that accident.

At a hospital in Fresno. You went back to Fresno after that accident because your mother got too sick to take care of you."

I pull my lips in. Hands clench into fists.

She says, "I'm waiting. Just say it. To me. You don't ever have to say it to anyone else."

I swallow and I hear the rain coming down.

She says, "I saw your mother's death certificate. Pneumonia."

I take a hard breath. Then another.

Genevieve says, "I'll give you all of me. Just say it. For us. And I'll give you all of me."

I feel us in that car. I swallow again and I'm hydroplaning. My hands are small again. It's that day in Pasadena. The day we had that accident in the rain. I close my eyes and see that wall coming at us so fast. The shattered glass sprays all over me. I get tossed. My momma's blood dripping. I scream for her. I am but a child. A terrified child who wants his momma.

That is where it ends in my mind. Right there.

But Genevieve is right. That is not where it ended.

Then my momma coughed. She moved her hand. Reached for me.

Her lips moved and she tried to ask me, "Baby, you okay?"

All I could do was cry.

By then people had run over to our car. The rain coming in and spraying my face.

Momma lost a lot of blood. She had to get a transfusion. Ended up getting bad blood.

Back then nobody wanted to touch you. Ignorance complicated by rumors. I was a child and my grandparents didn't understand. They kept away from me, just like they did my mother. Momma was cremated. Funeral homes didn't risk themselves with AIDS bodies back then.

And my grandparents threw away their old dishes. They bought two sets. One for them to use. Another for me to use. No hugs. No kisses. No love. They threw me behind a glass wall while I watched my mother wither and die a slow death that I did not understand.

Never wanted to see another dead body after that.

Never wanted anybody else to have to go through what I went through.

It was different then. Not much better now. But harder before it became celebrity driven. The word gets around school, the rumors begin, the ignorance spreads, nobody wants to touch you. Nobody wants to be your friend. You're ridiculed, left alone for fear that you may breathe on them and sentence them to death. You are left devoid of human contact. Left devoid of love.

Even by your grandparents. Even by the ones you need to love you unconditionally.

I wipe my eyes and look at Genevieve.

Her hair is in ponytails. Her teeth, crooked. The clothes she wears are ill-fitting, old rags. I look down at my hands. They are small. So small. As are my lace-up tennis shoes.

We are children.

I struggle with my words, manage to say, "Two years after we had that car accident . . ."

I pause. My voice is so young, that of the child I used to be.

I say, "AIDS killed Momma. That's how she died. She wasn't on no drugs. She needed some more blood and those people gave her some bad blood. Blood that had that . . . had that disease in it. They said they didn't know. And they said if Momma didn't get that blood . . ."

A moment passes. Genevieve says, "That's so sad."

I look at Genevieve. At LaKeisha Shauna Smith. She's thirteen, five years

415

older than I am now. Hair in those pony-tails. A brown-eyed girl in hand-me-downs. She says, "Dag. Why that so doggone hard to say? My momma was killed by my daddy and I can say that."

"I wanna . . . when I grow up I wanna make sure nobody else get that."

"Why don't you tell nobody the truf then?"

"Because people stupid."

"Uh-huh."

"Talking about people doing it with monkeys and it being a funny-people disease."

"They don't say that no mo'."

"I wanna 'member my momma the way she looked when she was alive."

Silence.

I shrug and stare at my little hands. "Because if I say that then I 'member how she looked before she died. I want to 'member her how she looked before . . . before that . . . before. I wish we had made it to the museum. I sho' wanted to see those buffalo soldiers."

"Bet that would've been a whole lotta fun."

"But we didn't make it. Almost made it down there. Almost."

I close my eyes and open them again.

We are once again adults.

Genevieve says, "I still think you're brave."

"No, I'm not. I'm a coward."

"You've always been brave to me."

I lower my head, wipe my eyes. I fold inside myself. Inside my dubious integrity.

I say, "We never made it to the Buffalo Museum. Never made it."

She says, "I know."

I cry. I give up my ghosts and I cry.

Genevieve's hand touches my shoulders. She hugs me.

I wonder who I would be if it wasn't for that day in the rain, if my momma had lived, if I had grown up in Pasadena and Houston, if Galveston had remained my playground.

"It's scary telling someone you care about, someone you love who you really are." Genevieve says that, her voice so clear. "I almost did in Fresno. Our first night. I sat there watching you sleep, staring out at those railroad tracks, thinking about all of this. I drank and got high to ease my anxiety. You woke up and I backed down. All I could think . . . keep thinking . . . thinking that, if you knew, you wouldn't be any different than the rest of them."

"I'm your husband."

"As I am your wife."

I rock.

She says, "People know your tragedies and they treat you like you're not human. Like you're a three-headed goat. A monster from some other planet. They keep reminding you of your pain. You see how they look at me? They're stuck on that person I used to be. They can't see that old life as just a moment in time that I've moved on from. It was a horrible life."

"Panic attacks. The way you burn trees. All of that makes sense now."

She adds, "The way I keep putting off having children."

"Yes. That too."

"The reason I didn't tell you in Fresno, one thought came to mind."

I look at her and wait.

She says, "If you know about LaKeisha, if you know about all that LaKeisha has left behind, if every time I look at you I see the creation of LaKeisha, then how can I be Genevieve? When you know it all, I don't know if I can look at you every day and stand to see LaKeisha's reflection in your eyes. And if we had children, and this is what they know . . . I do not want to look into my children's eyes and see a re-

418

flection of a life that I loathe."

She stands and walks away. Heads toward the graveyard.

I follow.

She wipes her eyes. "This would be a good time for you to turn around."

"Why?"

"It just would."

I catch up with her. I take her hand. We walk toward the DEAD END sign then turn right, walk between the trailer homes and head up the hill toward that graveyard.

I say, "I heard Delphinie was always gone. She ran away to Birmingham."

"Kenya told you."

"Yes."

"Delphinie would leave and she'd get homesick or broke, maybe she'd miss us. But she couldn't stay gone. Don't know what she was feeling. But she'd come back long enough to get pregnant by Gravedigger. They'd take up like she'd never left. She'd have a baby and leave it with Willie Esther, which was just like me having a baby because it all fell on me."

"Heard Willie Esther made her take one of you with her whenever she left."

"One time my mother took me and one of my brothers, J-Bo I think. When we got to the store she told us to hold hands and walk back home. Then she got in the car with some man who was down there waiting for her. J-Bo cried. I didn't. I watched her leave. I remember thinking, I'm going to do that one day, head down 411, see what's on the other side of this bubble, and vanish."

We walk slowly until we get to the fence. We pass by Willie Esther's trailer and walk on the other side of the fence. Move over burial ground and stop in front of Delphinie's tombstone.

Genevieve says, "I bought that tombstone. As soon as I got a job and could save some money, I bought that tombstone. Before then, Momma was in an unmarked grave."

"It's nice. Real nice."

We stand in silence.

"She had me when she was fifteen, then married Gravedigger the same year. She had six children by the time she was twenty-six."

"She only lived to see the age of thirty."

Genevieve nods. "We've both lived longer than our mothers."

I wipe my eyes, wipe away my own memories, and under the moon's light, I wait.

"I was her first child," she finally says. "Maybe I sealed her fate, kept her from her dreams. Always felt like I did. Jimmy Lee was last. He doesn't remember his mother. Or me."

"He was young."

"You're not listening to what I'm telling you."

"Okay."

She falls silent again. Then she looks back toward the library. Toward her memory.

"He was from Africa," Genevieve says then wipes her eyes with the palms of both of her hands. "The man in the yellow car, the man I saw that day, he was from Africa."

"The man who gave you your first joint."

She nods. "Yes."

"The man you watched drive away."

"He didn't drive away." She sets free a weary chuckle. "Not exactly."

"What happened?"

"I went with him. He drove away and I chased that car from the railroad tracks to 411. He stopped and took me with him. I was with him for six months. Lived with him. He had an apartment in College Park. Told people I was his cousin, but I don't think anybody believed it."

I swallow my discomfort. "Why didn't they?"

Like Kenya did before, Genevieve makes a motion at her arm, at her complexion.

I nod my understanding.

She says, "He sent me back when I got pregnant. I was thirteen and pregnant by a grown man. Thirteen years old. Having sex before I knew anything about my vagina."

I echo, "Pregnant."

"I left Odenville with him, stayed with him, got high with him, got pregnant by him, then he got scared and dumped my young ass back in Odenville. Drove me right back here in the middle of the night, had on the same tattered clothes I left here wearing. Left me crying. Facing that graveyard."

"He brought you back."

"Pregnant underage girl staying with a pedophile. Nobody believed I was his cousin. Being young and pregnant, too obvious. One phone call and his life would've been over."

"Why didn't you call and turn him in?"

"Why didn't you turn your pedophile in?"

I suck my bottom lip.

She says, "I loved him."

Silence.

"I was thirteen. Had been trained to cook three meals a day and clean up behind everybody and take care of a house filled with trifling lunatics. Being with him was wrong, I knew that, but that was easy. To me, at that time, compared to Willie Esther, compared to living under the iron hand of Lady Macbeth inside her tin Bastille, it was like heaven. I could check books out of the library and read as much as I wanted, could go outside and walk to the park, could see other black faces, could go places in the evening. Couldn't do much in the daytime, but I could read and watch television. Could watch whatever I wanted to watch until he came back home."

"And when he came back home?"

She sighs. "My pedophile. I hated him in the end. A few days later he came back to check on me, talked to my mother while Willie Esther gave him the evil eye. I have to give him credit for that. He came back to check on me. But still, how I hated him for bringing me back. For dropping me off, for putting me out of his car, for leaving me facing that damn graveyard. Hated him so much."

Silence.

Again she whispers, "How I hated him."

Miles away, lightning dances in the sky. Another storm will be here soon. I say, "Genevieve."

Silence.

"I used to dream about going to Africa, even before I met him. Willie Esther would laugh at me. Momma would laugh at me. That's how we've been conditioned. You tell people you want to go to Africa and they laugh. When I was growing up a black man would rather be called a nigger than an African. If you called a black man a nigger, he'd just call you a nigger back. But if you called somebody an African, watch out. You had to be ready to fight. Amazing how we are taught to be ashamed of who we are. How we shun our truths in hopes of social acceptance."

"You wanted to go to Africa."

"Yes. Ask me what part?"

"Where?"

"Kenya."

I repeat, "Kenya."

"Kenya. The name I gave my daughter."

I groan and die a thousand deaths.

I open my mouth, prepare to lay my own burdens down.

I'm falling apart.

My composure crumbles.

The hole that has been unearthed for a new tenant, I want to throw myself inside.

I say, "Genevieve, no Genevieve."

424

Genevieve puts her finger to her lips, asking me to hush.

"She calls you her sister."

"Not *her* sister. She calls me *Sister*. Out of spite."

I crumble.

A light flickers on and off. On and off. The source is Grandpa Fred's front porch.

The town is resting. But like a Roman god, that stern and legless warrior is up watching his land. If nothing else, the epitome of Neighborhood Watch.

Genevieve says, "He's waiting."

"For what?"

"Me. Us."

"Genevieve, I need to say something."

She puts her finger to her lips again.

I hush before I start my confession.

She asks me if I remember the day Grandpa Fred called, if I remember when I gave her that news. That she went out and jumped in the pool. It was a few days ago, not that many hours behind us, but she speaks as if it were a lifetime ago.

Like all tragedies in my life, I remember.

"I jumped in the pool. I was going to kill myself."

"Why would you kill yourself, Genevieve?"

"To make sure Willie Esther was dead."

Once again I do not understand.

Grandpa Fred coughs. He has come out on his porch, cigarette in hand. He coughs hard and strong. He gags and I see bits and pieces of him floating away like cancerous insects, each fleeing and leaving less and less. And I imagine that skeleton, Death, standing near, that scythe in his left hand, a bony finger teasing the edges of Grandpa Fred's face.

Again the sky rumbles. Dark clouds move to cover the moonlight.

Genevieve says, "I'll be right back."

"Where are you going?"

"I'm going to the church. I'm going to see Willie Esther."

"Her body is there?"

"Yes. The storm came and that kept the funeral home from taking her away."

"You sure?"

"Grandpa Fred told me. Wait over there until I get back."

I look at him, again scratching the side of his face with his nub.

I say, "I'll go with you. Make sure you're okay."

"I have to go make sure she's dead."

I stress, "Willie Esther is dead."

She firms her voice. "What if she isn't?"

I don't argue with her.

She takes a breath. "I want to see her

alone. There are things I have to say to her."

"Some things shouldn't be said inside a church."

"I'll ask for forgiveness before I leave."

Genevieve heads across the grass, walks by graves. She stops and looks at the open spot, the place where Willie Esther will be put to rest. She spits then moves on.

Light rain starts to fall.

I walk backward, letting the sound of Grandpa Fred's cough guide me as I watch Genevieve head toward First Baptist. She heads around toward the front and vanishes.

I turn and face him.

He extends his hand. His face-to-face apology.

With my soft hand I shake his rough hand.

He smiles, shows those four long teeth.

Our business is done.

He says, "Rain coming back."

Then I roll him back inside his home. His windows are closed. The cigarette stench is the strongest I've ever experienced. Billows of cancer dance around my head.

A battle is taking place on his big-screen television. Guns and airplanes and bombs.

I look at his old furniture and older decorations on his wall.

He coughs a good cough.

Willie Esther's obituary rests in his lap.

When Grandpa Fred is done coughing, he takes a pull from his cigarette, stares at the obituary, and shakes his head. He gets emotional. Then he says, "Willie Esther didn't have nobody for over fifty years and never gave me the time of day. No sir. I wasn't good enough for her. I didn't really care about what happened to her down in Lower Alabama, or about who her folks was. No sir. She lived right next door to me for years, never gave me the time of day."

I look at him, his handlebar moustache gray while his hair is dyed black. His clothes clean, pressed. I see an old man who is trying to look young again, trying to clean himself up for a woman's approval, doing the best he can to look good for her funeral.

I understand why he is telling me this. These are the confessions of a dying man. He is telling me what no one knows.

I ask, "So, you had a thing for Willie Esther?"

"When we was young we used to talk." Cough. "Was almost friends."

"You asked her out?"

"More times than I can 'member." He nods. "Then our chirren went and had chirren."

"You didn't want to see Gravedigger with Delphinie."

"Didn't seem right, not at the time. No sir, sure didn't. I coulda helped Willie Esther if she wasn't so doggone evil to me. I'll make sure she'll have a nice funeral. That's all I can do."

I motion at his cigarette, say, "You're going to be right behind her."

He inhales, blows smoke away. "That don't bother me none. We all gonna be right behind her. We all gonna die one day. I just hope when it's my turn I do it well."

"So you and Willie Esther were almost friends."

I shake my head and cough, feel my insides deteriorating.

"Yessir. She'll be nicer to me on the other side of the fence. When I get over there, I'll have both arms, my legs. She'll look at me then. She might even wanna dance, if I ask her."

I wonder what it was like for him, to live across the way from a woman he loved, a woman who rejected him on a daily basis, to watch their kids have what he never could.

Then to have his son kill his daughter-in-law, the child of the woman he loved.

To sit on this porch and see the police come take his son away.

Then have to face the family of the woman his son murdered every day.

To have to look out that window at Delphinie's grave every day.

To know that death was the demise of any hope he had between him and Willie Esther.

I think of Kenya. My wife's daughter.

Like dried dirt, again, my insides crumble.

Grandpa Fred clicks on another light, this one illuminating his space, his shrine.

My mind has been too preoccupied to take in this space.

Then I look up over Grandpa Fred's head, over his handlebar moustache and bloated body. My mouth creaks open as my eyes widen and take in that huge red, white, and blue flag.

It covers the wall facing east. The sight sends a shock through my body.

I think I understand why his grandchildren did not walk next door to visit him.

I know why Kenya's father took her away from here.

The thirteen stars on that flag speak their own truth.

Part of him still fights a war that was lost a long time ago.

Maybe Grandpa Fred reminded Willie Esther of all the things she wanted to forget.

I don't know. Only guessing. I only know how I feel at this moment.

Like running to the Interstate.

A coarse voice says, "Grandpa Fred."

I jump, as does he.

He calls out, "Who that?"

"Genevieve."

Genevieve is outside the door. He tells her to come inside from the rain.

She says, "You know I'm not coming in there."

My eyes go to that polyester flag as I rise.

I push his wheelchair though the nicotine haze and go back outside.

The air seems so much fresher now.

Genevieve's face is red, skin the complexion of sorrow and hate. Flushed. Her eyes are swollen. She's been crying. Her voice is almost gone. She's been screaming.

She looks at me. Sees that I have been, once again, stunned.

She asks Grandpa Fred, "Did you get what I asked you to get?"

"Look on the side of the house."

"Thanks, Grandpa."

"You not coming back tomorrow?"

"No. We're done, me and Willie Esther."

"They made her up real pretty, didn't they?"

Genevieve pauses. "She's so small. I thought she was huge. But she was so tiny."

We walk away, shoes crunching grass and gravel.

That cough follows us.

Then he calls out, "Will I ever see you again, Jenny Vee?"

She pauses. "I doubt it, Grandpa. I guess this is our good-bye."

"Come back when they put me over yonder. Could you?"

She nods. Her lie is one of the kindest things I've ever seen her do.

He says, "Help me say your name 'fore you go. Wanna make sure all of 'em say your name right from now on."

She almost smiles. "John."

He repeats, "John."

"Vee."

He coughs. "Vee."

"Ev."

He nods. "Eve."

"Not Eve. Ev."

"Ev. John. Vee. Ev."

She smiles.

He laughs, that handlebar moustache moving up and down as those four teeth dance.

"Take care of yourself the best you can, Grandpa."

"Research Man, you take care of John. Vee. Ev. She the best thing I done ever done. She might not be mine directly, but she part of me. The only thang I done done right."

She smiles, then she goes back and gives him a hug.

On the side of the house are three two-gallon cans. All three filled with gasoline.

Without asking any questions I pick up two cans as Genevieve picks up the last one.

I follow my wife to the trailer, get ready to step into the abyss of her remembrance.

The door is unlocked. She hesitates.

I say, "Genevieve. Are you having an attack?"

"Lot on my mind." Genevieve looks

back at the church. "They say when a soul dies a baby is born. Do you think that is true?"

"I don't know. Why?"

"I'm pregnant."

Two words and nothing else matters. Nothing matters but the life that is in her stomach. Whatever problems we have, they no longer matter to me. Boy or girl, I want my child.

"How long have you known?"

"That evening Grandpa Fred called and you answered. I was coming in from the doctor."

"You were happy."

"I was. Very. The same day Willie Esther dies, I find out I'm pregnant."

"Why didn't you tell me?"

"Wasn't sure what I wanted to do. This wasn't the . . . this wasn't . . ."

"The plan."

"No. It wasn't."

"Genevieve. All the smoking herbs. The wine."

"Before I could tell you, you told me Willie Esther was dead. And all of this . . . all of this came back. We might be done with the past, but the past is never done with us."

Now I understand her reaction at that

moment, that pain that washed over her.

She asks, "What if this is her inside of me?"

"It's not, Genevieve."

"What if it is?"

I snap, "It's not."

Her breathing changes.

I ask, "Are you having an attack?"

"I had one at the church. A small one. I'm okay now. It's nothing."

She sets the can of gasoline on the floor, on that spot where her father killed her mother. She goes to the wall, removes the picture of Jesus, then she hands it to me, asks me to set that picture outside. Leaves Martha Stewart and Ronald Reagan on the wall.

I stand there holding a picture of Jesus. He stares at my guilty eyes.

She says, "I have not been a good wife."

"You have, Genevieve, you have. I have to tell you about Kenya."

"Kenya is expressive. I envy her. She's passionate. She lets herself go."

She looks at me as only Genevieve can.

She says, "Jesus."

"What?"

"The picture of Jesus that you're holding."

I take that picture to Grandpa Fred. He

smiles without coughing.

He tells me that he will take good care of that indelible image.

He says, "Soon as that gets going, y'all hie on down to the highway."

By the time I get back inside, Genevieve has gone through the cabinets. All the hard liquor that Willie Esther has accumulated over the years, all the hard liquor that people have brought as a sympathy gift, she has taken every bottle out and lined them up like soldiers. Even now she is meticulous. She has two bottles in her hand, pouring the alcohol over the carpet, soaking that carpet then taking more bottles and pouring alcohol all over the sofa. She takes to the bedroom. I take Willie Esther's things out of the closet. I pour scotch and rum over as much as I can. Genevieve adds gasoline to those clothes, douses what Willie Esther has left behind.

I walk through the trailer, breaking windows with a flashlight.

Genevieve looks at me, confused.

I say, "Fire needs air to breathe. No air, it might go out before it gets started."

She nods.

Then she pours gas in the bedrooms. In the bathroom. Down the hallway.

She saturates the spot where her mother died.

She says, "Fire is the devil's only friend."

We stare at each other. She knows.

I ask, "Do you want me to stay in here and burn for what I've done?"

Her voice cracks. "Would you?"

"Yes."

"Then I will stay too."

"Why?"

She raises her hand, shows me her wedding ring.

She is my wife.

She has told me that countless times before. I understand her now.

She loves not like I, but the way Paul speaks of love in Corinthians.

Again she cries. We take shallow breaths. We stand in the middle of fumes.

She says, "I came downstairs this morning. For breakfast. You and Kenya were walking down the hallway. Saw you vanish into a conference room. Saw the door close. I stood outside that door, wondering what to do. Felt as if I were eavesdropping. I went back to my room. Waited. Then I was going to go back downstairs. I stood in front of Kenya's room. I heard."

"Forgive me."

"Forgive me for what I did not tell you."

She says that as if Kenya is both of our sins. Our last secret revealed.

Genevieve takes out a book of matches.

She repeats, "Fire is the devil's only friend."

Grandpa Fred is still on his porch as we walk our road to purgatory, that picture of Jesus and Willie Esther's obituary in his lap, a fresh cigarette in his hand, his nub waving good-bye.

He calls out, "Hie on outta here, Research Man. Take John. Vee. Ev. And hie."

The sky rumbles and rain falls as we hurry down Wellington Road, flames climbing high into the night. Like a sacrifice. There is no sound of Satan laughing. We look back and there is no image of Willie Esther rising out of the fire. Just a lot of smoke and the crackling of flames.

Rain starts to fall in steady streams.

When we make it down to the Exxon, both of us are wet. An F-150 is there waiting.

Bubba Smith stands next to the truck. Wearing worn jeans, old boots decorated with paint, and a plaid shirt rolled up to his elbows. His baseball cap has a picture of Dale Earnhardt.

He says, "Was out here listening to the

radio, this talk show I likes."

I ask, "Anything good?"

"People saw Flight 93 in flames while it was in the air and two military aircraft circling it."

My broad smile greets his. I ask, "Flight 93?"

"The one that went down over Pennsylvania. Nine-Eleven. We shot down our own plane. I'll ride a donkey before I get on a plane."

He opens the passenger door for us.

His rugged hands smell like ours, of gasoline and conspiracy.

Inside the truck my wife leans over and kisses me.

Bubba Smith says, "I got some ice water and some beer if y'all want some."

The sound of a fire engine punctuates the night air. Its flashing lights brighten my world as I put my hand on her stomach, rub her belly, stir up our son or daughter.

There is hope.

Bubba Smith and my wife talk about family, about Pell City and Sharkey County.

I close my eyes and think.

When we pass the exit for the airport, Genevieve leans to me, whispers in my ear, "Let's not go home tomorrow."

"What do you want to do?"

"Let me take you to Houston."

"To Houston."

"Let me take you to see the buffalo soldiers. Let me do that for your mother."

My face turns warm, throat tightens, and tears fall.

She wipes my eyes.

Genevieve.

ZHAWN-vee-EHV.

Over and over I say her name in its original language.

Allow it to drip from my tongue like warm butter.

The light of my life.

The fire in my loins.

Acknowledgments

☺

Right now I'm at the Marriott Waterfront in Baltimore. It's snowing. My flight is canceled and I'm snowed in. Freezing rain. Sleet. Stuck here for three days. Why am I telling you this? I have no idea. It's five a.m. PST so my brain isn't in gear yet. My editor told me to do my acknowledgments. I wanted to watch a movie on SpectraVision. *Sideways.* Heard it was good.

Here I go.

The book you're holding in your hand, or hands, or maybe opening with your feet if you have those skills, as are all my other novels, is a work of fiction. Odenville, Alabama, is a real place. You can pop out to my Web site (*www.ericjeromedickey.com*) and see the actual photos of the areas I used in the novel. I'll leave those pictures posted for a while. The same for the photos I took while staying at the Tutwiler

Hotel in Birmingham. Same smoke detector. ROFL. I take a lot of photos as I work, but this is my first time actually posting any. I have no idea what made me think about doing that.

The characters in this novel are not real. No matter how real they sound, no matter how much they remind you of someone, they are not real. This is another work of fiction. Fiction means not real. For real. It does. Look it up. Surprised me too. Made me scream.

☺

Why Odenville?

When I was in Birmingham, on tour for *Drive Me Crazy*, I caught a taxi to the airport, and the driver (don't really remember who he was), during a casual conversation (people in the South love to chit chat, even at five in the morning) said he was from, well, Odenville. Told me that Odenville was about thirty miles outside of Birmingham; think he referred to it as a good old prison town. Something about the driver was interesting. Honest. And that left me curious about his hometown.

While I was working on this novel, I flew back into the heart of the Bible Belt, drove down I-20 and found my way into Odenville four times. Drove down 411 and stopped at Frogs, listened in on a conversation about God and dinosaurs, then went down to BSC and chatted with the people who worked there. Bought Yoo-hoos and a ton of "props" from the Exxon on Alabama and Route 411, things that I sat on my desk as I worked, most of which appear in the story.

Damn. Outside my hotel window, there is a woman running with her dog in the snow.

I have to note that there is more to Odenville than is in the novel. I drove around (like a location scout) and found the spots I wanted to use, the *specific* settings, everything from the park to the railroad tracks, took notes on everything I wanted to use. I almost used a different side of Odenville, the road that cuts through heading toward Georgia, a peaceful area with very few homes and a wonderful forest, an area that has a spectacular sunrise and sunset, but I saw the graveyard. I sat parked on that road and stared for a while. Imagined the characters in a scene at that particular spot. And with Genevieve's past . . . the graveyard, the trailers, the church . . . well, that was what I needed.

Once again, I do not know any of the residents of Odenville. This is not their lives.

I visited Odenville's library, sat around there for a few hours flipping through local papers, reading articles on the town's history. Mary Banks, the town librarian, was very helpful in handing me history books and resource materials. She was a very kind woman. I thank her for that. I remained anonymous while I was there, so that means she is as polite to strangers who drift in as she is to the people she knows. I was pleasantly surprised to find a copy of one of my novels, *Liars Game*, smiling at me from the shelves. One of Walter Mosely's novels shook its pages and said hello to me as well. And they had brand-new CDs for a buck. CDs for a buck. Kindness, smiles, and brand-new *CDs for a buck*. That, my friend, is how the world *should* be.

I must note that as I went places, I didn't tell anyone who I was or what I was up to, just sort of blended in and drove around the best I could. Took in the five senses of each area. I have to admit that when I drove down 411 and saw a Confederate flag in the window of a business, I was tempted to bust a U-turn . . .
☺

(Note: This just occurred to me. And trust me on this one, people do not recognize writers. Well, unless you actually have a book signing and there are posters of you all over the joint. Forget the Witness Relocation Program. The best place for a writer to hide out is at a bookstore, especially the ones that have comfy sofas and coffeehouses attached, and the best place to remain unseen is right in front of his/her books. Believe me on that one.)

The same detail applies for the scenes that take place in Fresno, California, and in Pasadena, Texas. I visited those places. In Fresno, I stayed at the hotel mentioned in this novel. And in Pasadena, Texas, I rode Spencer Highway in the rain.

Hopefully, I described all of those places with accuracy. If not, forgive me.

Time for the shout outs.

Lon, thanks for insight and input on the issue of abuse. Thanks for meeting me at B&N and chatting for a while. Peace to you.

Stephanie McKinney, thanks for all the input on your job. Thanks for answering all of my e-mails without hesitation. Hope I got it right! The chicken and waffles are on me.

Jennifer Burford, thanks for . . . for . . . what the hell did you do? Oh, yeah, you gave me the info for what's-his-face. LOL.

Thanks for reading bits and pieces of this novel. Now, get back on your computer and finish that book.

Sheila Williams in B'ham, thanks for taking all of my calls and e-mails. And thanks for giving me directions around B'ham.

Sara Camilli, my agent since day one, thanks once again. We're up to eleven now. Only eighty-nine to go.

Lisa Johnson, Kathleen Schmidt, Betsy DeJesu, and all the wonderful people in publicity, thanks for all the hard work.

Julie Doughty and Brian Tart, my wonderful editors, I love working with you guys! It's nice to have a team who understands what you're trying to accomplish.

Lolita Files, author of *Child of God* and (soon to be released) *Book*, thanks for taking my e-mails at the ass-crack-of-dawn, and thanks for all the input and insight, thanks for helping me get 'Bama right. I'll pass on the mountain oysters. ROFL. Anyway, it's all about the details. And thanks for looking at so many damn changes. Thanks, thanks, thanks.

Yvette Hayward, my NYC speed-reading friend, thanks for reading this in all of its stages. If only I could read as fast as you . . . I mean, damn!

And for the rest of the peeps who had a hand in this bowl of literary soup, here ya go.

I wanna thank _____ for _____ because without them I'd be _____ at a _____ in _____.
You're the best of the best.

Damn. Still snowing.

Clicking the heels on my Nikes . . .

Still snowing. All flights still canceled. Well, better to be on the ground and wish you were in the air, than to be in the air and wish you were on the ground.

Guess I'll click on SpectraVision and watch *Sideways*.

☺

January 30, 2005
Baltimore, MD
Marriott, Waterfront
Room 1834
6:40 a.m. PST

About the Author

Originally from Memphis, Tennessee, Eric Jerome Dickey is the author of ten best-selling novels, including *Drive Me Crazy*, *Naughty or Nice*, *The Other Woman*, and *Thieves' Paradise*. In a July 2004 profile, the *New York Times* hailed Dickey as "one of the few kings of popular African-American fiction." Dickey writes full time and lives in southern California.